She set her fingers on his chest, straightening the collar of his tailored shirt. "That's okay—I don't think I could even begin to describe my first impression of you."

He caught her hands. "But it's changed?" he asked softly.

"The jury is still out," she told him. It wasn't, though. Not really. He was dedicated. He was...noble, even, she thought. He was Elven, she was a Keeper. Elven could be anything, and he had chosen, like her, to protect and serve.

There were a million reasons she should back away. They were embroiled in a horrible situation together, surrounded by death and tragedy, by a threat to everyone and everything they knew, to the entire world of the Others and the city where they all hid in plain sight.

And yet the worst of it was that she was worried not for her world but for her heart and soul.

And not a drop of the fear tearing through her could save her.

Dear Reader,

Welcome to the world of THE KEEPERS: L.A. I hope you enjoy this new four-book foray into the world of the guardians of the supernatural known as the Keepers. Writing these books—joined for this go-round by Harley Jane Kozak and Alexandra Sokoloff, two very good friends—has been a true labor of love.

When Harley and Alex and I began to think about this second go-round, our first concern was…where else? And, again, the answer came to all of us at the same time: Los Angeles, City of Angels, City of Dreams.

And a city where at any given time you might see any kind of performance, any kind of costume, any kind of *anything* happening right there in broad daylight—or the dark.

I'm actually in L.A. as I write this. Contestants for *The Voice* are scurrying around my hotel, all of them filled with hopes and dreams. And naturally, to sustain all the dreamers in the city, you have the exclusive clubs, the new "it" places and all the people who own and run them. And then there are those with the true power: the producers, the agents and the directors, who are thrilled—and sometimes challenged—by the choices the producers make.

What better place for a few new Keepers—a bit disconcerted by their sudden call to duty—to govern those denizens wearing masks beneath their masks?

I hope that you'll have as much fun reading about these new Keepers as we had writing about them.

Thank you, and enjoy!

Heather Graham

KEEPER OF THE NIGHT

HEATHER GRAHAM

First published in Great Britain 2013
by Mills & Boon, an imprint of Harlequin (UK) Limited,
Eton House, 18-24 Paradise Road, Richmond, Surrey TW9 1SR

© Slush Pile Productions, LLC 2013

ISBN: 978 0 263 90394 2
ebook ISBN: 978 1 472 00578 6

089-0313

Harlequin (UK) policy is to use papers that are natural, renewable and recyclable products and made from wood grown in sustainable forests. The logging and manufacturing processes conform to the legal environmental regulations of the country of origin.

Printed and bound in Spain
by Blackprint CPI, Barcelona

New York Times bestselling author **Heather Graham** has written more than a hundred novels, many of which have been featured by the Doubleday Book Club and the Literary Guild. An avid scuba diver and ballroom dancer and a mother of five, she still enjoys her south Florida home, but loves to travel as well, from locations such as Cairo, Egypt, to her own backyard, the Florida Keys. Reading, however, is the pastime she still loves best, and she is a member of many writing groups. She's currently vice president of the Horror Writers' Association, and she's also an active member of International Thriller Writers. She is very proud to be a Killerette in the Killer Thriller Band, along with many fellow novelists she greatly admires. For more information, check out her website, theoriginalheathergraham.com.

Sometimes in life we get to meet people and in a few minutes we feel we've known them all our lives. I've known both Harley and Alex now for years, but from the time I met them I felt that I'd known them since childhood. To my prized and beloved cohorts on this Keepers journey, Alexandra Sokoloff and Harley Jane Kozak. I cannot remember a time when we weren't friends, and I certainly can't imagine not having you in my life.

Prologue

Perception, to paraphrase the old saying, is nine-tenths of the law.

And so the world happily—well, mostly happily—accepts the truth of that. And, perception, of course, is the main duty of those born to be Keepers and maintain order among the paranormal races.

As centuries slipped by, man became a "show me" species and lost his belief in what he couldn't see plainly with his own eyes, and that was good for all the decent and law-abiding creatures. As the twenty-first century progressed, populations exploded. Human beings covered the earth, with birth rates at an all-time high.

And other *beings* flourished, too, learning how to coexist in a world where the magic of the earth and skies was no longer recognized, and human credence was more and more limited to one particular sense: sight. Many people began to lose faith not just in the unexplainable or unknown, but even in their own omnipresent God.

While those of an...unusual bent had once headed strictly to places like New Orleans, where even many among the human population believed themselves to be vampires or other denizens of the night, many places in the world became the destinations of choice for the *truly* different. The well-known among the races—vampires, werewolves and shapeshifters—were ready to expand their territory, as were Others who had once chosen to remain in their native lands, the Elven, gnomes, leprechauns, fairies and more.

With that expansion came the need for an international council, the first of its kind, to keep order, and Keepers from across the world were selected to meet at a secret rendezvous in order to construct a code that would be universally accepted. They would serve as the last word when it came to events that could disturb the status quo, because even the Otherworld races considered the most vile and beastly in human mythology were trying to blend in and survive.

With so many of the most experienced Keepers serving on the council, some of the most promising young Keepers were thrown into difficult situations with little warning.

And since so many of the paranormal races still liked to settle where the abnormal was the norm, where theatrics abounded, even the most absurd people and situations frequently went unnoticed, it was no wonder that the population of the Otherworld exploded off the charts in one particular place: La-La Land, also known as Hollywood, California.

City of dreams to many, and city of lost dreams for too many others. A place where waiters and waitresses spent their tips on head shots, and the men and women behind the scenes—the producers—reigned as the real kings.

So many of the paranormal races—the vampires, the shifters, the Elven and more—traveled there, and many stayed, because where better to blend in than a place where even the human beings hardly registered as normal half the time? With so much going on, no one set of Keepers could control the vast scope of the Greater Los Angeles Otherworld, and so it was that the three Gryffald cousins, daughters of the three renowned Gryffald brothers, were called to take their place as peacekeepers a bit earlier than had been expected.

And right when L.A. was on the verge of exploding with Otherworld activity.

Hollywood, they were about to discover, could truly be murder.

Chapter 1

There was blood. So much blood.

From her position on the stage, Rhiannon Gryffald could see the man standing just outside the club door. He was tall and well built, his almost formal attire a contrast to the usual California casual and strangely at odds with his youth, with a Hollywood tan that added to the classic strength of his features and set off his light eyes and golden hair.

And he was bleeding from the throat.

Bleeding profusely.

There was blood everywhere. It was running down the side of his throat and staining his tailored white shirt and gold-patterned vest.

"Help! I've been bitten!" he cried. He was staggering, hands clutching his throat.

No! she thought. *Not yet!*

She had barely arrived in Los Angeles. This was too soon, far too soon, to be called upon to take action. She was just beginning to find her way around the city, just learning how to maneuver through the insane traffic—not to mention that she was trying to maintain something that at least resembled steady employment.

"I've been bitten!" he screamed again. "By a vampire!"

There were two women standing near him, staring, and he seemed to be trying to warn them, but they didn't seem frightened, although they were focused on the blood pouring from his wound.

They started to move toward him, their eyes fixed on the scarlet ruin of his neck.

They weren't concerned, Rhiannon realized. They weren't going to help.

They were hungry.

She tossed her guitar aside and leapt off the stage. She was halfway to the group milling just outside the doors of the Mystic Café when she nearly plowed into her boss. Hugh Hammond, owner and manager, was staring at the spectacle.

"Hugh," she said, trying to sound authoritative and confident. "Let me by."

Hugh, a very tall man, turned and looked down at her, weary amusement in his eyes. He wasn't a bad sort, even though he could be annoyingly patronizing at times. She supposed that was natural, given that he had been friends with her father and her two uncles. Once upon a time he'd been a B-list leading man, and he was aging very slowly and with great dignity.

He was also the Keeper of the Laurel Canyon werewolves.

"Hugh!" she snapped.

"By all means, Miss Gryffald, handle the situation," he told her.

She frowned and started to step past him, refraining from simply pushing him out of the way. This was serious. Incredibly serious. If a vampire was ripping out throats in broad daylight, in front of witnesses…

"Stop!" someone called out.

Another man, dark where the victim was blond, not quite as tall, his face lean and menacing, broke through the crowd and addressed the bleeding man. "Give in to me! Give in to me and embrace the night. Savor the darkness. Give your soul to me and find eternal life and enjoy eternal lust. Drink from the human soul, the fountain of delight, and enjoy carnal delights with no fear of reprisal."

She was ready to shove through the crowd to reach the victim's side and defend him against the newcomer, but Hugh had his hand on her arm. "Wait," he whispered. "Rhiannon, take a look at what they're wearing and how they're acting, and *think about it.*"

She was dying to move, but she stood still, blinked and heeded Hugh's words.

The two young women reached for the victim's arms, holding him up as the dark man spoke. One licked her lips in a provocative and sensual manner.

"Lord, forgive me," the bleeding man pleaded. "God, help me, for Drago comes and would have his terrible way until none but monsters walk the earth."

Drago walked forward threateningly, then stopped suddenly and turned to the crowd. He grinned pleasantly, and menace became humor as he said, "If you want to see any more, you need to listen up."

Where there had been silence, as if people were frozen with fear, there was a sudden eruption of laughter and applause.

"Thank you! Thank you!" the "victim" announced, lifting his hands to silence the crowd. "I'm Mac Brodie, actor at large. The diabolical Drago is portrayed by the illustrious Jack Hunter, and..." He turned to the sensual vixens at his side. "Erika is being performed by the beautiful Audrey Fleur and Jeneka by Kate Delaney. Please, everyone, take a bow."

They did. Drago was darkly handsome, and both young women—Audrey, a brunette, and Kate, a blonde—were extremely pretty. They, like the two men, were in Victorian attire, but in their case it was Victorian night attire. Beautiful white gossamer dresses, with gorgeous bone corsets beneath, and silky pantalets.

Mac continued to speak. "Please, join us at the Little Theater on the Hill this evening or anytime throughout the next three months, where we're presenting *Vampire Rampage,* which will soon begin production as a major motion picture, as well. We ask that you come and tell us what you think. Shows start at eight o'clock every night except Sunday and Monday, but to make up for that, we do have matinees on Wednesdays. Thank you!"

He bowed low, lifted his head and waved to the appreciative crowd.

Hugh stepped up close behind Rhiannon. "Actors," he said, sounding tired, as if he knew the profession and its attendant promo stunts far too well—which of course he did. "This is Hollywood, Miss Gryffald. Everyone's a bloody actor. Get used to it. You've got a lot to learn about life out here." He smiled down at her in that patronizing way that made her crazy, and shook his head. "Looks like your tip jar just disappeared."

Rhiannon turned quickly toward the stage. It was true. The lovely little tip jar her great-aunt Olga had made for her was gone. Along with her tips. And they hadn't been half bad today; a lot of people had thrown in bills instead of nickels.

She wanted to scream. Worse, she wanted to run back to Savannah, where so many people— and…Others—survived on the tourist trade alone that they behaved with old-fashioned courtesy and something that resembled normal human decency.

But Hugh was right. This was Hollywood, where everyone was an actor. Or a producer, or a writer, or an agent, or a would-be whatever. And everyone was cutthroat.

It's Hollywood, she told herself. *Get used to it.*

Go figure that the Otherworld's denizens would be starstruck, too.

"I'm calling it quits for the day, Hugh. I'm heading home."

He lifted her chin and stared into her eyes. "Calling it quits? That's what they sent us? A quitter? It's up to you, but I'd get up there and play if I were you. You can't quit every time there's a snafu. Lord above! We need Teddy Roosevelt, and they send us a sniveling child."

"I'm not a sniveling child, Hugh. I just don't see the sense of going on working today. Since there's certainly no imminent or inherent danger—"

He interrupted her, laughing. "Imminent or *inherent* danger? The world is *filled* with inherent danger—that's why you exist, Rhiannon. And imminent? How often do we really know when danger is imminent? Did you think being a Keeper was going to be like living in a *Superman* comic? You see someone in distress, throw on a red cape, save the day, then slip back down to earth and put your glasses on? How can you be your grandfather's descendant?"

Rhiannon felt an instant explosion of emotions. One was indignation.

One was shame.

And thankfully, others were wounded pride and determination.

"Hugh, I know my duty," she said quietly. "But my cousins and I were not supposed to take over as Keepers for years to come. No one knew that our fathers would be called to council, that the population explosion of Otherworlders in L.A. would skyrocket the way it has and we would need to start our duties now. It's only been a week. I'm not quitting, I'm adjusting. And it's not easy."

Hugh grinned, released her chin and smoothed back her hair. "Life ain't easy for anyone, kid. Now get up there and knock 'em dead."

She looked around the place and wondered drily if it was possible to "knock anyone dead" here. It was basically a glorified coffee shop, but she did need to make something of herself and her career here in L.A.

She'd left Savannah just when Dark As Night,

her last band, had gotten an offer to open for a tour. Her bandmates had been incredulous when she'd said that she was moving, and distressed. Not distressed enough to lose the gig, though. They had found another lead guitarist slash backup singer before she'd even packed a suitcase.

Wearily, she made her way back to the stage. Screw the tip jar. She didn't have another, and she wasn't going to put out an empty coffee cup like a beggar.

She could not only play the guitar; she was good.

Unfortunately, given the recent twists in her life, it seemed she was never going to have the chance to prove it.

She stepped slowly back up on the stage. Earlier the crowd had been watching her, chatting a bit, too, but and enjoying her slow mix of folk, rock and chart toppers.

Now they were all talking about the latest Hollywood promo stunt.

Rhiannon began to play and sing, making up the lyrics as she went along, giving in to her real feelings despite her determination not to be bitter that she was suddenly here—and with little chance for a life.

I hate Hollywood, I hate Hollywood, oh, oh,
I hate Hollywood, I hate Hollywood, oh, oh,
oh, oh.
Everyone's an actor, it's a stark and fright-
ening factor,
I hate Hollywood....
And I hate actors, too,
Oh, yeah, and I hate actors, too.

Okay, her cousin Sailor was an actress, and she didn't hate Sailor, although she wasn't certain that Sailor was actually living in the real world, either. She was too much the wide-eyed innocent despite the fact that she'd grown up in L.A. County—and had also spent a few years pounding the pavement trying to crack Broadway and the New York television scene. Maybe the wide-eyed innocence in Sailor was an act, too. No, no, Sailor really wanted the world to be all sunshine and roses. And, actually, Rhiannon loved her cousin; Sailor always meant well. And now, according to the powers that be, she and Sailor and another of their cousins, Barrie, a journalist with a good head on her shoulders, were to take their place as Keepers of three of the Otherworld races right here in L.A.

Oh, yeah, yeah, yeah, yeaaaah, I hate Holly-
wood,
And I hate actors, too.

If anyone disagreed with her lyrics, they didn't say so. No one was really listening, anyway. And maybe that was the point. Easy music in the background while the coffee, tea, latte, mocha and chai drinkers enjoyed their conversations.

Polite applause followed the song. Rhiannon looked down, not wanting the audience to see her roll her eyes.

At ten o'clock Hugh asked her to announce that the café was closed for the night. She was shutting her guitar case when one of the coffee drinkers came up to her, offering her a twenty. Surprised by the amount of the tip, she looked at him more closely and realized that he was Mac Brodie, the actor who had been covered in fake blood earlier.

She looked at the twenty but didn't touch it, then looked back into his eyes.

Elven, she realized.

Six foot five, she thought, judging that he stood a good seven inches over her own respectable five feet ten inches. And he had the telltale signs: golden hair streaked with platinum, eyes of a curious blue-green that was almost lime. And, of course, the lean, sleekly muscled physique.

She lowered her head again, shaking it. *"Elven,"* she murmured. "It's all right. You *did* ruin my night, but that's okay." She made a point of not looking directly at him. Elven could read minds, but most of them had to have locked eye contact, so looking away made it possible to block the intrusion. And, luckily, the process was hard on them, so they didn't indulge in it frivolously.

"Keeper," he said, drawing out the word. "And new to the job, of course. Sorry. I saw that look of panic on your face. I'm assuming you're here for the bloodsuckers?"

She stiffened. In Savannah she'd been a fledgling vampire Keeper, apprenticing with an old family friend who'd kept the city peacefully coexisting for years, but she'd always known that one day she would take her father's place in L.A.

As she'd told Hugh, this had all been so sudden. There hadn't been a warning, no "Tie up your affairs, you're needed in six months" —or even three months, or one. The World Council had been chosen, and in two weeks a core group of some of the country's wisest Keepers was gone and their replacements moved into their new positions. And there was no such thing as calling the Hague for help. No Keeper business could ever be discussed by cell phone, since in the day and age they lived in, anything could be recorded or traced.

So the new Keepers were simply yanked and resettled, and the hell with their past lives.

"Yes, of course, Keeper for the bloodsuckers," Mac said, his tone low.

"Some of my best friends are bloodsuckers," she said sweetly, looking quickly around. She'd been about to chastise him for speaking so openly, but the clientele was gone and the workers were cleaning the kitchen, well out of earshot. Of course, he might know exactly what she was thinking even without her saying it aloud. Some Elven were capable of telepathy even without eye contact, so she braced her mind against him. In fact, she knew she was playing a brutal game. It cost an Elven dearly to mind-read, especially without locking gazes, but it cost the target a great deal of strength to block the mind probe, as well.

There were a lot of Others in L.A. County. One thing they all did was keep the secret that they were…unusual. It was the key to survival—for all them. History had taught them that when people feared any group, that group was in trouble.

"Same here," he told her. "I'm fond of a lot of vampires."

She stared at him for a moment. He was undeniably gorgeous. Like a sun god or some such thing. And he undoubtedly knew that Elven usually got their way, because they were born with grace and charm—not to mention the ability to teleport, or, as they defined it, move at the speed of light.

She was annoyed. She had no desire to be hit on by an Elven actor, of all things, but she didn't want to fight, either. All she wanted was to make her point. "I don't want money from a struggling actor," she said. "You don't need to feel guilty. I'm fine. I work because, Keeper or not, I still have to pay the bills. But Hugh gives me a salary, so go do some more promo stunts. I'm fine."

"You're more than fine," he said quietly. "And I'm truly sorry that we ruined the evening for you." He offered her his hand. "I'm Mac. Mac Brodie."

She hesitated and then accepted his hand. "Rhiannon. Rhiannon Gryffald.

"It's a pleasure, Miss Gryffald. And am I right?" he asked her.

"About?"

"The vampires?"

"Are you asking me so that you could avoid me if I were Keeper of the Elven?"

"Hey, we Elven have spent centuries keeping the peace because we're strong, sure of ourselves, some might say arrogant—" he smiled "—and we can talk almost anyone into almost anything. I'm asking you out of pure curiosity," he told her. "And because I'm trying to make casual conversation—and amends. I really am sorry."

Rhiannon waved a hand in the air. "I told you, it's all right. However, it has been a long day, and I would like to go home now."

"No nightcap with me, eh?" he asked.

He was smiling at her again. And like all his kind, he had charm to spare.

That's why the Elven fared so well in Hollywood. They were almost universally good looking. Tall, and perfectly built. They were made for the world of acting.

She realized, looking at him, that he was exceptionally godlike. She was surprised, actually, that he bothered with small theater at all. He would have been great in a Greek classic, a Viking movie or a sword and sorcery fantasy. He was lean, but she knew that he was strong—and would look amazing without a shirt.

Then again, he'd announced that the play was going to turn into a major movie. Maybe he was sticking with it for the stardom it might bring.

"No nightcap," she said. "I'm simply ready to go home."

"Perhaps you'll consider letting me buy you that apology another time?"

"Doubtful," she assured him.

He pulled a card from his pocket and handed it to her. "Well, be that as it may, you really should come see the show."

"Thank you, but I really don't enjoy a mockery being made of my—my charges," she told him.

He leaned closer to her, and the teasing, flirty smile left his face. He almost appeared to be a different person: older, more confident and deadly serious.

"No, you really *should* come see the show," he

said. "My number is on the card, Miss Gryffald. And I'm sure you know L.A. well enough to find the theater."

He turned and walked out the door, nearly brushing the frame with the top of golden head.

Puzzled, she watched him go.

Hugh appeared just then. "Still here? I'm impressed," he said.

"I'm leaving, I'm leaving," she told him.

"I'll see you tomorrow. And be on time."

The man could be extremely aggravating. Werewolf Keepers were often like that, she had discovered. But then, the more experienced a Keeper was, the more he or she often took on the characteristics of a charge to a greater or lesser degree. She suspected that Hugh could become a wolf at the drop of a hat.

With her precious Fender in hand, she left the café. She heard Hugh locking the door behind her.

She headed to the ten-year-old Volvo that her uncle had left for her use, set her guitar in the trunk and started off down the street. Her song really hadn't been half bad. "Hollywood, oh, I hate Hollywood," she sang as she drove.

* * *

Brodie nodded to the attendant on duty and proceeded down the hallway of the morgue, past rooms where dozens of bodies in various stages of investigation were stored.

That was one thing about L.A. that wasn't so good. The city was huge, and the number of people who died on the streets, many of them nameless and unknown, was high. Possibly even sadder were the ones whose names were known—but whose deaths went by unnoticed and unmourned.

Of course, the morgue also housed the remains of people who were known and loved—but who had died under circumstances that ranged from suspicious to outright violent.

That night, however, he passed by the autopsy rooms, remembering all too clearly the one he'd entered when he was sixteen, a room filled with corpse after corpse wrapped in plastic shrouds—so many dead. His father had arranged it after discovering that Mac had left a party after drinking. Luckily he had only creamed the garage door. But it might have been a person, and his father had made sure he knew what the consequences could have been.

He reached a door marked Dr. Anthony Brandt, Senior Pathologist.

Tony undoubtedly knew that he was coming. Tony knew a lot. He had an amazing sense of smell that had served him well as a medical examiner. He could smell most poisons a mile away.

Before Brodie could tap on the door, Tony had answered it. "I was expecting you tonight," he said.

"Oh?"

"We've gotten another body that I think belongs to your killer."

"Where did he leave his mark this time?" Brodie asked.

Tony just looked at him, ignoring the question. "You still doing the show?" he asked.

"Yep."

"I saw that the cast included a Mac Brodie. That's you, I'm assuming. Not much of an alias," Tony said.

"None of the other actors actually know me. Being Mac Brodie instead of Brodie McKay works all right—if anyone looks me up, the captain has made sure that they'll find my online résumé and all the right information. Makes it easier if someone who does know me calls me either Mac or Brodie."

Tony mused on that for a minute. "You're not the only one going by a stage name, are you? I noticed a Jack Hunter in the credits."

Brodie shrugged. "You're right—that's Hunter Jackson. Obviously the cast and crew know who he really is—they're just sworn to secrecy."

"So he *is* the well-known director?"

"Yes. The play is his baby, really. He found the script and decided to produce it, then sell the film rights. The play was written by a friend of his, our stage manager. Name's Joe Carrie. Nice guy, about forty—and definitely human."

"So you don't think he's our murderer?" Tony asked.

Brodie shook his head. "No, and there's no proof the killer's even involved with the play itself. He could just be a theater buff. But the play does seem a solid place to start, at least. So, anyway, what makes you think our killer is responsible for this corpse?"

"Exsanguination, for one thing."

Tony was an interesting guy; he looked like what you would expect a werewolf to look like in human form. He was big and muscular, with broad shoulders and an equally broad chest. He had a head full of thick, curly light brown hair, and when he was on vacation, he grew a beard that would do Santa proud.

"And?"

"There's never anything obvious about the marks he leaves behind, but this time it looks like they're on the thigh. This is one clever vampire. He makes sure that he disposes of the bodies in a way that will lead to the most decay and deterioration in the shortest time."

"Want to show me the body?" Brodie asked.

"I thought you'd never ask."

Tony led the way down the hall to one of the autopsy rooms.

It was a large room, big enough for several autopsies to take place at one time. Now, however, the room was quiet and dim, and only a single body lay on a gurney on the far side of the room.

Strange, Brodie thought. He was Elven, although the Elven were pretty damned close to human in a lot of ways, maybe more human than they wanted to be. And he was a detective, often working undercover in some of the grittiest neighborhoods of a tough town where bluebloods crossed paths with derelict drug dealers. But despite both those things, he'd never gotten over the strange sensations that nearly overwhelmed him at an autopsy. Life—flesh and blood—reduced to sterile equipment and the smell of chemicals on the air. The organs that sustained life ripped from the body to be held and weighed and studied. It was just somehow...wrong, despite the fact that the work done here was some of the most important that could be done for the dead and the living both.

Tony pulled down the sheet that covered the victim, and Brodie stared first at the face, his jaw hardening.

"You've seen him before?"

Brodie nodded. "It's hard to tell, really, the body is so decomposed. But I think I recognize him. I think he was at the first performance of the show."

"Any idea who he is?" Tony asked.

"No, he was just a face in the crowd. Second row center. Have you gotten a hit off dental records? What about fingerprints?"

"Look at the hands," Tony told him, pulling the sheet down farther.

Brodie did, and he felt his stomach lurch sharply, even though he'd expected the scene that met his eyes.

The killer had chopped off the fingers.

Tony nodded toward the body. "Just like the other two. And here's what I found—you'll need that magnifier there." He pointed.

Brodie picked up the small magnifying glass that Tony had indicated, then walked down to join Tony by the foot of the gurney. Tony slipped on gloves and moved the thigh. The skin was mottled and bruised looking.

"No lividity?" Brodie asked.

"The discoloration and bloating you see are because he was dumped in a pond out by one of those housing projects they never finished off Laurel Canyon—suspiciously near your theater," Tony said. "But use the magnifying glass and check out his thigh. There are marks. They're tiny, and they're practically buried in swollen flesh, but they're there. And, of course, the body was pretty much drained of blood. There *is* a slash at the throat, but despite the damage and decay, I believe it was postmortem."

Despite his feelings about autopsy and corpses, Brodie donned gloves, shifted the dead man's leg and peered through the microscope, searching for the telltale marks, then looked up at Tony.

"Third body in two weeks with the same marks and same method of disposal," Tony said.

"And I *know* I've seen this one at the theater," Brodie said wearily.

"And the killer dumped them all close to that theater," Tony told him. "Your captain seems to have been on the mark."

Brodie nodded. "Yeah, without his insight the victims might have fallen on to the big pile of cold cases, with no leads to go on. The captain is…a smart guy."

"Guess that means you stay undercover," Tony said. "Too bad L.A.'s three best Keepers have been called to council. This is one hell of a mess."

Brodie thought about the stunning young auburn-haired woman with the big green eyes he had seen at the café. She'd rushed to what she thought was a crime scene like a bat out of hell. She'd been ready, he thought. But she wasn't ready *enough*. She loved her music too much. In a way, he understood. It was difficult to realize that you could—*had to*—lead a normal life, then let it all go to hell when necessary.

He wished to hell that Piers Gryffald, Rhiannon's

father and the previous Keeper of the Canyon vampires, was still there.

But he wasn't.

And the body count was rising.

Driving in L.A. was not like driving in Savannah. People in Savannah moved at a far more *human* pace. Everyone in L.A. was in a hurry, which seemed strange, because often they were hurrying just to go sit in a coffee shop and while away their time, hoping to make the right connection. Some hopefuls still believed that they could be "discovered" in an ice cream parlor, and God knew, in Hollywood, anything could happen, even if the statistics weren't in their favor.

At least coming home—to the house that had been her old summer home and was now her permanent base—was appealing. She had to admit, she loved the exquisite old property where she lived with Sailor and Barrie. Each of them had her own house on the estate—the compound, really—that had been left to their grandfather, Rhys Gryffald, by the great Merlin, magician extraordinaire, real name Ivan Schwartz.

Somehow during his younger years, Merlin had

learned about the Keepers. He'd longed to be one, but only those born in the bloodline, born with the telltale birthmark indicating what they were destined to become—werewolf Keeper, vampire Keeper, shapeshifter Keeper and so on—could inherit the role. Since he couldn't *be* a Keeper, Ivan did the next best thing: he befriended one. In fact, he had become such good friends with Rhiannon's grandfather that he had first built him a house on the property, opposite the guesthouse that already existed, and then, on his death, Merlin had willed the entire compound to him.

Good old Ivan. He had loved them all so much that he had never actually left.

The House of the Rising Sun, the main house, loomed above her as she drove along the canyon road, and she had to admit, it was magnificent. It wasn't as if she hadn't known the house all her life. Her grandparents had three sons—her father and her two uncles—and her dad had been mentored by a Keeper in Savannah, which had turned out to be a very good thing, since he'd fallen in love with her mother, a musical director for a Savannah theater. But then he'd returned to L.A. and assumed responsibility for the Canyon vampires—and she shouldn't have had to take over for another zillion years, give or take. She had grown up in Savannah, where her mother had kept her job, and her father had traveled back and forth on a regular basis. Despite the distance, her parents enjoyed one of the best marriages she had ever seen. And she'd grown close with her L.A. family, because she'd spent summers and most holidays there at the House of the Rising Sun. Sailor had always lived in the House of the Rising Sun itself, except for her acting stint in New York.

Barrie was now in Gwydion's Cave, the house Merlin had built for their grandfather, and she herself had the original 1920s guesthouse, called Pandora's Box.

Pandora's Box. A fitting name for all of L.A. in her opinion.

The main house really was beautiful! Regal, haunting and majestic, high up on a cliff. The style was Mediterranean Gothic, and it seemed to hold a thousand secrets as it stood proud against the night sky.

As a matter of fact, it *did* hold a thousand secrets. All right, maybe not *a thousand,* but a lot of them. Like the tunnels that connected all three houses. And the little red buttons that looked like light switches and were set randomly around the three houses. Little red buttons that set off alarms in all three residences, in case someone in any one of them needed help.

The property could only be reached via a winding driveway that scaled the cliff face, and the entire property was protected by a tall stone wall. She had to open the massive electric gate with a remote she kept in her car or else buzz in and hope someone was home to answer.

Grudgingly, she had to admit that she loved the House of the Rising Sun and living on the estate wasn't any kind of punishment. It was still breathtaking to watch the gate swing wide to allow entry to the compound, and then awe inspiring to see the beautiful stone facades of the houses appear.

Sometimes she wondered why Merlin had bothered with the wall. The Others that the Keepers were assigned to watch weren't the type to be stopped by walls or gates. But then again, Merlin had lived in the real world with its real dangers, too, as did they—although calling the surreal world of Hollywood "real" seemed like a contradiction in terms.

She clicked the gate shut behind her and drove forward slowly, noting that Barrie's car was parked on the left side of the property, while Sailor's, unsurprisingly, was not. Since there was no garage—all the available land had been used for the houses—she assumed that if Sailor's car wasn't there, neither was Sailor herself. Barrie was determined to save the world, not only by overseeing the shapeshifters but also by practicing the kind of hard-hitting journalism that could bring about change in L.A., if not the world, so, she tended to keep reasonable hours. Sailor, Keeper of the Elven, was determined to rule the world from the silver screen, which meant she was likely to be out and networking at all hours.

Still thinking about the way the Elven had handed her his card and told her that she *should* see the play, Rhiannon pulled into her usual parking place and exited the car, bringing her guitar with her as she headed for Pandora's Box. Slipping her key into the lock, she shoved a shoulder wearily against the door, stepped in and flicked on the lights.

She was tired. And she worked in a café, for God's sake. She should have brought home a gourmet tea to sip while she unwound, but after only a few minutes with Mac Brodie she had been too disconcerted to think of it.

She set her guitar case in its stand and headed into the kitchen. There she quickly brewed a cup of tea and added a touch of milk, then headed back out to the living room to sink into the comfortable old sofa and lean back. She closed her eyes.

"No, you really should *come see the show...."*

There was a tap at her door. She listened for a minute without rising. She was tired. And frustrated. And, she had to admit, unnerved.

An Elven had come to her and told her that she needed to see a vampire play.

Why?

It was just a play, a pretense. No vampires were out there killing people. Or other vampires, or anyone else. If they were, she would have heard about it on the news, wouldn't she?

The tapping became more persistent. Rhiannon forced herself to rise. It could only be one of a very few people at this time of night. Maybe Sailor had come home early and might listen to the story of Rhiannon's night and give her some advice.

It wasn't Sailor or even Barrie who stood at her

door. Merlin had come by to visit. "I hope I'm not disturbing you?" he asked anxiously.

Yes, you are, she almost said, but she refrained. Merlin was a ghost. If he wanted to, he could be anywhere—perched on the end of the grand piano in the living room, day and night, if he felt like it. But he was a polite ghost, one who had learned to manifest corporeally. He had mastered the art of knocking on doors to announce his presence and behaved at all times as if he was not only living but a gentleman. He had maintained his old room in the main house, and he was careful to be the best possible "tenant." They all loved him, but Sailor, in particular, was accustomed to living with him— both before and after his death.

They had all sobbed at his funeral—until they realized that he was standing right there with them, comforting them in his new and unearthly form.

"Come in, Merlin, please," she said. "Have a seat. My home is your home, you know. Literally," she added with a warm smile.

Merlin had always been so good to her family, and it had been a two-way street. Her grandfather had saved him from jail when a shapeshifter had impersonated him and perpetrated several lewd crimes while posing as the noted magician. Her grandfather had been the shapeshifter Keeper and had worked with a friend on the police force—a werewolf—to prove that someone had been impersonating Merlin, and ensure that the proper person was caught and punished.

She stepped back from the door, sweeping a hand wide to indicate that he should join her.

Merlin stepped inside, looked around and sighed with happiness. "I'm so glad that you girls are living here," he told her.

He walked to the sofa and sank onto it, looking like a dignified and slightly weary old man. Which was exactly what he had been when he'd died. He'd lived a good, long life that had left him with a charmingly lined face, bright blue eyes and a cap of snow-white hair. Having him around really was like having a grandfather on the property.

"And we're glad to be here," Rhiannon said.

What a liar she was, she thought. She'd been about to get her big break when she'd been called home and been told that she was an adult and the good times were over. Her responsibilities had crashed down upon her with no time for her to think about it, to say yes or no. Suddenly all three

Gryffald brothers were being sent overseas and their daughters were taking their places, and that was that.

Of course her father and her uncles hadn't been given a chance to say yes or no any more than she and Sailor and Barrie had.

The brothers had been summoned to serve on the new high council of Keepers at the Hague, a council that would act as a worldwide governing body for the Otherworld and the Others.

"Are you fitting in okay?" Merlin asked her, sincere concern in his voice.

"Of course." She forced a smile. None of this was Merlin's fault. Or her father's. He'd tried to be so fierce when he'd talked to her. *You are the Keeper for the vampires, Rhiannon. They are powerful and deadly, and yours is a grave responsibility.*

At the time, of course, all she'd seen was that her band was finally getting a real break—and she wasn't going to be there to experience it.

Merlin nodded thoughtfully. "I was just wondering…I mean, this *is* L.A. It's not as if there isn't plenty of murder, mayhem and scandal on a purely human level."

"Merlin, what are you talking about?" she asked wearily.

"You might want to talk to Barrie. There have been a few mysterious deaths lately."

Something hard seemed to fall to the pit of her stomach. This couldn't involve her. Not already.

"Mysterious deaths?" she asked.

Merlin nodded. "They haven't gotten a lot of coverage, because none of them have been on one of those trashy reality shows or even made Hollywood's D list. These poor people have gone from this world unnoticed and unknown."

"Like you said—this *is* L.A.," Rhiannon said, frowning.

"Well, speak to your cousin, because she's got contacts who have told her a few things. There have been three similar deaths, and all three corpses were discovered in a similarly advanced state of decay."

"And?" She whispered the word, as if that could keep her fears from becoming real.

"The cops have been trying to keep the details out of the papers, but someone leaked one important fact," Merlin told her grimly.

"And that fact is…?" she asked.

He winced. "I'm sorry, Rhiannon. The corpses were almost bone dry, sucked dry of…"

"Of?" she asked, even though in her heart she knew the answer.

"Blood," Merlin said gravely. "Sucked dry of blood."

still days. She knew she wouldn't sleep if she

Chapter 2

To a lot of people in L.A., it wasn't all that late.

But to Rhiannon, after her wretched shift at the café, nothing sounded more welcome than her bed and a pillow.

Still, she knew she wouldn't sleep if she didn't try to talk to Barrie, though with any luck Barrie would already be in bed and wouldn't answer the knock at her door.

To Rhiannon's dismay, Barrie was up.

A single light was on in Barrie's living room, where she had been sitting on her sofa and working. Her laptop was sitting on a pile of newspapers and magazines.

Barrie definitely tended to be a workaholic.

She had a good job in her chosen field, but she still wasn't where she wanted to be in her career. At the moment she mostly got stories that ran under headlines—often handed to her whether she liked them or not—like "West Hollywood Woman Reveals Secret Behind Amazing Weight Loss."

Barrie was a crusader; she had strong opinions on right and wrong. She wanted to be where the action was. She wanted to get off the crime beat and into issue-based investigative journalism, but her Keeper duties would always have to take precedence, and that was a problem.

Rhiannon sympathized with her. She knew how difficult it was, trying to have a real career and deal with this sudden shift in purpose.

"Hey, I didn't expect to see you tonight." Barrie grinned and rolled her eyes. "Merlin, maybe—sometimes he forgets the time. Thought you'd come home exhausted and ready to crash."

"Am I interrupting?" Rhiannon asked her.

"No. Yes—but it's all right, honestly." She sighed. "I'm trying to come up with a story and an angle no one's thought of yet, so I can take it to my boss and maybe—finally—get a green light."

"Good luck," Rhiannon offered.

"So, how did things go at the café tonight?"

"They sucked. Totally sucked. Some actors staged a vampire attack right out front to publicize their play and nearly gave me heart failure—and in all the fuss my tip jar was stolen."

"You're right. That sucks. Want a cup of tea?"

"I just had one, but sure," Rhiannon said.

Barrie led the way into the kitchen.

All three of their houses might have been curio museums, filled as they were with Merlin's collections from a lifetime of loving magic—and the bizarre. The main house held the bulk of it, because it was so large, with five bedrooms upstairs, a grand living room and a family room that led out to the pool. Tiffany lamps were everywhere, along with Edwardian furniture, and busts and statues, and paintings that covered the walls. Pandora's Box had a Victorian feel, with rich, almost stuffy furniture, and a collection of sculpted birds, with the largest being a magnificent gesso rendition of Poe's raven. It also boasted a few of Merlin's old coin-drop fortune-teller machines.

Gwydion's Cave, Barrie's house, was decorated with old peacock fans, marble sideboards and rich wood pieces from the decadent days of the speak-easy. The service she used for tea was Royal Doulton. As she entered the kitchen, Rhiannon caught sight of herself in one of the antique hall mirrors, and though she knew it was distorted by the old glass, her own image troubled her.

She had the shocked look of someone who had stuck a finger in a live socket.

Barrie hummed as she boiled water and then looked at Rhiannon. "Something more happened than what you're telling me, didn't it? I always think of you as the go-getter among us. Nothing fazes you. But tonight you look…fazed."

"What if that attack had been real? Would I actually have been able to do anything to stop it? I guess we didn't think we'd be handling this kind of thing so quickly," Rhiannon said.

"None of us did. But it's not like we had a choice."

"I know. I just want to play my music, you know? It's all I've ever wanted. I missed my shot with the band, but at least I get to play at the café, you know? And that's what I was doing when those idiots interrupted."

"Listen to you, being so whiny."

"Whiny?" Rhiannon protested indignantly.

"Yes, whiny. 'Everybody but me gets to play in the band, while I'm stuck in a coffee shop playing for tips.' Buck up, buttercup."

"All right, all right, I have been whining. A little bit. But, honestly, I just wish…I wish we'd been a little better prepared. I mean, my dad is in great health. I never thought…"

"You never thought you'd have to be a Keeper until you were old and gray. I know. Neither did I. But here we are. So, what else is bothering you? Because I know there's something."

"All right, I came here to tell you, so…one of the actors was an Elven. I saw him when I was closing up my guitar case for the night. He came up to me and chatted, and I—I wasn't exactly rude, but I felt like he was comparing me to my dad and it bugged me. You know that Keepers all over the state put us down all the time. 'The Gryffald girls. What a shame their fathers were *all* put on the council. There used to be *good* Keepers in the Canyon.' So I guess I was a little rude. But really, I don't want to get all warm and cozy with the Elven—I'm going to have my hands full with the vampires."

"I understand all that," Barrie said calmly. "So, why are you so upset?"

"Well, he invited me to see his show. Like I want to see some ridiculous play about a bunch of vampire attacks. I brushed him off. But he knew who I was, and he said, 'No, no, you really *should* see the show,' or something weird like that, and when I got home…" She paused for breath.

"When you got home?" Barrie prompted.

"Merlin dropped in on me. And he told me that I should speak to you—that there have been three recent murders in L.A.—"

"Only three?" Barrie interjected drily.

"Three in which the bodies have been found drained of blood and decayed and…I don't know. Merlin just said to talk to you."

"Oh," Barrie said.

"Oh?" Rhiannon repeated. "Come on, Barrie. You must know something. You work at a newspaper, for God's sake."

"You know all they give me is fluff," Barrie reminded her.

"Yes, but you're there and you must hear things."

"I don't remember anything that sensational, but maybe the police are keeping the details quiet. I do remember hearing about a John Doe found in a lake near some half-built apartment complex. That might have been one of your victims. I'll see what I can find out," she promised. "So—when are you going to see the show?"

"Now that Merlin's talked to me? Tomorrow night," Rhiannon told her, then sighed. "Hugh told me not to be late tomorrow night. He's going to give me a buttload of grief, not to mention dock my pay."

"Tell him you can't be there—that you have Keeper duties and that's it. I've seen you in action. You're great fighting other people's wars—fight this one for yourself. For all three of us," Barrie added. "We have to prove ourselves. You might as well start tomorrow night with Hugh."

As Barrie poured hot water into the teapot, they heard the sound of a car door slamming. "Sailor's home," she commented.

"So she is."

"I'll get another cup."

Rhiannon walked to the door and opened it just as Sailor was about to knock.

"Hi," her cousin said.

Sailor spoke with a cheerful voice and had a

perfect smile to go with it. Rhiannon thought that while they were all decent looking, Sailor was their true beauty. It made sense that she was so passionate about being an actress. She had both the talent and the looks.

Maybe it had to do with the fact that Sailor had been destined to be Keeper of the Canyon Elven. Elven were beautiful, Rhiannon reminded herself drily, thinking of Mac Brodie.

Guilt bit into her. Several times she'd caught herself feeling impatient with Sailor for not taking their calling seriously, but hadn't she wanted to deny it herself? And now she was facing her first real challenge—because even if the murders proved to have nothing to do with the Canyon vampire community, standing up to Hugh was going to be no picnic—and all she wanted was to run away.

"I saw the light, so I thought I'd stop by," Sailor said.

"Come on in," Rhiannon said.

Sailor swept past her and headed straight for the kitchen. "I had a great night—I mean a *great* night. I went to this fantastic party at the club—Declan Wainwright's club, the Snake Pit."

Declan Wainwright was the shapeshifter Keeper

for the Malibu area. They'd known him forever, though Rhiannon wasn't sure she would actually call him a friend.

"Declan told me he was going to ask you to play there a few nights a week. Well, he didn't tell *me*. He's kind of an ass to me. I'm not A-list enough for him, so mostly he ignores me. But I was with Darius Simonides, and he told Darius that he was going to talk to you. Pretty great, huh?"

"It's nice that you spent some time with Darius," Rhiannon said, filing away the potential offer of employment to consider later. Darius Simonides was Sailor's godfather and a big-deal Hollywood agent, but as far as Rhiannon could tell, he hadn't done much for her. At least not professionally. There was also something…slimy about him, she thought. Maybe it was because he was so…Hollywood. In his line of business, double-talk was really the only talk. Maybe that was at the heart of her reaction to him, but she still didn't trust him.

"Not only that, we hung with Hunter Jackson, too—do you know who he is?"

"Hunter Jackson," Rhiannon repeated, trying to

remember why he sounded so familiar. "I've heard the name," she said.

"He's a director," Barrie said.

"He's *the* director these days, and he says that he has a role for me in a big-budget vampire thriller he's going to start filming in January. He and Darius actually invited me to the Snake Pit tonight to talk to me about it." Sailor beamed. "And it turns out there's a reason why Darius has kept his hands off me."

"That's good to hear," Barrie muttered sarcastically.

"I mean as far as my career goes," Sailor said. "Darius is a sweetie—people just think he's tough because he's so powerful. The thing is, he wanted me to make my own way, to prove I could succeed on my own before he stepped in. But tonight—it was wonderful!" Sailor looked rapturous. She drew a breath, and Rhiannon was sure she was going to go on some more about her amazing night, but instead she said, "Barrie, you have artificial sweetener, don't you? I don't want to gain an ounce right now."

Rhiannon decided that she would once again

have to rethink Sailor's role in ensuring the safety of the world.

"I have everything I can think of for anyone's choice in tea," Barrie said. "Dig into the cabinet and help yourself."

"So, tell me more," Rhiannon said, genuinely happy for her cousin and momentarily putting aside her fears for the fate of the world.

Sailor turned to her, beaming. "The two leads will be major A-list actors. I don't know who yet. But what I'll make for just a few days' work will pay my bills for months."

Rhiannon lowered her head. At least one of them would be making a decent income, though if what Sailor had said about the offer to play the Snake Pit was true, she would be earning some real money, too, even if Hugh got mad enough to fire her. She looked up quickly, frowning. "Hunter Jackson... I remember reading something about him." She looked at Sailor. "He's a vampire, right? But he's the responsibility of the West Hollywood Keeper, Geoff Banner."

"Yes," Barrie said. "And he's the perfect person to direct a vampire thriller. The movies always have it wrong. Like all that crap about how vampires can't go out during the day."

"Seriously," Rhiannon agreed. "But no one wants to hear that the only problem is their eyes are exceptionally sensitive to light, so they always wear sunglasses—something that seems to be expected in Hollywood, anyway." She met Sailor's eyes. "You did know that he's a vampire, right?"

Sailor stared at her, indignant. "Of course I did. I'm the one who really grew up here, remember? I know the lowdown on almost everyone. Am I supposed to suddenly be suspicious of him because he's a vampire? And of all people who might be down on vampires, it shouldn't be you!"

"I'm not down on vampires," Rhiannon said quickly.

"Then what's your problem?" Sailor asked.

"I just wanted to make sure you knew what you were dealing with, that's all," Rhiannon said.

Sailor looked at her as if she knew Rhiannon doubted her abilities—and her competence in the face of a crisis. "Yes, I am well aware, thank you. And if you come across any Elven, I hope you'll try to be a little less judgmental."

Failed that one, Rhiannon thought. But she kept silent.

"Hey!" Barrie said, lifting a hand. "I get that we're all a little jittery right now, with our new responsibilities and all, but it's important that we get along. The world respected our fathers, but we're going to have to prove ourselves. And that will be a lot easier if we respect each other."

"Yes, you're right," Rhiannon said softly.

"There's nothing to prove, at least not right now," Sailor said. "Thanks to our dads, everything in the Canyon is running smoothly." She turned to Rhiannon. "Can't you just be happy for me?" she asked.

"I'm sorry. I *am* happy for you," Rhiannon said. She hugged Sailor, who resisted for a moment then eased up and hugged Rhiannon in return. "I'm sorry. It was a bad night for me," Rhiannon said.

"Her tip jar was stolen," Barrie explained. "Among other things."

"Those bastards stole your tip jar!" Sailor said, straightening, her protest loyal and fierce.

"It's all right," Rhiannon said. "I'll live." She an arm around Sailor's shoulders. "We need to go home. Barrie has an early morning, as usual." She turned to her other cousin. "Night, Barrie, thanks for listening."

"Hey, wait," Barrie said, following Rhiannon and Sailor to the door. "Rhiannon, I'll see what I can dig up tomorrow. And also, I was thinking that Sailor and I should go see that play with you."

"You don't have to," Rhiannon said.

"Play?" Sailor said, perking up. "What play?"

"Vampire Rampage," Rhiannon said.

To Rhiannon's surprise, Sailor's jaw dropped. "You're kidding, right?"

"No, not at all. They pulled a promo stunt in front of the coffee shop tonight."

Sailor's eyes were wide. "The movie—the one I've been asked to be in—is called *Vampire Rampage,* and it's based on the play. Yes, let's all go. It will really help me to see the original."

"And to think, I was just hoping it might keep someone alive," Rhiannon said.

Sailor turned slowly and stared at her. "What's going on?" she asked.

"An Elven actor stopped by the café tonight, and he told me that I really need to see the play. And then Merlin told me tonight that three murder victims have been found drained of blood. So now I'm kind of worried that a vampire, well, you know…."

Sailor stared at Rhiannon for a long moment, and then reached out and pulled her into a hug. "Oh, I am so sorry! You know…maybe someone has been itching to break the rules and waited until our fathers were gone, figuring that—"

"We'd be ineffectual," Rhiannon said wearily.

Barrie and Sailor were silent.

"Well, I don't intend to be ineffectual," Rhiannon said. "So tomorrow night, the three of us, the theater…"

"We'll be ready," Sailor assured her. "It will be great."

"All I can think about is three bodies drained of blood—and I've barely been here a week," Rhiannon said.

"We'll get through this. We'll help you get the answers," Barrie said. "Right, Sailor?"

"Right," Sailor agreed.

Rhiannon left Gwydion's Cave and headed back to her own house. The moon was out, shining down and creating a crystal trail across the surface of the pool.

Three bodies drained of blood.

Tomorrow she would get out her dad's list of helpful contacts in the city. She had to get into the morgue and see what she could find out, and then, tomorrow night, the play.

"Vampire Rampage," she murmured.

She reached into her pocket and fingered the business card the Elven had given her, then pulled it out and looked at it. *Mac Brodie, Actor.* And then it offered a cell phone number. It was curious that an actor's card didn't have his website and résumé listed.

She thought about calling him, then decided to wait until she'd seen the show. She might be a novice Keeper, but she was going to have to be strong and prove that she could be as effective as her father.

Because she was very afraid that there was already a vampire on the rampage in L.A.

Brodie sat at his desk at the station, reading over the files on his desk.

The first body had been discovered three weeks ago at the bottom of the molding pool at an abandoned house off Hollywood and Vine—the owner had gone into foreclosure and no enterprising real estate mogul had as yet snapped up the place. The victim, who was in his twenties, remained unidentified, despite the fact that they'd combed through missing person reports from across the country. Of course, he'd been missing his fingers and though the morgue had taken dental impressions, they were worthless when there were no records with which to compare them.

The dead man must have had friends or family somewhere, but apparently none of them had reported him missing. Then again, young people often took off to "find themselves," so their nearest and dearest didn't always know they were missing.

Because of the fetid water where the body had been dumped, the soft tissue had been in an advanced state of decomposition. Despite the mess he'd had to work with, Tony Brandt's report stated that he'd tentatively identified the puncture marks at the throat that had led to exsanguination, which he listed as cause of death. Because the body had been in the water and then in the morgue for several weeks—and because it was a John Doe—the case had ended up at the bottom of a pile of open cases that had gone cold.

There was one interesting fact, though. A waterlogged playbill had been discovered in his pocket.

Ten days ago, with the discovery of the second body, two files had landed on Brodie's desk. His captain was concerned. The second file contained another John Doe. This one had been found in a small man-made lake in Los Feliz—near a rehearsal hall that had been rented to a local theatrical group, the same group now performing *Vampire Rampage*. Once again dental impressions had been taken, and they were still hoping to make a match. Also once again, no fingerprint identification was possible because there were no fingers.

That body had also been decaying for some time. It was in fact so decayed that Tony Brandt could only find the suggestion of puncture marks in the jugular vein. But the similarities had been enough for Brodie's captain to decide that the two murders might be the work of a serial killer, and that it was time to get to the truth.

Captain Edwin Riley knew something about the Others and the Otherworld. He was one of the few individuals trusted by the city's Other community, being the son of a practicing Wiccan and high priestess who'd been targeted for death. Brodie didn't really know the whole story, and the captain didn't like talking about it, so he didn't pry. But it had something to do with a religious cult that had decided his parents were devil worshippers, and that they needed to have an accident—one that would remove them from the earth.

They'd survived the accident, thanks to Brodie's father, then a young Elven, who had seen what was happening and jumped from his own car in time to rescue the Rileys' car before their car went over a cliff.

Most human beings had no idea about the existence of the Others, but the captain knew about Brodie, which made him the logical choice to find out what was happening.

The next thing he knew, he was auditioning. There had been an opening in the cast because an actor had suddenly and, from the cops' point of view conveniently, left, sending Jackson Hunter an email stating that he had to get back to Connecticut and stop the love of his life from marrying another man.

It had seemed a weak link—joining the play— but it was better than nothing, and the theater was the only connection, however vague, between the murders. He'd been suspicious that the missing actor might be one of the John Does in the morgue cooler, but Adam Lansky, in the police tech assistance unit, had tracked him down, and he was indeed back in Connecticut. Whether he'd stopped the love of his life from marrying another man or not, Brodie didn't know.

Tonight, after seeing the third corpse on Tony Brandt's autopsy table, he was more convinced than ever that the killer was somehow involved with the play. Not only had the corpse been found in the lake that was just past the parking lot and a stretch of overgrown brush behind the theater, but there was the fact that he'd actually seen the man in the audience.

Three John Does, all of them connected in one way or another to the theater and *Vampire Rampage*. And, he was very much afraid, to a real vampire, too.

All right after the three strongest peacekeepers in the area had left.

And in their place…

Three untested…girls.

Brodie stood and walked to the rear of his bungalow apartment in central Hollywood. He could see the crescent moon rising boldly in the clear heavens. He tried to tell himself that the fact that the bodies had been drained did not definitely mean that the killer was a vampire. The victims might have been drained so that their deaths *appeared* to be the work of a vampire. And God knew, there were plenty of crazy humans who *thought* they were vampires. And there were dozens of reasons for draining a body of blood, starting with…

Hunger.

Like it or not, he had the feeling that a vampire was guilty.

All he had to do was find him—and kill him.

Obviously he couldn't count on any help from the new Keeper, Ms. Rhiannon Gryffald, and yet the case definitely fell under her jurisdiction. He'd given her his card, damn it, and she hadn't even bothered to call him. Okay, so she didn't now he was a cop. But still, she should have realized that something important was up—something she, as a Keeper, needed to investigate.

He gritted his teeth, wondering just how many corpses they would find before the killer was unmasked.

Chapter 3

Rhiannon wasn't as close to Darius Simonides as Sailor was, but their families had always been involved, so she was confident enough to head for his office late the next morning, despite the fact that she had no real idea of what she was about to say. She hadn't seen him since she'd come to town to take over her father's duties, so she could just chat, of course, and hope something useful came out of it.

Darius was a powerhouse; his offices were chrome and glass, impeccably modern. Head shots of his A-list clients covered the walls, along with movie posters. Artistic little Greek columns held statues of movie scenes. The offices were elegant, as they should be. Darius had earned his reputation.

She made her way past the guard on the first floor and up the broad marble staircase to the second floor, aware that security cameras followed her all the way. When she reached Darius's office she was stopped by his secretary. She smiled when she saw the woman; she had known Mary Bickly from the time she'd been a child. Mary was no-nonsense. She had iron-gray hair and a manner to match. No one saw Darius unless she chose to let them in.

"Well, hello there, Rhiannon," Mary said, rising and coming around her large desk, her arms outstretched for a hug. Rhiannon quickly accepted. "Welcome. I understand that you and your cousin Barrie have moved to Los Angeles. It was quite bizarre, the way your families all moved to Europe. Did they go back to Wales?"

"No, no, my father and his brothers were always close, and I guess they just decided that they'd tour Europe together. My dad has always been fascinated by the Hague, so that's where they're spending most of their time." Not only was Mary human, but she had no idea that Darius was a vampire. It was amazing, really, that the Others were so heavily represented in L.A., and yet most of them managed to remain completely below the radar.

"Well, I know that Darius misses your father and his brothers, but I'm sure he'll be delighted to see you. He's in a meeting right now, if you can wait a few minutes? Would you like some coffee, dear?"

"I don't mind waiting, and you needn't bother—" Rhiannon began.

"No bother. The little pod maker thing is right there, on the shelf. Go help yourself."

"Thanks."

Rhiannon walked over and selected something that promised to be "bold and eye-opening, the best breakfast blend." As she played with the coffee-maker, the inner door to Darius's sanctum opened. She turned quickly, and to her surprise she saw not just Darius and Declan Wainwright, but one of the men who had destroyed her evening at the Magic Café. Jack Hunter, she remembered. Aka "Drago." And right behind them, another man. Mac Brodie.

Darius saw her just as Declan did, and both men offered her broad, welcoming smiles.

Jack Hunter stared at her curiously, as if he felt he should know her but didn't.

Nice to be remembered, she thought, then caught

Mac's eyes. From his expression it was obvious that he, at least, definitely remembered her.

And the way he looked at her...

She was surprised to feel heat burning inside her. He unsettled her. Well, he was Elven, of course. But she should have been immune, and it annoyed her that she wasn't. Despite that annoyance, she felt her pulse thudding, the blood rising in her throat.

"Rhiannon! Sailor was saying that you and Barrie had moved to L.A.," Darius said, striding toward her, arms open wide. He was a little over six feet, a striking man with sharp hazel eyes, dark, slightly graying hair and an air of power that was unconsciously seductive. She had no idea how old he was; he definitely retained a dignified sexual appeal, but his face bore the character of centuries.

"Yes, Darius, we're both living on the estate. I was hoping that I might see you, just quickly, because I know you're incredibly busy." She turned to Declan and said, "I got your email this morning, and I'd love to play the club on weekends."

Darius introduced Mac next.

"No need for introductions, Darius. Ms. Gryffald and I met last night. In fact, we had a brief but very…interesting conversation." He met her eyes. "I do hope you'll think about what I said."

"Certainly. I'm weighing its importance," she said pleasantly.

"I think—for you—the importance could be high," he said.

He spoke lightly, but she felt his eyes on hers in a way that made her uncomfortable. Afraid that if he looked for too long he would read far too much, she quickly lowered her gaze.

He turned away to address the other men.

"I hate to meet and run, but if you'll excuse me, I have to be somewhere." He nodded curtly at Rhiannon then. "I meant what I said last night, as well as just now. Think about it."

And then, with a wave, he was gone. Rhiannon stared at his retreating back, feeling a bit as if she'd just been run over by a very attractive truck, then realized the men looked as stunned as she felt by his abrupt departure.

Darius shook his head as if recalling himself to the present and turned to Jack Hunter

"Hunter Jackson, meet a very dear friend of mine, Rhiannon Gryffald," he said. "Jack is adapting a fantastic vampire play for the screen. Rhiannon, Hunter Jackson."

Hunter took her hand and smiled at her, his eyes bright with amusement. "It took me a moment to recognize you, but we almost met last night. I must say, Ms. Gryffald, you're a courageous young woman. Everyone else was screeching and screaming, and you rushed out like Joan of Arc on a mission."

The others laughed. Rhiannon forced a smile, not feeling the least bit amused.

"I believe you were introduced last night as Jack Hunter," she said, frowning, not the least bit impressed that she was meeting the illustrious director Hunter Jackson. Sailor was going to be thrilled, though.

"You've unmasked me, Darius," Jackson said, then turned back to Rhiannon. "Like a lot of directors, I started off with an acting career, and I decided to direct and star in the stage version of the show myself. A little bit of ego going on there, I'm afraid."

"You should be careful with your promo stunts, Mr. Jackson," she said. "I'm just a musician. What if there had been a cop there last night and he'd pulled a gun on you?"

"It's not likely, Ms. Gryffald," Hunter said, and shrugged. "This is Hollywood. The cops usually know a show from the real thing." He looked at Darius and laughed. "So I take it that *this* charming Miss Gryffald is *not* looking for a career on the big screen?"

Darius shook his head. "Musician, as she said."

Hunter turned back to Rhiannon, grinning. "Good for you. Because—my ego speaking again, I'm afraid—aspiring actresses always feel the need to suck up to me, and it can get pretty tiresome."

She forced a pleasant smile. "I'm sure that when you choose a star for one of your productions, you base your choice on talent and not just because she sucked up to you."

"Such a diplomat," Hunter said, but he was laughing.

Rhiannon realized that she ought to be nice to the man; she wanted to know why one of his actors had insisted that she come to the show. She managed to keep her smile in place. "My cousins and I are going to see the show tonight," she told him.

"That's great. Is one of the cousins you're referring to Sailor Gryffald?" Hunter asked.

She nodded.

"I'm glad. She'll get a good feel for the material by seeing the play. It's not just a horror story. It's about the many different kinds of hunger that can drive us, even ruin our lives, and about what we're willing to do for love. Of course," he said thoughtfully, "it's about redemption, as well."

"It sounds interesting," Rhiannon said.

"It's a musical," Darius said. "You're going to love it, Rhiannon."

Declan smiled. "They're going to film some scenes at the Snake Pit," he said.

She nodded, trying very hard to keep a pleasant smile glued to her lips. She might have accepted a job offer from the man, but she didn't trust shapeshifters. They were pranksters. And when they went bad, their ability to shift into any guise meant major trouble. Their Keepers could be just as... shifty, and Declan definitely was.

"Sounds just great," she finally said, knowing how lame she sounded.

"Gotta go," Declan said. "I'll see you Friday night?"

"Yes, thank you."

He shook hands with the other men and started toward the stairs. As he was leaving, Hunter said, "Well, I'd best be on my way, too, Darius. Ms. Gryf-fald…a pleasure. And please, come see me back-stage tonight. I'd love your opinion on the show."

"I'm not really a theater expert, but I'd be de-lighted to see you after the show," she said.

"Any audience member is an excellent theatrical judge," he said. "I'll see you later." He gave them both a wave and left.

Darius looked at Rhiannon assessingly, and she could see that he was well aware that she hadn't just dropped in on him for a casual chat.

"Shall we enter the inner sanctum, my dear?" he asked.

She nodded. "Thanks."

Mary had returned to her desk while the others talked, but she spoke up then. "Darius, shall I hold your calls?"

"Yes, please, Mary," Darius said. "Thank you."

Rhiannon grabbed her coffee and followed Dar-ius into his office. It was huge, with massive win-dows that looked out over the city. In addition to the requisite designer chairs in front of a chrome and glass desk, the room boasted a comfortable sofa against a wall, a full stereo and wide-screen system and a wet bar. There was also a bathroom—all chrome and glass and marble. Darius easily could have lived there and sometimes did, despite the fact that he had a fabulous mansion in the Hollywood Hills.

"Drink?" he asked her.

"I've got coffee. I'm fine," she told him.

"I'll help myself, then," he said.

He reached into his refrigerator, which was filled with his "specials." Mary didn't fill his refrigerator; his assistant, Rob Cantor, took care of that chore. His specials looked like Bloody Marys, but they would have gagged a vegetarian. His blood came from a meatpacking plant he owned in west Texas.

"Sit," he told her, taking his own chair behind the desk, easing back and planting his feet on the shiny surface. "You doing okay?" he asked her once she'd taken a seat.

"I'm all right, yes, thanks," she told him.

"You can't be all right if you're here to see me so soon. What's the problem?" He took a sip from his glass, sighed and seemed to sink back farther in sensual delight.

"I saw a piece of the play last night, Darius. Your friends staged it right in front of the Mystic Café."

"How is that old dog Hugh Hammond?" Darius asked, laughing at his own joke.

"As growly as ever," Rhiannon assured him.

Darius enjoyed that. He didn't reply, but his easy smile deepened. He took another sip of blood and then looked at her. "And…?"

"Your play—or movie," she said.

He frowned. "What about it?"

"Darius, it's about a vampire on a killing spree," she said.

"Oh, please!" Darius said. He was clearly irritated. He swung his feet down and stared at her hard across the desk. "What? I'm going to stop the world from making vampire movies?"

Rhiannon drew a deep breath. "It's come to my attention, Darius, that three bodies have turned up in the area, drained of blood."

He arched a brow. "Really?"

"Really."

"Then you're not doing a very good job, are you?" he asked her.

She froze but refused to let him see her reaction in her expression. Instead, she leaned closer, staring at him. "The first body appeared before I ever arrived, Darius, and the second when I had just gotten here. But now there's a third."

"Then I suggest you bring it up at the local council meeting," he told her. "I haven't heard anything about this."

She didn't know that much herself yet, but she decided to fake it. "It sounds like a serial killer—a vampire serial killer—is at work."

"How dramatic, Rhiannon. Maybe you *should* have gone into acting," he said. "Bodies drained of blood. If you're accusing me of covering up for someone—which you had best not be—remember that I've been making my way by playing the human game for a very long time now. I love my life, and I'm not about to jeopardize it. If I did know of any suspicious vampires, I'd let you know. But I don't. Period."

"I didn't accuse you of anything," she said.

He continued to eye her suspiciously. "Did you come to me for help?"

"Yes, I suppose I did."

That, at least, mollified him.

"You still need to bring it up at the council meeting," he told her. "But I think it's pretty unlikely that a vampire's really behind this. I'm not the only one out here who is extremely happy. We make movies. We have a great supply of blood—I bring a lot of it in from my home state, where people are always lined up to donate—booze and women. We live in peace out here. All of us, not just the vampires. I know a dozen gorgeous Elven who are big successes in this business—I get them roles, they make me money. Wcrewolves, shifters and all the rest…things work for them here in L.A. This is a city where we get along."

"It's also a city where lots of people don't make it," she reminded him. "Waitresses remain waitresses. Valets remain valets."

He lifted a hand. "I still don't see it, Rhiannon. I really don't." He leaned toward her. "What makes you think the murders have some connection to the play?"

"I never said they did," Rhiannon said. That was true; she hadn't said any such thing. She had suggested that both the play and movie might be in bad taste—for a vampire, at least—but that was all.

Suddenly she didn't want to tell him about Mac

Brodie's insistence that she see the show. She wasn't sure why. Maybe because it seemed that Darius, like everyone else, didn't have any faith in her. Maybe it was because the two men knew each other, and until she knew how well, she didn't want to take chances.

And on top of that, she was a *Keeper*.

Which meant, for the time, as she felt her way forward and dealt with situations as they were thrust upon her, she was going to learn to *keep* things to herself.

She rose, determined not to make an enemy. "Darius, thank you. I'm glad I can look to you for help. I *will* bring this up at the council meeting."

"It's going to be your first," he told her. "I'll be happy to introduce you."

"Thanks."

"Thursday at midnight, the old church off Bertram," he told her.

"I'll be early," she promised.

He escorted her out of his office, giving her a hug. Moments later she found herself out on the street, wondering what to do next.

The answer was obvious. It was time to pay a visit to a werewolf.

* * *

Dr. Anthony Brandt arrived in the reception area of the morgue in his clean white coat.

He smiled when he saw Rhiannon, as if he were actually happy to see her. "Well, look who's come to see me," he said, then gave her with a hug she was sure was intended for the benefit of the receptionist. She knew Tony—she'd known him since she was a child. He thought she was spoiled and had felt free to tell her parents so on occasion.

"It's so nice to finally see you, Tony," she said, her tone filled with artificial warmth. "You could have called me, you know."

"Well, I was thinking that you'd just arrived, that you were busy," he said.

As in, too busy to do what you should have been doing—being a good Keeper!

"I'm here now," she said.

"Well, then, come on back to my office," he told her. "Sign in first, though. You'll need a visitor's pass."

She got her pass and then followed him down the hallway.

His office was neat—sparse, actually. His desk held his computer and a stack of files, bookshelves lined two walls, while a single window looked out on the city. L.A. and life were all around him, but Tony lived in the realm of the dead.

"Have a seat," he told her.

He'd closed the door as they entered. She took a chair in front of the desk and leaned forward. "Don't go giving me that superior-than-thou look. I just got to town. If there was a problem and you knew about it, it was your responsibility to tell me. I shouldn't have had to rely on the grapevine to tell me about these murders—and the condition of the bodies." She stared challengingly at him. "You would have called my father."

He was quiet for a minute. "Yeah, I would have," he said quietly.

"Tony, I know you're a werewolf and you don't officially owe me anything, but can't you help me— the way you always helped my father?"

He looked a little abashed. "All right, Rhiannon, I'm sorry."

"Thank you. I'm learning, Tony. I can use all the help I can get."

He lifted the files on his desk and riffled through them, then produced three and handed them to her.

"John Does, all of them. We can't get IDs on any of them."

"Did you find anything on the bodies? Any DNA from the killer? What about the bites? Any saliva?" Rhiannon asked.

"You know as well as I do that if they were bitten by a vampire, there would be no DNA. Vampire DNA disintegrates almost instantly. But, beyond that, all the bodies were found submerged in water and massively decomposed."

"No fibers, tickets, wallets, anything?"

"Totally empty pockets. All I know for sure is that they were bitten and exsanguinated."

"Is that what you put on the death certificates?" Rhiannon asked him.

He shook his head, indicating the reports. "The bodies *were* drained of blood, but due to the condition in which they were found, I couldn't determine an absolute cause of death. In fact, the really strange thing is that there was water in the lungs, so it's a crapshoot as to whether they drowned or died from blood loss, but whatever happened probably happened in the water. Or maybe they were just this side of dead when the killer tossed them in the water. No way to know, really."

"You're sure you found puncture marks?" Rhiannon asked, flipping through the files. There was information the police had given the medical examiners, and there were outlines of the male bodies, with notations and drawings. She looked back up at him. "It looks like they were tiny...you'd think that they'd be obvious. Vampire marks aren't usually as tiny as pinpricks."

"The fact that the flesh was so swollen around would have compressed them and made them harder to see. Still, there's nothing usual about these cases."

"I'm assuming you have a contact in the department?" she said.

"I have a lot of police contacts, but I don't think they'd appreciate my sharing their names. For now, you've got what you need to go on, so don't go barging into the station, telling one and all that you're the new vampire Keeper—especially since most of the bodies look like vampire victims."

Rhiannon had never actually ever been in a morgue in her life; even coming into the reception area had seemed difficult. Now...

You're at the morgue, she told herself. *This is what you're supposed to be doing, seeing the dead.*

She rose and followed Tony, who led her to a chilly room holding what appeared to be massive file cabinets, except that she knew they weren't. Each drawer contained one of the county's dead—those who still needed an autopsy, and those who were waiting....

To be claimed? Or because they were unclaimed? Either way, it was sad.

She slipped into the white gown, mask and gloves Tony handed her, despite the fact that she had no intention of touching the bodies. She tried to appear professional.

But, no matter what her resolve, she wasn't ready for what she saw when he opened the first drawer.

The body was recognizable as human, but just barely.

"John Doe number one," Tony said. "He's our oldest, dead about a month. As you can see, the decomp is very bad. And, as you can also see, his fingers are missing."

Rhiannon willed herself not to gag. Despite the mask and the chemical smells in the air, the scent of decomposition was overwhelming. The flesh appeared absolutely putrid. His eyeballs were missing, and the flesh of his face was so puffed up that she couldn't have recognized anyone in such a state—even her own mother.

"The fingers...were they eaten by some creature? Or maybe they...rotted off?" she asked.

He shook his head. "There are telltale signs that a blade was used to remove them."

"So no one could make an ID?" she asked.

"It certainly makes it impossible to search the fingerprint database," he said.

She swallowed hard. "This seems like the work of a madman."

Tony looked around, but they were alone. "Or a hungry vampire, breaking the rules, attacking humans and trying to remain anonymous by making sure we can't ID the victims and connect them to him."

She stared into his eyes. "Yes, the killer *could* be a vampire. But it's far from certain. Do you have anything else to show me?"

Tony reached out and turned the head. "Here, right here. As the report said, they're tiny and surrounded by swelling, but the puncture marks are here. Now let's move on to John Doe number two."

He shut the drawer and didn't even glance her way as he led her to the next. The second body was in no better shape. Again he showed her what he had determined to be puncture marks and pointed out the missing fingers. The third body was the worst. He swept the sheet all the way down to show her the thighs, and at that point she thought she was going to black out or at least vomit.

Somehow she managed not to do either.

"Alcohol? Drugs? Had they been doing anything prior to their deaths? Stomach contents? Can their last meals be traced?" she asked.

Tony looked at her for a moment, then nodded. "All three men had been drinking. They were just above the legal limit, for whatever that's worth. I'm afraid that their last meals had been well digested, suggesting that they'd been drinking rather than eating during their final excursions into the wilds of the L.A. nightlife. Or day life. I don't have a time of death—I can't even guarantee a *day* of death. Water is vicious on human remains. And it's summer, so…" His voice trailed off.

Rhiannon silently willed him to close the last drawer. He did so, and then walked her back out to the hallway, where she dropped her lab coat, mask and gloves into the appropriate disposal bins.

She hadn't needed the gloves. She'd known she wouldn't.

She could still smell the terrible stench of death. She steeled herself against it. Had the hall smelled so strongly when she had arrived, or was the scent engrained in her forever?

"No poisons in the tox screens, right? You would have told me," she said.

"Nothing our screens have detected so far."

"Thank you, Tony," she said stiffly.

He nodded. "I'll let you know if…anything happens. And you'll return the favor?"

"Of course," she told him.

"Where are you going from here?" he asked her.

"To prepare for a night at the theater. I'm going to see a new vampire play. One of the actors told me I should see it." She tried not to think about how much she was actually looking forward to seeing Mac Brodie again—no matter how hard she tried to convince herself she didn't care. "And then I found out about the bodies."

"Yes, Rhiannon," he said after a moment, "I believe you *should* go to the theater. I think it will be a very enlightening evening for you."

Chapter 4

Brodie stood by the lake that lay about a hundred and fifty yards behind the theater. He knew that if he turned and faced the theater he would see a service station to the left, beyond the parking lot. To the right there was a warehouse. The lake itself was man-made. It had been dredged to build the housing project on the other side; however, the contractors had apparently run out of funds. The entire shore was overgrown, the lake itself green with alga, and, as twilight fell, the scene was forlorn.

He had already walked the area, carefully surveying the ground, but any clues that might have been left behind were long gone.

But he hadn't come to see if the crime scene unit had missed anything; he had come to figure out why the perpetrator had chosen this location.

The killer had method. He drained his victims of blood, then discarded the bodies in water, which washed away any biological evidence, making it impossible for the M.E. to tell if the punctures had been inflicted by the fangs of a vampire or a sharp, probably metal, object of some kind.

All three locations where the bodies had been found were lonely, derelict—perfect for leaving a body without being seen, and with a reasonable expectation that it wouldn't be found for days or weeks, if ever.

It chafed Brodie no end to realize that he'd been working at the theater when the last victim had been dumped.

Frustrated, he hunkered down and skipped a stone across the lake. He had no leads. The bodies were giving them nothing—not even identities. The crime scenes had been cleansed by nature long before any first-on-scene officer could examine them.

The only possible connection between the victims and their killer was the play. He thanked whatever stroke of luck had led to the role being open just when he needed it. His natural Elven abilities had seen to it that he'd landed it without any trouble.

In his mind, his abilities made him a good cop. Unlike so many of his kind, he'd never yearned for the stage; he'd longed to keep order. He hated realizing that he and so many Others would be loathed and feared if their true natures were known by the general populace. He believed in equality, and that meant he believed in the law, as well, not to mention simple decency. Everyone deserved respect, the right to live, to seek happiness and to enjoy the freedom to follow their dreams.

He turned away from the lake. He wasn't particularly fond of water. Elven were creatures of the earth. They didn't melt or anything, but they hadn't populated the new world until the airplane had been invented—they couldn't be away from solid ground for the time it took an ocean liner to make it across the Atlantic. They lost strength and eventually died if they didn't feel the power of the earth beneath their feet.

He glanced at his watch. It was almost his call time, and he prided himself on never being late. He made a point of talking with his cast mates every night, though so far his investigation hadn't netted him anything. He hadn't been sure about the connection to the play at first, but now he was. Instinct, perhaps. Which meant he had to be close to someone who at least knew what was going on—even if they didn't know they knew.

As he reached the cast entrance, he noticed that an old Volvo had pulled into the parking lot. Three women emerged.

The Gryffald cousins had arrived.

He was pleasantly surprised. Rhiannon hadn't called him, but at least she was coming to see the play.

He watched Rhiannon Gryffald as she stood by the driver's door, surveying the area. Her eyes were on the lake. She didn't see him as she studied the water.

She'd found out, he thought. She knew bodies had been found drained of blood. And she knew *where* they had been found; he could tell from the way she was looking at the water.

Yes, she definitely knew. Which meant she *definitely* hadn't come to see *him*. Damn it.

Intrigued, he stood by the rear door for a moment. He recognized Sailor Gryffald, of course. She'd grown up in L.A. and had often accompanied her father when he'd met with the Elven elders. She was an actress.

He hoped that she wouldn't recognize him, though of course she would know that he was Elven. Her interest in being a Keeper had been minimal when he had last seen her, so hopefully she hadn't paid any attention to him.

He smiled, taking a moment's pride in his people. She was the Elven Keeper, so by definition she possessed a bit of Elven charm. She didn't seem to have a passion for her hereditary responsibilities, but maybe that didn't matter so much. The Elven tended to be peaceful. They brooked no interference and could fight when drawn into battle, but they tended to live according to a philosophy of "Do as you will but harm no others." It was unlikely that she was going to have to solve a massive Elven crime spree.

Barrie Gryffald was now the Keeper of the shapeshifters. They were mischief-makers, and if any race was prone to misbehavior, it was them. But from what he knew, Barrie was a serious young woman, dedicated to becoming an investigative reporter.

For a moment he swept his concerns about the situation and the Gryffald cousins from his mind. They were all standing together, looking out at the stagnant lake. They were close to one another in height, and they all had varying shades of the same sleek hair. They looked like three Muses as they stood there, young, still naive and hopeful, and beautiful.

And, he feared, ineffectual.

He opened the stage door and came face-to-face with Bobby Conche, the tall, leanly muscled shape-shifter who'd been hired to take care of security. Bobby was from the Malibu area and fell under the jurisdiction of Declan Wainwright. He loved the theater, but as a fan, not a participant. He loved to guard the stage door, because it meant he got to see new productions in rehearsal. He knew, of course, that Brodie was Elven.

He didn't know he was cop.

"Hey, Bobby, thanks. I think I have some friends coming tonight. Three young women, the Gryffald—"

"Yeah, yeah, the Gryffald girls, the new Keepers," Bobby said, and grinned at Brodie. "Glad I'm with the Malibu pack—takes new Keepers a while to learn the ropes, you know?" Bobby nodded. "I'll make sure they find their way to you."

"Thanks," Brodie told him, then left to start getting ready for that night's performance.

Mac Brodie was a good actor. Damn him.

Not that Rhiannon had really expected anything else. Elven were known for their ability to charm—and to make others see them as they chose to be seen.

Vampire Rampage took place in modern London, but it was a riff on Bram Stoker's *Dracula*. It opened in a sea of mist, and then a car appeared. Mac Brodie, as Vince Anderson, stepped out, along with Lena Ashbury, who was playing a character named Lucy. They were lost in Transylvania, seeking her old family home, while on an extended honeymoon, and poor Lucy—who had dreamed of finding her distant cousins—was now terrified. Their rental car had died; the sound of wolves howling filled the air with a plaintive and spooky symphony. The writing was good, the dialogue occasionally funny as Lucy dreamed of the Transylva-

nian Automobile Association coming to the rescue.
And then the fog thinned, revealing lights in the
darkness, and they headed off to the house they
saw in the distance.

The house was, of course, Drago's ancestral
castle, where they were greeted there by Nickolai
Drago and his household, which included an eerie
butler and several sinfully sexual maids, all the
action accompanied by a winning combination of
dialogue and duets. Drago was charming, assuring Lucy that he would help her find her relatives
in the morning, then having the newlyweds shown
to a room. Later that night, however, Lucy rose
and wandered downstairs to Drago's lair, where
he proceeded to turn on his supernatural charm.
Meanwhile, two of the sexy maids—Rhiannon recognized the actresses she'd seen outside the Mystic
Café—broke in on Vince and attempted to seduce
him. Rhiannon found her attention riveted on him
with an intensity she couldn't fight as he escaped
his would-be seducers and broke in on Drago and
his wife. The audience was left to wonder if the
vampire's teeth had or hadn't sunk into Lucy's lily-
white throat.

In the morning Vince tried to convince his

wife, who had no memory of the night's events, that they had to get away, because there was something evil afoot in the castle. Lucy, however, was clearly under Drago's spell, and refused to leave. That night Vince lay awake and waited, and when he heard the howling of the wolves in the forest, he saw Lucy awaken as if in response to their call. He followed her downstairs and managed to get her out of the castle without running into Drago, who was waiting with fangs bared. Vince dragged her through the forest, until they finally came upon an inn, where they were welcomed and warned that those who go to the castle were usually never seen again. Lucy met her long-lost cousins, who warned her that she had to be vigilant and avoid Drago and his castle at all costs.

Rhiannon tried to think why Mac had been so insistent that she see the show, because while she'd certainly enjoyed it—and him—she hadn't found anything so far that seemed relevant to the murders. Of course, maybe the problem was that she had been paying too much attention to Mac and not enough to the play.

There was a fifteen-minute intermission. As Rhiannon rose, she noticed that Sailor was still staring at the stage.

Her cousin looked up at her, rapt. "Isn't he magnificent?" She lowered her voice. "Imagine, Hunter Jackson playing Jack Hunter playing Drago. I can't believe the press hasn't pointed that out yet. I mean, someone besides me must have recognized him."

"I'm sure he'll be recognized once the show finishes previews and the reviewers descend. It's probably all part of his plan to start a major buzz about the whole project. He wants huge box office numbers when the movie opens. Clever, really," Rhiannon admitted.

"I am beyond excited. I'm going to be playing Erika, the upstairs maid."

"I wonder how the current upstairs maid feels," Barrie said drily.

"They're not using any of this cast for the movie," Sailor explained. "The show is going to keep running while the movie is being made. They're expecting to open on Broadway and hoping for a long run. After that, touring companies, if all goes well. It's not as if any of this cast will be out of a job."

"Still," Rhiannon said, "I wonder how they

feel about not even getting the chance to be in the movie."

Sailor sniffed. "Well, certainly not angry enough to go around killing innocent strangers as if they were real vampires," she said. "They're working. In Hollywood, if you're not waiting on tables, you're a success."

A few minutes later, out in the lobby after Sailor decided she wanted a glass of wine, Rhiannon idly scanned the crowd. She was startled to see that Declan Wainwright was there. He must have known that he was going to be there that night when he'd seen her at Darius's office, but he hadn't said a word.

Not that he looked as if he really wanted to be found. He, too, seemed to be watching the audience members as they milled around, but unlike her, he was leaning against a support wall, mostly hidden from view.

Declan was a shifter Keeper, and he'd worked hard to take on the abilities of his charges. With enough concentration, he was capable of shifting. If he really hadn't wanted to be seen, he could have come to the show as anyone.

He could even have come as the proverbial fly on the wall.

Of course, shifting was taxing and exhausting. Maybe he was just here because he had an interest in the show. But why hadn't he mentioned that he was coming?

He hadn't seen her, so she walked up behind him and cleared her throat.

He whirled around in surprise. For a moment he looked disconcerted. Then he smiled. "Ah, there you are. I was looking for you and your cousins. How are you enjoying the play?"

"I love it. The songs are excellent," she said. "I didn't know that you were coming tonight."

He grinned at her. "I didn't know if I'd make it or not. The Snake Pit doesn't get busy 'til late, but I lost a manager a few weeks ago, and if I don't have someone I can trust going in to open, I don't like to be away. But I found someone to handle it, so I'm here to get a feel for how they're going to be using the club when they film there." He shrugged. "I'm hoping the film's a big hit. We do extremely well, but it's a fickle world. One day the lines are out the door. The next day you've been dropped for the newest thing down on Sunset or Vine."

Rhiannon smiled. "Declan, the Snake Pit has a built-in clientele."

It did, of course. Otherworld denizens flocked there by the dozens—especially vampires, who really liked the nightlife.

Declan shrugged. "I know. But I have to say, it would be pretty cool to be as well known as the Viper Room."

"Maybe not, given the deaths associated with it."

He waved a hand dismissively. "Death happens everywhere, Rhiannon. You must be aware of that. Deaths don't happen because of clubs, they happen because people—and Others—can get out of control." The lights began to flicker, indicating that intermission was over. "It's always good to see you, Rhiannon," he said, inclining his head slightly.

There was something old world about him, she realized. And she was lucky, getting a chance to perform at the Snake Pit. Not only was it a well-known venue, but it had after-hours and then it had *after-hours.* The club was a success in the world at large—and in the Otherworld, as well.

He turned and walked back into the theater. Rhiannon walked back toward the snack bar, but her cousins were gone. She quickly returned to her seat, just in time for the lights to go down once again.

Act II brought Vince and Lucy back to L.A., where they returned to their jobs in Hollywood, Lucy in animation and Vince in casting. Vince believed they'd gotten away clean, but shortly after their return he was visited at work by one of Drago's maids, and then another maid turned up as a barista in his favorite coffee shop. He realized that Drago was not far behind.

In the next scene the vampire arrived at Lucy's studio looking for work as a sketch artist. Vince found out when he showed up to take her home and saw sketches of characters that looked like Drago—and Lucy. Afraid, he called on an old friend—Dr. Van Helsing—who told him about vampires and explained that there was only one way to save Lucy from Drago.

The customary climax brought a twist. Vince had allowed himself to be infected by the vampire barista in order to fight Drago. Van Helsing met them in a Hollywood wax museum's chamber of horrors with a priest in tow, and Drago was put down. The scene ended with Vince and Lucy happy and still together—although they both had to adjust to a new lifestyle, since they'd both become vampires. Hand in hand, they headed off to a blood bank, starving after their exertions.

The finale had Drago rising again after the couple had departed, and he had a fantastic solo number—before dining on one of the policemen left to guard the "crime" scene.

Rhiannon didn't think it was the best show she'd ever seen—and she still wasn't sure what deeper meaning she'd been meant to discover—but it had certainly been entertaining.

The audience rose to give the cast a standing ovation, and she politely rose, as well. She noticed that Sailor was still staring at the stage as if hypnotized. "Hey," she said, and nudged her cousin. "It's over."

"Oh, my God, I'm in love with it," Sailor breathed.

"It did have a few twists," Barrie commented.

"There was a lot that was the usual," Rhiannon said. *And,* she thought, *a lot that could only have been written by an Other, someone aware of what was and wasn't real. Vampires didn't need to wait for night to come out, and while they—like everyone in California—enjoyed sunglasses, they weren't blinded by the sun. They could sleep pretty much*

*wherever they wanted—after all, you couldn't get
dirt from a mausoleum.*

*Perhaps those were the points Mac had wanted
her to notice? But why?*

"I can't believe I'm going to be in the movie!"
Sailor said, still wide-eyed with awe.

"Let's head backstage," Rhiannon said.

"Can we?" Barrie asked.

"I don't see why not," Rhiannon said. "After all,
I was practically ordered to be here."

They walked out the front door and around to
the stage entrance. Rhiannon felt someone walk up
and slip an arm through hers. Startled, she turned
to see that Declan Wainwright had joined them.

He gave her a grin and a shrug. "Safety in numbers," he told her.

She arched a brow at him but couldn't resist the
blatant attempt to make her smile. "Sure, safety in
numbers."

Declan turned to greet Sailor and Barrie, but his
tone was merely polite, as if he had no real interest
in them. Barrie nodded and said hello in return, but
Sailor actually gritted her teeth and turned away.

At the stage door, Declan spoke to the guard,
greeting him familiarly. "Hey, Bobby."

"Hey, Mr. Wainwright," the guard said. He was tall, fairly young and muscular. He smiled—clearly he knew Declan well—and Rhiannon realized he was a shapeshifter.

"Bobby Conche is with the Coastal shifters," Declan said softly, introducing them. Given that she was now a shifter Keeper, it made sense that Bobby stared at Barrie longest. He grinned. "Welcome, ladies," he said. "Just walk on in."

They walked along a hallway that ran parallel to the stage and stood to one side to wait, their eyes on the dressing room doors.

A moment later Mac Brodie came around a corner. His face was scrubbed clean of stage makeup, and his golden hair was still slightly damp. He walked toward her. "Miss Gryffald, I'm delighted to see that you took me up on my invitation. And these lovely ladies must be your cousins, Sailor and Barrie."

"Yes, Sailor, Barrie, please meet Mac Brodie. And of course you know Declan."

"Of course," Mac said, smiling and shaking Declan's hand. Their eyes met and seemed to convey an unspoken message, which disturbed Rhiannon.

They knew something she didn't. Exasperating! How could she work when everyone kept secrets from her?

"Nice to see you here. And, Barrie, Sailor—a pleasure," Mac said. "So, what did you think?"

"I thought everyone was wonderful," Sailor said. "Especially Drago." She frowned slightly. "Do I know you?" she asked him.

"I hope you feel that you do—that's the ultimate compliment for an actor," Mac said.

"Really?" she asked.

"So I hear," he said, and shrugged.

"One thing amazes me," Sailor said, then lowered her voice to a whisper. "I had no idea that Mr. Jackson was playing the role himself."

"He's a multitalented man," Mac said. "Come on, I'm sure you want to tell him yourself how much you enjoyed the show. And he'll be delighted to hear it. We're having a bit of a celebration tonight, because things are coming together so well. You can meet everyone."

He led them down the hall to a door marked Jack Hunter/Mac Brodie. Mac opened the door, and they entered.

The entire cast was there, everyone in civilian

clothes. Hunter Jackson was seated in front of his dressing table, and the others were gathered around him. Champagne was flowing, and hors d'oeuvre trays covered every available surface. Hunter was laughing up at Audrey Fleur, the brunette playing Erika. Kate Delaney, the blonde who played Jeneka, was chatting with the actor who had portrayed the innkeeper. "Lucy," real name Lena Ashbury, was chatting with the actress who had played the innkeeper's wife. The buzz in the room didn't stop when they entered; apparently this group was ready to party with any and all comers.

"I've got to talk to Hunter," Sailor said, and walked over to the director.

Kate, bearing three glasses of champagne, walked over and welcomed them, then handed glasses to Rhiannon and Barrie, and then Declan. "Mac, you can grab your own champagne. And you must all be friends of Mac. Oh, wait! I know who you are," she gushed to Declan. "I've seen your face in the paper. You're Declan Wainwright, and you own the Snake Pit."

"Guilty," he said.

"Now I wish I was going to be in the movie," Kate said, smiling.

She made a good vamp, Rhiannon thought. Vamp, in the old-school sense, not vampire. The woman was definitely human.

Declan introduced the women, and Kate continued playing hostess.

"So nice to meet you, Barrie, Rhiannon," she said, and smiled, lifting her champagne glass, a slight knot of confusion tightening her brow as she asked Rhiannon, "Are you, um, with Mac?"

Mac, who had gone to get some champagne, slipped close to Rhiannon's side. "Yes," he said, before she could protest.

Rhiannon got the impression that Kate wasn't pleased by his answer. She wondered if Mac had ever given the woman any reason to feel proprietary, then reminded herself that Elven had a talent for engaging people on a sensual level even without intending to. And when they *did* intend to... Well, they were extremely sexual beings, and the numbers of them that now populated L.A. bore witness to that fact.

"I've seen *you* before, too," Kate said. "Somewhere."

"Rhiannon sings at the Mystic Café," Mac explained.

"I've never actually been in there," Kate said. Then, having decided that Mac was interested in Rhiannon, so there was no point making a play for him, she turned to Declan. "Of course, I *have* been to the Snake Pit," she enthused.

"I'm going to introduce Rhiannon to the rest of the cast," Mac said to Declan as Barrie wandered off to check out the canapés. Once again Rhiannon had the uncomfortable feeling that the two men were sharing information she wasn't privy to.

"What the hell is going on here?" Rhiannon demanded as they walked away, standing on tiptoe and whispering in his ear. She steadied herself with a hand on his shoulder and was annoyed by the jolt of lightning that seemed to sweep through her as she touched him. *Elven!* She hated knowing he had that kind of power over her. She wanted to snatch her hand away, but he caught it, and Elven were strong. She couldn't have pulled free without creating a scene.

He leaned down and whispered back, his lips close to her ear, "Not the time to ask." His tone carried a warning.

"I want answers," she said.

He told her softly, "Smile. Kiss my cheek. I'm

trying to buy you entry around here as the woman I'm seeing. Go with it."

She kissed his cheek. Her lips felt as if they were on fire.

Worse.

She felt *hungry*.

"Ah, the lovely Rhiannon," Hunter said. "So—I said I wanted your opinion. What did you think?"

"I particularly loved the musical numbers," she told him honestly.

"I thought you might," he said. "And?"

"I like the twist at the end, too. I think you're going to be a success on stage *and* on screen," she told him. That was honest, too. A show didn't have to be brilliant to make it big; it just needed the right ingredients. Hunter Jackson would see that this one did.

Rhiannon felt someone close behind her.

Vampire.

She turned. Audrey Fleur was standing there. She smiled at Rhiannon, then dipped her head in acknowledgment that Rhiannon was a Keeper.

"Hi," Audrey said cheerfully.

"Hi, I'm Rhiannon—"

"Gryffald. I know. I just met your cousins. It's

great that you came to the show. Mac brought you, of course."

"Yes, good old Mac," Rhiannon said, and shot him a look to be sure he didn't miss her meaning. "I didn't know that you would be having a celebration."

"I'm sure that's why he brought you and your cousins tonight," Audrey said. She clinked her champagne glass against Rhiannon's. "This is our last night of previews. It's a big deal for us. We're crowing with delight—except for Mac. He acts like it's just another day's work for him."

Mac shrugged. "I just know the game, Audrey. One day you're hot, one day you're not." He smiled to take any sting out of the words. "Now, if you'll excuse us, I want to show Rhiannon around the theater."

She smiled, far too aware of him slipping his arm through hers as he led her out of the dressing room and toward the back of the theater.

"Where are you taking me?" she asked him.

"First, to meet Joe Carrie. The playwright. He's out onstage."

"Shouldn't he be at the party?"

"He should, but Joe's a funny guy. Kind of quiet, not a big party animal."

He took her hand and led her along a narrow passageway and out onto the stage. "Joe?" he called.

There was a man onstage, pad in hand, talking to several others about where to reset props for the next performance.

He was tall, dark and probably about forty-five.

When he turned to look at Rhiannon, she knew. *Vampire.*

"Joe, meet Rhiannon Gryffald. Rhiannon, our playwright and stage manager, Joe Carrie."

Joe Carrie immediately stopped what he was doing, a broad smile on his face. He came forward and shook Rhiannon's hand enthusiastically. He looked around and lowered his voice. "Piers Gryffald's daughter? Great to meet you. You're the new Keeper for the Canyon vampires, aren't you?"

"Yes, and it's great to meet you, as well," she said.

"What did you think?" he asked anxiously. "Factually speaking, I mean. Bram Stoker didn't have it so wrong, really. Most of all, did you have a good time tonight?"

"Yes, of course, I especially love the musical numbers," she said.

He beamed. "Thank you!"

"Rhiannon's a singer, so I thought you two should meet," Mac said. "I'm going to show her around a bit more now, Joe."

"Enjoy," Joe said, still smiling.

"Where to now?" Rhiannon asked as Mac led her away.

"Outside," he said.

She didn't know why she felt such a sudden surge of dread.

Yes, she did. She knew she was going to hear more about the murders.

She wanted desperately to get away from him. Maybe it was because he had way too much of the legendary Elven charm, and she was afraid that when he told her bad news she was going to curl up against him in the hope that he could somehow make all the bad stuff go away.

"You coming back?" Bobby asked when they reached the door.

"We'll be back before the party breaks up, I promise," Mac assured him.

"Where are we going?" she asked again as he

practically dragged her toward the rear of the parking lot—and the lake beyond. She was going to be strong, she decided. Strong as befit the Keeper he didn't think she had the capability of being. And *he* needed to know that she was strong, as well. "You do realize that I have the ability to wrench someone's head off if I need to, right?"

He paused at that. She didn't think he'd meant to be rough—Elven were just over endowed with strength as well as charm. She found herself being spun around to face him and read incredulity in his eyes.

"You think I intended to *hurt* you?" he demanded. "Why, you...brat! I'm trying to *help* you, you little idiot. This is your jurisdiction—you should have stopped this!"

"This? You mean the murders? Yes, this is my jurisdiction—and has been for a whole week, which means the killer started working before I even got here, not to mention that he chose victims who wouldn't be missed and was careful to hide his crimes. And you know what else? If you knew what was going on, you could have called me. You know, picked up a phone, introduced yourself and explained that there was a matter that required my attention. And what's it to *you,* anyway? You're an Elven. Do you know who one of the victims is or something? Have you lost a friend, a fellow actor... what? Don't you dare get mad and put me down when you have me running around in circles for simple information!"

"First off, Miss Gryffald, I don't have any information on who the dead might be. And I didn't call you because we'd never met, and it was more important that you see the play, because I think the play and the murders are related, and that's why I'm even in the damned thing."

"What do you mean that's why you're in the damned thing?" Rhiannon demanded.

"I'm not an actor, Rhiannon. I'm a cop. My name is Brodie McKay, not Mac Brodie. I'm working undercover, and before my captain gets impatient with the fact that I haven't discovered a damned thing yet and brings in more cops who aren't part of the Other community, I could really use some help— from the vampire Keeper."

Rhiannon stared back at him, feeling like a fool.

He was a cop.

Working undercover.

He could have told her that earlier. Or that hairy

bastard of a medical examiner might have mentioned it. They were withholding information as if she didn't matter—and then getting mad when she didn't perform up to their standards.

She straightened her shoulders and smoothed down her wounded pride, dredging up her strength and determination. "Thank you for the information," she said, then stared at him for a long moment, shaking her head. "You're Elven, so why don't you just read minds until you find the connection?"

"Whoever is doing this knows how to be careful. It's almost impossible to get into the subconscious, and so far all I'm getting is people running lines and bitching because so-and-so has a bigger part. Most or maybe all of it is legit. If the killer *is* here, I'm being blocked," he told her. "I need the killer to slip up—and having the vampire Keeper actually involved just might provoke that."

"Well, the vampire Keeper might have been involved already if the cop had seen fit to tell her what was going on," she retorted.

Then she turned and started heading back to the theater, moving with as much dignity as she could manage.

"Hey!"

She didn't want to halt her perfect exit, but she did. Turning around sharply, she asked, "What?"

"I didn't bring you out here for a tryst. I thought you might like to see where the last victim was discovered," he told her, sounding weary.

"Is that going to help us at all?" she asked.

"I don't know. I'm not the vampire Keeper," he replied.

She walked back to him. At that moment she hated the crystalline hypnotic power of his eyes, eyes that so often seemed to mock her.

"No. It won't help me—certainly not at this point. If there was something to be discovered there, either the crime scene investigation unit or *you* would have found it by now. On the other hand, hearing the truth from everyone rather than being taunted will help a hell of a lot. If you don't have anything solid for me, excuse me. I'm going to go home and sort out the lies and omissions from the truth. Somehow I don't feel that I'm going to get any assistance with that from the people who should be helping me. Good night, Mac—or whoever the hell you really are."

This time she completed her exit, relieved to see

that Sailor and Barrie were already at the car. She unlocked it and slammed her way in.

Barrie might have questioned her mood, but Sailor was still going on and on about the play.

Rhiannon turned up the radio, but Sailor didn't notice. With the cacophony rising in her ears, Rhiannon drove as quickly as she safely could, fighting the urge to scream the whole way home.

Once she was home, Rhiannon headed up to bed, thoughts about the night swirling through her head. Brodie McKay was absolutely the most annoying man she had ever met.

He could have just told her right away that he was a cop. No—she had to meet him while he was pulling a ridiculous stunt in front of her place of work.

Her pillow took the brunt of her anger as she curled into bed, but her mind continued to race. Aggravated, she tossed and turned for hours. Then, somehow, she drifted into sleep.

Somewhere in her mind, darkness turned to a soft swirling silver mist, and in that mist, he was walking toward her.

He was shirtless. She groaned, longing to touch the sleek and shimmering contours of his well-muscled chest. He walked fluidly, a small smile curving his lips as he approached her. He was coming to taunt her, of course, to make a comment about her lack of prowess as a Keeper, to tell her...

But he didn't speak. When he stopped directly in front of her, she could feel the heat that emanated from him, could feel his breath.

He was Elven.

Perfect face, beautiful and yet masculine, with strong cheekbones and a stronger jaw, a full mouth, and those eyes of his...eyes that read her mind, delved into her soul.

Still without speaking, he lifted a hand and cupped her face, and she knew that when he looked into her eyes, he could tell that she was waiting, longing, for him to do more.

And then his lips touched hers. She could feel the sense of power and passion that lay beneath his gentle touch. Her arms lifted without conscious thought on her part and wound around his neck. The kiss deepened; it was simmering and liquid, and ignited a fire inside her.

And then he touched her, truly touched her.

His hands slid over her flesh, and their clothing was magically gone. She ran her fingers down the hard length of his back and over his buttocks as she felt him crushing her to him. The silver mist formed a bed, and they fell back on it together. He broke the kiss and straddled her, and his eyes continued to hold hers as he lowered himself again, capturing her mouth. His hands were amazing…Elven hands. They caressed her midriff, teased her breasts.

She arched toward him, trying to deepen the kiss, but he pulled away. Then his lips moved to her collarbone and her breasts, then lower still. She could barely breathe as he teased her in every imaginable and intimate way, until she was whispering his name, then crying it aloud as she threaded her fingers into his golden Elven hair and drew him back to her. At last they were making love, and she was twisting and writhing in awe and wonder, the world nothing but the heat and fire of the man in the silver mist….

She cried out.

And woke herself from her dream.

She realized she was lying alone in her bed and groaned out loud, humiliated—and desperately glad that she lived alone and that Merlin was far too polite to have glanced into her bedroom. Her cheeks burned with embarrassment—even though she was by herself.

She threw her pillow across the room.

"I hate Elven!" she announced to the empty air. "Hate them, hate them, hate them!"

She shuddered and glanced at the clock on her bedside table. 5:00 a.m.

What the hell. She rose, strode into the bathroom and took a very cold shower.

Chapter 5

Back at the station house, Brodie handed a copy of the full audition list for *Vampire Rampage* to Adam Lansky, one of the department's research techs.

The younger man looked at the size of it and then looked up at him. "And you want me to...?"

"I want you to track down the people on that list and make sure they're alive and well," Brodie told him.

Adam was the best at searching through the internet for clues, and he had figured out how to access almost every database imaginable. If there was a code, Adam could crack it. Brodie had long ago decided it was best if he didn't always know how Adam got his information.

"I don't even know who our victims are," Brodie told him. "Maybe this will help."

Adam frowned. "You think the dead men are actors who didn't make the cut? Maybe I haven't lived in L.A. long enough, but wouldn't a rejected actor want to kill an actor who *did* get into the play, not vice-versa?"

"I think," Brodie told him, "that the killer is involved with the play somehow. I think that he might have gotten to know some of the people on that list to find out who might not be missed for a long time. If we can go through the list and find out who's missing, I might be able to find out who the victims are, and if I can find out who they are I might have a chance of finding out who's killing them and stopping the violence before it escalates."

Adam nodded. "Any order? Alphabetical?"

"Start with the top page—the group that made the callbacks. The people who made the final cut had a greater chance of getting to know each other."

Adam nodded again. "I'm on it."

As Brodie headed back to his desk in Homicide he noticed that Bryce Edwards, an old werewolf working in vice now, was leading in a guest. A guest—not a detainee, since she was walking without benefit of handcuffs.

It was Rhiannon Gryffald. Visiting Edwards. Well, he should have suspected that she would find a way to circumvent him. Then again, maybe he hadn't gone about things in the right way or the right order. Maybe he felt more bitterness than he'd realized that all this was happening just when Piers Gryffald had gone off to join the World Council.

He watched as she went into Edwards's office. The old wolf was a lieutenant now. She sat in front of his desk in a tailored dress suit and appropriate heels, looking to all the world like some kind of a completely competent businesswoman.

Pain-in-the-ass Keeper!

As he watched, one of Edwards's men rushed in, staring at her with puppy-dog eyes. Brodie gathered that the man was asking if he could bring her something to drink, and Rhiannon, with one of her alluring smiles, was assuring him that she was just fine.

Should he walk on over? he asked himself. Or let her ask a vice detective what he knew about a string of murders?

Without giving himself time to question his decision, he walked into the office to join them. "Good morning."

"Hey, Brodie!" Edwards said, greeting him. "Come on in. You two should meet, if you haven't already. This is Rhiannon Gryffald, Piers Gryffald's daughter. Rhiannon, this is Brodie McKay, homicide."

Rhiannon stared at him. "Good to see you, Detective," she said.

"Good to see *you*, Miss Gryffald." He turned to Edwards. "We've met," he explained.

"This is the man you need to talk to," Edwards said. "Come on in, Brodie, come on in—and close the door." He kept speaking as Brodie complied. "We've had a long history of working together, you know," he began. "The police—and the Keepers. We need to maintain that tradition."

"I know," Brodie said. "And I think that Rhiannon and I are ready to continue that tradition now. At least, I hope so."

Rhiannon looked at him and nodded. "Thank you. I'd just come by to see Uncle Bryce, but I'm glad you're here."

Uncle Bryce? Yes, Brodie supposed, that was... kind of right. Bryce had been instrumental years ago in helping out an old magician, the same magician who had built the House of the Rising Sun and befriended Rhiannon's grandparents.

"Perhaps we should discuss where we are with the case at the moment?" Brodie said.

"I'd like that," Rhiannon told him.

Brodie stood and opened the door for her, and they both looked back at Bryce Edwards, who had a fatherly grin on his weathered face.

"Thanks," Brodie and Rhiannon said at the same time.

He ushered her out. "Let me grab my coat," he said. "We should go somewhere where we can really talk. The office is too hectic—and even though there are a fair number of Others on the force, it's just easier to talk out of the office."

"I know where we can go," she told him. "My place." She smiled and winked. "I'll drive."

"Let me get my files," he said.

Five minutes later they were out on the road, heading to her home in the Canyon. He'd known the old Keepers, but he'd never been out to the estate. He was curious; there were fantastic rumors about the place, which was supposedly still filled with all kinds of magical paraphernalia. It was well guarded—against human interference, at least. Despite the famous internal alarm system and the wall that surrounded the property, it was easily accessible to most Others. Despite that, as far as he knew, no one had ever tried to breach the walls.

But that, he thought now, *was because of the extraordinary strength of the Keepers who had once lived there.*

Rhiannon—who maneuvered the tricky California freeways like a native—broke into his thoughts as they reached the compound and she pushed the button that opened the gate. "You look worried," she said.

"I was just thinking," he said.

"Thinking that…?"

"That this should be a very safe place to live."

"That it should be—but isn't?" she asked. "And of course you're also thinking that the Canyon is due to erupt into violence—because my cousins and I are just girls, and weak."

He shook his head. "No, I'm thinking that evil exists no matter what, and that there is an evil element out there that will put you to the test just because you're new."

She smiled as they drove onto the property. "That one is mine," she said, pointing. "Pandora's Box."

"Very nice."

"It's the original guesthouse. Gwydion's Cave, where Barrie lives, is across the pool, and of course the main house is impossible to miss. Sailor lives there. She has since she was a child."

Rhiannon parked, and they exited the car. She walked to her house and he was glad to see that she had locked the door, even though this was a gated compound. She opened it, and he entered her inner sanctum.

The old magician's legacy was immediately obvious in the three fortune-teller machines in the living room. The first was an old Gypsy, the second a magician, and the third an ethereal ghost dressed all in white.

Statuettes and curios filled the shelves that lined the walls, along with countless books. He glanced at the spines and saw that most were on pagan religions, Druids, witchcraft and the occult. Others were magicians' manuals, and the collection was rounded out by an eclectic mix of world history, modern mysteries and fantasy.

He noted a number of guitar stands, each one

holding one of her precious instruments. There was also a beautiful old grand piano in the center of the room. His gut told him that the piano had been there long before she took over the house, and that the guitars were her own property, brought with her when she made the permanent move to L.A.

"So...stuffy? Creepy?" she asked him, aware that he was assessing the place.

"Cool. Very cool," he told her.

"I like it very much. I've put up a few pictures, but honestly, I haven't been here long enough to really put my stamp on the place. But it really is nice. The three of us might have struggled just to afford a lousy apartment in a so-so part of town, but instead we have beautiful homes of our own," she said. "So sit. The sofa is comfortable, and there's the big coffee table there for the files."

"Sure. Thanks." He sat down and spread out the folders he had brought.

She sat down next to him, and he started to talk.

"Victim one, victim two, victim three. I didn't know anything about the first murders—it went to a good cop, a guy on night shift. But when the second body was discovered, my captain brought both cases to me. He saw the link to the theater, so I took the part in the play to see if I could find out anything. And then the last victim was found just behind the theater, which pretty much clinched it—especially when I realized I'd seen him in the audience one night."

The crime scene photos were horrible, but she didn't flinch. And after what she had said last night, he was certain she'd been to the morgue.

"The killer is taking the fingers," she said.

He nodded. "Usually you take fingertips because you're trying to hide the victim's ID, and it's certainly feasible that this killer took the fingers for that reason. But he didn't destroy the teeth, not that that's helped us any. So far there's been no way to get a viable sample of the killer's DNA, because the bodies have been too degraded by the time they were discovered." And I gather you've seen Anthony Brandt down at the morgue, so you probably already know that the victims were drowned while they were being sucked dry of blood, or maybe right after they'd pretty much been drained."

She nodded, staring down at the files. "So they're all still unidentified."

"Like I said, I saw number three at the theater, watching the show."

"And he was killed in the lake behind the theater," she said.

He nodded, watching her face. She looked so serious, biting her lower lip as she carefully studied the crime scene photos. The Gryffalds really did have beautiful eyes. They were like prisms, catching the light in all kinds of fantastic patterns. At first he'd found her annoying...irritating....

And now... Now he couldn't stop thinking about her. The Elven were blessed with charm and the ability to use it to get what they wanted. But with it came a heightened sexuality. They loved the carnal pleasures, and he suddenly felt as if her allure was almost overwhelming.

It was easy for Elven to satisfy their sexual urges, thanks to their charm, but at least they accomplished it with respect for morality. It was an unwritten Elven rule that only those who wished to be seduced were charmed into relationships, whether for a night or for a longer time.

But Rhiannon was a Keeper, and Keepers were all but taboo. They weren't to be treated lightly.

People were being murdered, he reminded himself harshly. He needed to keep his mind on the case.

And still the subtle scent of her perfume was seducing him almost to the point where resistance would be futile.

He stood and walked over to one of the fortune-telling machines. She barely seemed to realize that he had walked away, which was more than a little disappointing.

"I had a talk with Darius Simonides yesterday, after you left," she said. "You know, of course, that he's a vampire."

"A vampire who lives by the rules. He wants to be a Hollywood success story far more than he wants to be a vampire," Brodie said.

"I wasn't accusing Darius of anything," she said. "I just felt that he might know something, that he might have heard something. And what about Hunter Jackson? And Declan Wainwright?"

"What about them? A human and a Keeper, a shapeshifter Keeper," he said. "Both well-known and respected."

"And both involved in the play," she reminded him. "So, what's happening with your investigation? Where have you gone with it?"

"Right now I have someone working on the audition sheets, tracking down everyone who tried out for the show and didn't make it."

"You think a disgruntled actor is doing this?" Rhiannon asked, and laughed suddenly.

Her smile, he realized, was radiant. His eyes had wandered down to her curves, and he forced them back to hers.

"I'd like to think it's an actor," she told him, still laughing. "They suddenly seem to be the bane of my existence."

"I'm sorry we ruined your night at the café," he told her.

She shrugged. "This is far more important. Of course, when I told Hugh Hammond that I wasn't coming in last night... Honestly! One minute he thinks I'm a total disaster as a Keeper, but the next, when I'm trying to do what a Keeper should do, he gives me a lecture about my obligation to my job and how I need it to survive in the real world."

"He's old guard. He'll come around. Maybe he's disappointed that he wasn't asked to be on the council while all three of the Gryffald men were," Brodie suggested.

Rhiannon shrugged. "Maybe. But I still have to make a living, and that means I still have to work with him," she said. "So—tell me about the victims. Do they have anything in common?"

He nodded. "All three of them were around thirty years old, the prime age to audition for the show. If I'm right that they were all among those who auditioned, then we know for a fact that the killer is somehow involved with the play."

"What about the cast?" she asked him.

He nodded, taking a seat again, this time a few feet away from her.

Not far enough. The soft, subtly sexual scent of her perfume still reached him.

"Here's what I think," he told her. "Joe Carrie's a vampire and thrilled to have his show being produced. Hunter Jackson's human; and I admit it, I think he's willing to do a hell of a lot to make *Vampire Rampage* a part of horror history, but I can't see a human as being physically capable of these murders. Lena Ashbury's another human, and as far as I've been able to ascertain, she's just a struggling actress who's delighted to have gotten the part. Then we have the two maids. Kate Delaney is human, and I can't find anything suspicious about her. Audrey Fleur is a vampire, and, she knows I'm

Elven, of course, but again, there's nothing to cast suspicion on her."

He stopped and took a breath, then went on. "I've dismissed the old couple at the inn, the cousins and the backup dancers and singers. They're all human, so it's doubtful that they're involved. There are techs and seamstresses, stage managers...but I haven't discovered a single thing that would lead me to believe that any of them is the killer, either."

Rhiannon nodded. "What about Hunter Jackson? I know you don't think a human could have done it, but if he's willing to do anything to make this show the biggest thing since The Beatles, would he resort to murder just to show that vampires might be out there?"

"I *have* thought of that. I've searched his dressing room, and I've followed him, and I haven't seen him do a single thing that would suggest he's capable of murder," Brodie told her. "If we could pinpoint the time of the murders, I'd be able to trace people's movements and know if they had alibis. But with the bodies left in the water to accelerate decomp, it's impossible for Tony to determine time of death, so it's also impossible to eliminate anyone."

Rhiannon sighed. "And it could just be...a vampire on the rampage. Taking advantage of the fact that my father is gone, and that…and that the Canyon vampires may now have free rein."

The idea had occurred to Brodie a number of times, but now he wanted to deny the possibility.

Now he wanted to defend her.

"I don't think so. I really don't. Whatever's behind this, it has something to do with the play. I'm certain of it."

"All right, so we need to follow everyone—except the humans—who has anything to do with *Vampire Rampage*," Rhiannon said. "That's not going to be easy."

"Maybe you can find us some help," he told her.

"How?"

"Make the announcement to the vampire community that the police are actively seeking a killer who's draining his victims of blood. Your constituents—most of them, anyway—will be outraged and more than happy to keep an eye out." He was quiet for a moment, shaking his head. "I know that in a lot of cities the Others all have meetings together. In L.A., maybe because of the sheer sizes of the different populations and the physical size of the city, every race has its own council meetings. Obviously,

Barrie and I can ask for help from the Elven community, and Hugh Hammond and Anthony Brandt can speak with the werewolves. And your cousin Sailor can help out with the shapeshifters."

"Maybe Barrie can get the press involved, too," Rhiannon suggested.

Brodie was thoughtful for a minute. "Let's hold off on that a bit."

"But one of the problems recognizing that a serial killer was at work was the fact that no one seemed to care about the victims," Rhiannon said. "If there's a big splash—"

"Let's just see what we can find out about our victims right now and follow the leads as we get them," Brodie suggested.

Rhiannon nodded grudgingly. "I'm going to have to go to work soon," she said, and grimaced. "I only work Monday through Thursday at the café. If I don't show up at all—"

"The Mystic Café is a good place for you to be," he told her. "You don't know what you might hear there. It's a favorite hangout for Others as well as human beings, so do your best to get to know the customers. And Hugh may be a pain in the ass to work for, but he's been a Keeper for a very long time, so he knows damn near everything. You can learn a lot from him."

She nodded again. "Should I meet you after the show tonight, so we can compare notes?"

"I'll pick you up from the café after the play. A lot of the cast and crew head to the Snake Pit after a performance. We can head over and show the world that we're an item, and you can also take a good look at where you'll be working on Friday."

"All right," she said. "And Declan is involved, too, in a way. They're going to film some scenes at the club, and he was at the play last night, too. What's weird is that he didn't tell me he was going to be there, even though I said *I* would be." She frowned. "Brodie, if any of the powerhouse guys—like Declan or Darius—*is* involved, you could be in real danger. They know what you are, right? That you're a cop, I mean."

"Yes, they do. But that's the point. I *am* a cop, Rhiannon."

"Yes, and you're Elven. But you're not…well, werewolves can rip a person to shreds, and shape-shifters—"

"Shapeshifters aren't really a threat. They can become anything, but they use up their strength to be it, though I admit Declan will bear watching. But please, don't go underestimating the Elven," he said.

He walked over to her, hunkering down so that he was almost kneeling in front of her. He took her hand, ignoring the electric jolt that ripped through him as he touched her. "Thank you for worrying, but I'm going to be fine. But we'll watch each other's backs, all right? Because, you know, I'm pretty worried about you, too."

She flushed. "I'm a Keeper."

"That's not going to protect you—not against a vampire who's truly on a rampage," he told her. "Keepers have been killed in the past, Rhiannon. Some of them by their charges, because they weren't prepared."

He stood quickly, unable to go on touching her or even be so close to her. A burning sensation was filling him, heating his blood to boiling.

He was a cop, he reminded himself. And she was a Keeper. This was a serious situation. Three men were dead already, with more to come if he couldn't stop the cycle of violence....

He stepped back. "You've got to get to work, and I have to check in at the station and then get out to the theater. I'll see you later, and you can tell me everything you overheard at the café."

She nodded and stood, as well. She seemed a little shaky, and when he reached out to take her shoulders, for a moment their eyes met.

Hers were deep, beautiful pools of green. He felt as if he was sinking, as if he were lost in the depths of an ocean.

She forced a laugh, stepping by him. "Sorry about that. Clearly I need more sleep," she said.

As he walked toward the door, Brodie found himself stopping by one of the fortune-teller machines. It was the Magician, an older man with bright blue eyes and a mischievous smile, dressed in a magician's traditional tux.

Brodie didn't touch the machine.

Suddenly the magician started moving, picking up a card in one white-gloved hand as eerie music played. The card dropped into the receptacle, as if daring Brodie to pick it up.

He glanced over at Rhiannon, slowly arching a brow in question and smiling.

"Faulty wiring. Mr. Magic goes off now and then by himself," she said.

He picked up the card.

"What does it say?" she asked him.

"'Remember to keep your enemies close, and as you do, beware of those you would call friend,'" he read aloud.

"Merlin, are you here?" Rhiannon called out.

Brodie was surprised; even when his opinion of her had been at its lowest, he had considered her sane.

There was no answer, and she didn't attempt to explain herself. She simply picked up one of her guitars and joined him, carrying the instrument as if she were carrying gold from Fort Knox.

He followed her out, and as she turned to lock the door she at last caught the way he was looking at her. "He's still here, you know."

"Pardon?"

"Ivan Schwartz. Merlin. He's still here."

"The old man who used to own the place? The magician? Are you telling me that he's still here... as a ghost?" he asked skeptically.

She laughed suddenly. "You're Elven. I'm the Keeper responsible for the Canyon vampires. We deal with werewolves and shifters on a daily basis. And you're going to doubt the existence of a *ghost*? Speak to me. Tell me what you're thinking. I don't want any more cover-ups and half-truths between us, please."

Brodie had to laugh, too. "Okay, for a moment I was thinking you were crazy. I didn't know who you were talking to."

"And now?"

"Now I'm curious to meet him."

She let out a soft sigh and smiled slowly. "I'll try to see that you get that opportunity," she said.

They were close again. Too close.

This time she was the one who stepped away quickly.

"Work," she said firmly, as if to remind herself. And then she led the way toward her car.

Brodie greeted the cast and crew as he went into his dressing room to change for the night's performance. He shared the room with Hunter Jackson, but the other man hadn't come in yet.

He was just finishing getting dressed when he heard the door open and turned, assuming that Jackson had arrived, but it wasn't Hunter Jackson who stepped into the room.

It was Audrey.

"Audrey? Do you need something?" he asked.

"No, I'm just ready and getting bored waiting," she told him.

She had perched on the chair in front of his dressing table. She was dressed for her first scene, and her costume was provocative, to say the least. Victorian finery in shreds, with plenty of heaving bosom. She was attractive and flirtatious, but so far she'd been professional, as well, even if her conversation was always full of innuendo.

Brodie buttoned his shirt and walked closer, ready to start on his makeup, but she didn't move from his chair.

"So you're seeing the vampire Keeper," she said. "My Keeper. But you know that, of course."

"Of course."

"Is that allowed?" she asked.

"She's the vampire Keeper. I'm Elven."

Audrey laughed, a sound that originated low in her throat and was meant to seduce. "Oh, yes, you certainly *are* Elven. I've been rather surprised that you haven't been acting like one."

"We're in a play together, Audrey. And, as you just commented, I'm in a relationship."

"Would that really stop an Elven?"

"Audrey…"

"I wouldn't mind a threesome. And I'll bet you wouldn't, either."

"Audrey, I don't know what you *think* you know about Elven, but we pretty much function the same way human males do," he told her.

That elicited another delighted laugh. "Then you're willing to bed pretty much anyone, under the right circumstances."

She stood and walked over to him, and before he knew what she was doing, she had slipped a hand down and grabbed his crotch. His reaction was purely physical.

"Oh, no, you are much better than other men," she assured him.

Was she really bent on seducing him? Or was something else really on her mind?

It was worth temporarily sacrificing some of his strength to practice telepathy, he decided.

But what he could read was purely carnal.

Nice dick. He'd be scrumptious if I could get him into bed. I'll bet he knows what he's doing, too. That would so relieve some of the boredom....

At this moment, at least, her thoughts weren't worth reading.

He caught her hand, glad of the strength of his

race, which was greater than hers in such a battle. He pulled her hand away and spoke to her gently. "Audrey, you're beautiful, you're sexy and I'm in a relationship."

Angry, she flushed and stepped away. "Are you *really* in a relationship? Or are you two really just snooping around to see what *I'm* doing?"

"What?"

"You heard me," Audrey snapped at him. "Yes, I can be a little wild at times. I do like three-ways, and yes, dammit, I really do like sex! And yes, I'm bisexual. That's not a bad thing—it just means I love everyone. So what if I organized an orgy at the Theater on the Square last month? Half the people in this city are having sex with anyone who'll look at them. If your little prude thinks she's going to come after me for my behavior, she'll have to clean out the whole city—not to mention the rest of the country!"

Brodie stared at her, ready to break out laughing. He fought the urge.

"Audrey, I swear to you that Rhiannon is not planning to chastise you for your sexual behavior. I sincerely doubt she knows about it, and if she did, I'm sure she'd say that so long as you're having your fun with consenting adults, more power to you."

She looked back at him, her anger fading, though she was still frowning slightly.

"You really don't want to get it on with me?"

Brodie pondered that question. Since he'd been here, he'd been focused on catching a murderer. He'd barely noticed Audrey's playful sexual innuendos on anything other than an intellectual level. And yet he'd seen Rhiannon and immediately responded with every fiber of his being.

Audrey was extremely attractive and sexual, but she just wasn't his type. Rhiannon, on the other hand...

"It's a real relationship, Audrey," he said quietly, and he knew it was true, even though they hadn't so much as kissed yet.

"Hmm," Audrey mused thoughtfully, studying him.

"She's only been here a week."

"It only took a few days," he told her.

She lowered her head for a moment and then looked back at him. "Then congratulations. What you have is rare. Anywhere, but especially here in

La-La Land. And I promise, I'll behave, and I'll even be nice to her. For you."

"That's great of you, Audrey," Brodie assured her.

As Audrey was going out, Hunter Jackson was coming in. He brushed past her in the doorway.

"Good evening, Hunter," Audrey said. There it was again: that sultry, sexual purr in her voice.

Hunter watched her as she walked away. "Damn, she's sexy," he said. Then he turned back to Brodie and said, "Hey, full house last night. And it was nice to meet your lady, Mac."

"Yeah, thanks. I heard it's another full house tonight," Brodie said. "Here's hoping for good reviews."

Hunter nodded, pleased. "This could be it, Mac. This could be the project that takes me from being successful to being legendary." He raised an imaginary glass. "Here's to another great night."

"To another great night," Brodie agreed.

A few minutes later Joe Carrie, in his role as stage manager, stuck his head into the room. "Curtain, gentlemen, ten minutes."

"Thanks, Joe," Brodie said.

Another night, another show.

And he still needed answers.

It seemed that her song "I Hate Hollywood" had earned her some fans the other night; she received a request to play it not long after she took to the stage.

The night was, in all, a great deal better than that night had been, at least musically speaking.

Yet as for making any progress toward learning the identity of the murderer, she didn't come up with any information at all. The clientele was virtually all human; the only Other she saw was Anthony Brandt, who stopped in after his shift at the morgue. She took a break while he was there and sat down beside him, cradling a cup of blended black tea that was delicious.

"Anything?" she asked him softly.

He shook his head wearily. "Tonight? Nothing to do with the murders. A woman in her nineties who had to have an autopsy because she died in her son's custody. The son is seventy and on oxygen himself, but by law…"

"And she died of…?"

"Pulmonary arrest," he said. "The son isn't going

to be far behind her. Heavy smoker—likely to blow himself up. He goes from his oxygen to a cigarette."

"Well, at least no one was murdered," she said.

"Yeah, at least no one was murdered. Today."

"I'm really angry with you, by the way," Rhiannon informed him. "Thanks a lot for telling me the truth about your buddy."

He flushed, looking down at his tea. "So," he said softly, "you've figured out that your Elven actor is a cop?"

"Yes, thank you, I've figured it out," she said.

"So?"

"We're working it," she said.

"Good," he told her.

"You could have just told me the truth, you know. Much easier on both of us."

"Maybe. Maybe not. Maybe you two had to learn to respect each other."

"Do you know anything else you haven't told me yet?" she asked him.

"No, do you?"

She nodded. "If it should come up in conversation anywhere, I'm with Brodie. Or Mac. The actor Mac Brodie. As in we're seeing each other," Rhiannon said.

"Good ruse," Brandt said. "I like it. You've filled Hugh in?"

"Yes, I had to. And he still gave me grief about taking last night off so I could see the play," she said indignantly.

It was almost as if she had given Hugh a cue. He walked up to where they were sitting and stared at her. "You're slacking off again."

Rhiannon looked at her watch. "I actually have sixty seconds of break left, Hugh. I'm not slacking off at all."

"Hey, Hugh, let's give the kid a chance here, huh?" Brandt asked.

"She's getting her chance," Hugh said. "She's working for me, isn't she? I'm showing her the ropes." He turned to Rhiannon. "This is Hollywood, kid. You fly or you die. Brutal, but that's the way it is. I'm doing you a favor toughening you up," he assured her.

"Thank you. Thank you ever so much," she said, then turned away and smiled at Brandt. "Brodie is coming by after the play. We're going to the Snake Pit, if you want to join us."

"Hey, don't mind if I do," Hugh said, as if she

had spoken to him. "Don't mind if I do at all," he repeated as he headed back behind the counter.

Rhiannon decided that she really wanted to write a song about how much she hated werewolf Keepers, but she decided that she wouldn't, discretion being the better part of valor and all. Instead, she sang songs she knew by rote, watching as Hugh came back and sat down with Anthony Brandt, then wound up deep in a heated discussion with him.

She couldn't help it. She wondered what they were talking about and whether it was something she should know, too.

Chapter 6

Brodie was grateful for one special Elven attribute that night: his ability to move like the speed of light. Since the theater, the Magic Café and his apartment were just different stops right off the 101, he left quickly after the show and stopped at his apartment for a shower. For some reason—maybe it had been his few moments of something like intimacy with Audrey Fleur and the realization they'd forced him to reach about his feelings for Rhiannon Gryffald— he'd felt the heat of the lights and the grease of his makeup a little too much that night.

He arrived at the Mystic Café to find that Rhiannon was ready to go.

"We should have met at the Snake Pit," she told him apologetically. "I have my car here, and also, I'd really love a quick shower. I feel like twenty varieties of Hugh's best Colombian beans tonight, for some reason."

"That's fine. I'll follow you to your place and wait for you. We don't need two cars at the Snake Pit. Parking off Sunset is a bitch."

"All right," she told him. "Thanks."

"Hugh will be at the Snake Pit tonight, too," she told him as they walked out to their cars.

"Oh?"

"Anthony Brandt stopped by, and I suggested he come. Hugh assumed that I was inviting him, too."

Brodie shrugged. "Maybe Hugh wants to keep an eye on you," he suggested. "Keep his newest employee safe."

"Hugh doesn't want to keep me safe from the wolves, he wants to throw me to them—or rather, to the werewolves," she said. "He gave me a speech about life being brutal—sink or fly, that kind of thing."

"In a pinch, I think he'd help," Brodie said. And

then he found himself wondering if that was true. Maybe Hugh was bitter about not being asked to be on the council and wanted to exact his petty revenge on Rhiannon, since she was handy. He decided to keep that thought to himself.

At his side, Rhiannon shrugged.

He followed her to the estate and up the drive to her house. "You all keep late hours," he commented when he saw that her cousins' cars were absent.

"Sailor is always schmoozing—and Barrie is always on the hunt for a good story she can use to make her name," she explained as she led him inside. She set her guitar case carefully in its place as they entered and indicated the living room and kitchen. "Make yourself at home. I promise, I'll be back down in ten minutes."

She raced up the stairs and he was left to wander the house. The fortune-telling machines fascinated him. He walked over to the Mr. Magician machine. "Any more fortunes for me?" he asked it aloud.

But it didn't answer, and no card dropped into the receptacle.

He could faintly hear the shower start to run above him. With his supernaturally acute hearing, he could hear it clearly. And with the sound of water splashing against tile came the visual. He could imagine her standing there, water cascading down on the naked beauty of her flesh, red hair streaming behind her. He could imagine being a bar of soap, sliding over that sleek naked flesh....

He gritted his teeth sharply. He might be Elven and still acutely aware of where and how Audrey had grabbed him earlier, and yet...

Audrey's blatant approach hadn't done a thing for him. All it had done was make him think of the redheaded Gryffald beauty who was up in the shower at this very minute. All he could think about was mounting the stairs and wrenching back the shower curtain. She would turn to him in surprise, of course, but he had a feeling she wouldn't really be surprised. She would be waiting for him, and he would see in the green depth of her eyes the look she had given him earlier....

"Good evening."

He was startled from his imagination-run-amok by an elderly man.

"I'm sorry. You *do* see me, right?"

Brodie blinked. Of course he saw the man, clear as day. He frowned sharply. "Who are you, and what the hell are you doing here?" he demanded, his hand dropping to the Smith & Wesson tucked into its holster at his waist.

"I'm so sorry. I usually knock. I'm Merlin, master magician. And who are you, please?"

Brodie paused, stunned into silence. He'd met all kinds of creatures in his life, but he'd never had a ghost come up and introduce himself.

"Sir, I can see that you are Elven, but even the Elven are far more attractive with their mouths shut," Merlin said.

Brodie came quickly back to life, instinctively offering his hand, then realizing that the ghost couldn't shake it. "Detective Brodie McKay, Mr. Merlin. I'm Rhiannon's guest."

"Finally! Thank the Lord above us, the two of you have connected," Merlin said.

Brodie decided not to broach the subject of just *how* he had imagined being connected to Rhiannon just moments before.

"Have you found out what's happening yet?" Merlin asked him. "With those murders?"

"No, sir, we haven't."

"What are you waiting for?" Merlin demanded indignantly. "You need to solve this case quickly. Men are dying—and you're doing Rhiannon a huge disservice. The girl just got out here, and you're behaving as if she should have done all your work for you by now."

"Merlin!" Brodie was startled by Rhiannon's sharp tone as he turned to look up the stairs. She'd been true to her word. Less than ten minutes had gone by, and she was transformed. Her hair looked like pure floating fire, and she had donned a short, sleek blue dress and matching high heels with lacy ribbons that tied around her ankles and drew attention to her long legs. The effect was truly wicked in the sexiest possible way.

"Hello, my dear. I was just introducing myself to your young gentleman here," he told her.

"He knows I'm a cop," Brodie said.

"And an Elven," Merlin added, looking at Rhiannon. His tone indicated that as far as he was concerned, *Elven* meant *beware*.

Rhiannon's attitude had shifted to one of amusement. She walked over to the ghost, and Brodie almost laughed at the way she seemed to take the older man by his nonexistent shoulders and bend to give him a kiss on the cheek. In her heels she was over six feet, and Merlin...wasn't.

"Thanks for worrying about me, Merlin. We're

heading out to the Snake Pit to see if we can pick up any information—and so I can see where I'll be working," Rhiannon said.

"Just be careful," Merlin said. He turned and studied Brodie again. "Vampires...they're cagey, and they're powerful. If your killer really is a vampire..."

Brodie smiled. "Elven aren't weaklings, you know."

Merlin nodded. "All right, then. My dear," he said to Rhiannon, "my apologies, but I feel it's my duty to your dear parents to look out for your welfare."

Rhiannon smiled. "You're a sweetheart, Merlin. But you don't need to worry when you see Brodie in the future, okay?"

Merlin nodded, though he still looked doubtful. "I'll be returning to the main house," he told her. "But remember, I'm very close, if you ever need me."

"Thank you, Merlin," she said with a smile.

Brodie kept an eye on the ghost as he led Rhiannon to his car. When Merlin rounded the pool, he seemed to vanish into thin air.

"You did say you wanted to meet him," Rhiannon reminded him.

"Yes, my first ghost," he told her as he opened the passenger door for her. Once he was in the driver's seat, he added, "Actually, it's good that you have a watchdog."

"I suppose. Though, come to think of it, I've always wanted a real dog. Something huge, like a Saint Bernard."

"Scottish deerhound," Brodie suggested. "Or a good old German shepherd would be good, too. They make great guard dogs. They aren't vicious, but they're loyal, and they know who belongs and who doesn't. And—"

"And like all dogs, they have extra senses that we don't have," Rhiannon said.

No, he thought, *because neither of us is a werewolf.* Then again...compared to the human population, he *did* have extra powers. And once Rhiannon had enough experience that she could take on some of the abilities of her charges, *she* would have extra senses, too.

He realized that he was afraid she wouldn't know in time when she needed to use all her innate abilities. He didn't have the right to dictate to her, he thought. And yet...

This situation had given him the *feeling,* even if he didn't have the right.

"Now that I know I'm going to be living here, I think I *will* look for a dog," she said.

He nodded. "I don't have a pet. I keep lousy hours. It wouldn't be fair."

She smiled. "When I get my pup, you can borrow him. How's that?"

"Sounds like a plan," he said, trying to speak lightly. He felt a catch in his throat. This was getting ridiculous. It was one thing to feel a strong sexual attraction. He was what he was—and she was a stunning woman. It was even all right to feel a little protective, whether she felt it was an insult or not. It was quite another to feel things that went beyond that.

A few minutes later he pulled off the freeway and was pleased to pull right up to the valet.

The attendant was one of the extremely tall leprechauns living in the L.A. area. The doorman was a shapeshifter. It was only natural that Declan Wainwright would employ so many of the city's Others.

As the valet took the car, Brodie stepped onto the sidewalk, where Rhiannon was waiting. He thought again that she looked absolutely breathtaking, and he wondered how the hell he had gone so quickly from finding her an annoying interruption in the functioning of his beloved city to seeing her as an exotic and nearly irresistible beauty.

She smiled; he took her arm. He felt magic in the air—unbelievable for an Elven who spent his days—and nights—dealing with the seamiest sides of the world, human and Other.

And then the moment was completely blown as a flash went off.

He turned to see Jake Reynolds, one of the paparazzi—and a gnome—snapping pictures from behind one of the ivied trellises that protected the front of the Snake Pit and added to its air of exclusivity.

Damn it! *Jake knew exactly who and what he was.*

He swore softly beneath his breath, ready to rip into Jake. Rhiannon set a calming hand on his arm.

"Let me," she told him softly.

He watched as she hurried over to the photographer. By then a small crowd was watching with interest. But, to her credit, Rhiannon seemed to be completely in control, smiling and laughing with Jake. But when she returned, she didn't have the photographer's memory card or camera.

"That damn gnome is going to blow my cover," Brodie told her.

She shook her head. "Smile over at the gnome. He's going to use your stage name. He wants a picture, so let him have one. He'll list Mac Brodie and Rhiannon Gryffald under the shot and sell it on the web. Everything's fine, and it will be great PR for the show."

"I don't trust gnomes," he said.

"We don't have a choice—unless you want to cause the kind of scene that will definitely create the wrong kind of publicity, not to mention give you away," she said.

"I still think he's going to out me as a cop," Brodie said, and he knew that his voice sounded like a growl.

"What if he does? All you have to do is say that you've always wanted to be an actor but didn't want to resign from the department." She touched his cheek as she spoke, and her fingers felt like silk against his skin.

Control yourself, he thought. He needed to get over her. Maybe he should sleep with the oversexed Ms. Audrey Fleur and get this out of his system.

"I'm all right," he said. He bared his teeth in a semblance of a grin. "I'm smiling at the gnome. See?"

"Good." She gave the gnome a beautiful smile of her own, waved and then they went on into the club.

Declan himself met them at the door.

"Welcome," he said, taking Rhiannon's hands and kissing her cheek. "I saw what happened," he said, and looked at Brodie. "Do you want me to do something about him?"

"No! I already told Brodie not to strong-arm him. That would only cause a bigger problem," Rhiannon said.

Declan grinned. "I wasn't going to strong-arm anyone. I was going to shift into cop form and demand he hand over his memory card."

"No need," she said. "I asked him to post it using Brodie's stage name, so it will only help with what he's trying is to do."

Declan nodded and looked at Brodie. "Some of the other cast members are already here. Do you want to join them?"

"Maybe later. I think we should make a point of being alone," Brodie said. "As if we're out for a romantic evening."

"Gotcha," Declan said, grinning, as they entered the club. "By the way, Rhiannon, you're going to be appearing in the Midnight Room. Shall I show you as soon as you're inside?"

"Yes, thank you," she said.

"Brodie," Declan told him, "your friends are in the Velvet Lounge. Tell Humphrey I said to give you a VIP table in the back."

"Thanks," Brodie said. He kept Rhiannon's arm through his as they made their entry into the club. As soon as they had been noticed, he made a point of caressing her cheek, feeling her eyes burn across his skin as he touched her. Then, looking for all the world like reluctant lovers, they parted.

He watched for a moment as Declan escorted Rhiannon up the stairs to show her the Midnight Room, which was only open on the weekends. He imagined he was going to be spending a lot of time at the Snake Pit now—so long as Rhiannon kept playing there.

She might be a Keeper, with the potential to take on the abilities of her vampire charges. But she was still human—with all the weaknesses that went with that.

Brodie approached the Velvet Lounge and found Humphrey, one of Declan's werewolf maître d's, at the door. He was a big guy, the kind that brooked no trouble. He greeted Brodie with a smile, listened as Brodie repeated Declan's words and then led him to a table in the back.

Everything was velvet and silk at the Snake Pit. The back tables were like intimate tents, surrounded by velvet curtains that could be drawn back for a view of the entertainment or pulled closed for privacy.

Brodie sat. Several tables away, toward a magician who was performing the usual hat tricks, he could see Hunter Jackson sipping champagne and enjoying the company of Audrey Fleur and Kate Delaney. Both women were beautifully dressed and didn't seem to mind sharing his attention. Bobby Conche was with them, sitting back and enjoying a drink, clearly enjoying the reflected glory that came with sharing a table with the cast. Strange, Brodie thought. In essence, shapeshifters were actors, capable of taking on any role. But this shapeshifter didn't want to be anyone else—he just wanted to be around those who did.

At another table he saw Darius Simonides, accompanied by Sailor Gryffald. She seemed to be in seventh heaven. Of course, she wanted to act, and Darius was a major player.

A moment later Rhiannon returned and slid onto the chair next to him. She noticed her cousin, and she didn't seem happy. "I can't believe Sailor's here with him again. I know he's her godfather, but…"

"He *is* giving her a part in a major movie," Brodie offered.

"And I still don't trust him," she said.

"He's one of yours," he said, then leaned forward and spoke softly. "Let's keep an open mind and look at tonight as a fact-finding mission. We could be going in the wrong direction entirely, thinking everything's connected to the play. Maybe you'll know more after the council meeting tomorrow night."

She nodded but looked unhappy. Before he could say more, a waitress came by. Elven. She was tall, striking and sensual.

"May I take your order?" she asked sweetly.

"Rhiannon?" he asked.

"Do you carry Harp?" she asked.

"Absolutely. What about you, sir?" the waitress asked Brodie.

"The same, thanks."

As soon as their waitress left, Rhiannon rose.

"Where are you going?" he asked her.

"I can't just pretend that I don't see them," she said. "That would be rude."

"Rhiannon, we're observing—" he began.

But she was already gone. He rose quickly to follow her. She headed first to the table where Hunter Jackson was holding court, sweeping over as if she were just saying hello, and she played the scene perfectly, stopping to speak for just a moment, then moving on. Then she moved on to the table where her cousin was sitting. Brodie noted the way Jackson's eyes followed her.

And he saw that Audrey noticed, too.

Darius rose when Rhiannon reached the table, and they traded air kisses. Sailor rose, too, and gave her a hug, but she didn't look happy to see Rhiannon.

He decided to join them. Sailor stared at him in surprise, and then looked from him to her cousin. "So you two really are a couple."

"Would you like to sit down?" Darius asked.

Brodie suddenly regretted joining them. He had only met the man that one time at his office, when he'd invited himself along with Jackson and Declan, supposedly to talk about the filming but really because he wanted to meet everyone who had any connection to the show. He'd been Mac Brodie, actor, then. He hoped Sailor knew only his cover story, or that, if she knew the truth, she would remember that he was undercover. She should. She was the Elven Keeper, so she must have some sense.

"For a moment, sure, thanks," Brodie said, sliding in by Sailor.

"Out with your godfather—how nice," Rhiannon told Sailor.

"We were having a lovely discussion about my future," Sailor said. "It was all about me," she said with a rueful laugh.

Rhiannon grinned at that. "I came to see where I was going to be working."

"You know, Rhiannon, there might be a place for you when we record the soundtrack," Darius said.

"That would be great—especially if it pays well," Rhiannon said.

Darius laughed. "Honesty. I like that in women.

How about you...Mr. Brodie? How do you feel about not being asked to be in the film?"

Sailor turned to him. "Seriously, Mr. Brodie, how *do* you feel about knowing someone else will play your role on the big screen?" She sounded genuinely curious. Maybe she'd forgotten what he did for a living, or maybe she really didn't know.

"I'm just happy to be working," he told her. "I don't have any problem with not being in the movie. Hunter Jackson won't be in it, either, and the whole project is his baby. Even the writer is stepping aside. He has consultation on the script, but that's it."

Sailor lowered her voice. "I feel a little awkward. I'm going to be playing Audrey Fleur's role in the movie, and I'm not sure she feels the way you do. We stopped by to say hello, and she was outright rude to me."

"This is Hollywood. People should be happy for whatever they get," Brodie said.

"But most of us aspire to be stars," Sailor said. "And I'm sure she was hoping this would be her big break."

"Sailor, are you worried about her?" Rhiannon asked.

"You may not believe this, but I honestly hate to hurt anyone," Sailor said.

"You're perfect for this role, Sailor," Darius said. "Stage and screen are different, and you shine on film. Besides, it was Hunter's plan from the start to do it this way. Lord, if I had to take a bullet for every unhappy actor in Hollywood, I'd be so riddled with holes there would be nothing left."

"And now, a volunteer from our audience, please," the magician called out, drawing their attention away from their conversation.

Hands went up all through the room. Audrey was waving wildly, but the magician ignored her and walked into the audience saying, "Sometimes the best volunteers are those who must be coerced onstage."

He was coming straight for them, announcing, "Tonight my good friend Declan Wainwright has given me permission to invite you all to visit the House of Illusion, where my fellow illusionists and I practice *real* magic. If you come on Sunday night, I promise you'll see the show of a lifetime."

When he stopped at their table, Brodie knew immediately that the tall, white-haired man was Elven. "I do hope you'll join us on Sunday night," he said directly to Brodie, who realized he'd seen the man at council meetings, though he didn't even know his name.

"My dear, you would make a wonderful assistant," the magician said.

He stretched out a hand, and Brodie thought he was reaching for Sailor, seeing as she was the new Elven Keeper.

But he wasn't offering his hand to Sailor. He was offering it to Rhiannon, who looked as if she wanted to crawl beneath the table.

"My dear?" the magician said. She stood reluctantly, accepting his hand, and they walked to the stage. "Now all I need you to do is lie down in this box…and then I'll cut you in half," he said.

Brodie had to stop himself from jumping to his feet and rushing to her side.

Sailor was clearly unhappy, too. "What's he doing?" she whispered. "I don't see why—"

"Just kidding!" the magician said. "If you would just enter this glass dome…and then, when you hear a question, I swear you'll know the answer."

He opened the door to the glass dome, and Rhiannon entered.

"Beautiful, beautiful!" the magician said, then

started soliciting questions from the audience and deferring to Rhiannon to provide the answers.

At the beginning, all the answers were amusing. One girl asked if she would find her true love, and the answer was, "Many times." That question segued into one from a pretty girl who asked if she would marry her boyfriend, and once again the answer was, "Many times." Then a young man asked if the pilot he had just shot would make it as a series. The response was, "Not this one, but it will lead to a movie role."

The next few questions all concerned Hollywood and the movies. And then a young guy asked, "Will I find my friend Jordan?"

The answer was, "He has already been found."

The man's gasp was frightening. He started walking toward the stage, his hand at his throat and his expression so intense that Humphrey the werewolf started toward him.

"Where? Where is he?" the man asked desperately. "I have to find him, I told him not to beat his head against the wall, but he loved that show, so he kept on trying…"

He didn't get any further, because Humphrey caught up to him. The magician seemed to realize that his session had veered from entertaining to all-too-real, and he helped Rhiannon from the answer box and asked that the audience give her a big hand.

As soon as he saw that Rhiannon was safely off the stage, Brodie hurried after the young man—then being escorted out by Humphrey.

He caught the two of them just outside the room. "Humphrey, may I?" he asked.

The werewolf shrugged. Brodie took the young man's arm and led him toward the door. "Who are you looking for? How long has he been missing?"

Miserably, the man looked at Brodie. "Jordan Bellow. We've been together since high school. He's an actor. A *good* actor. We're from San Francisco, and he came down here to audition for some vampire play. He left me a message about some kind of a tour, but he didn't say anything specific, and now he's not answering emails and his cell goes straight to voice mail. I don't know where to look or what to do."

"And you are…?" Brodie asked.

"Nick. Nick Cassidy," the young man said. "This was just a silly game, right? He hasn't really been found, has he?"

"I don't know," Brodie said, and hesitated. If he

did have the answer to Jordan Bellow's disappearance, his longtime lover wasn't going to like it. "Stay here. I'll be right back, and I'll see if I can help you."

He started back into the Snake Pit, but Rhiannon was already walking out in search of him. He practically collided with her at the door.

"Can you get a ride home with Sailor?" he asked her. "I'm going to take this man to the morgue and…find out if Jordan really has been found."

She nodded. "Of course."

"Before I go… How were you getting the answers?"

"They appeared in the glass, which isn't just normal clear glass. You were seeing a picture of the lower half of my body, while I had a computer monitor beside me," she explained. "I have no idea how the magician got the answers to show up there, though."

"Go talk to that magician. Find out who he is—and what he knows," Brodie told her. "But don't go talk to him alone—don't go *anywhere* alone. Sailor is going to have to give you a ride anyway, so make her stay with you. She's the Elven Keeper, so that might give you some clout."

"I'll be fine—go," Rhiannon told him.

Brodie rejoined Nick Cassidy.

"Where are we going?" Cassidy asked him.

"The morgue," Brodie said.

The magician had seemed a nice enough guy, and since she was going to be working at the Snake Pit herself, Rhiannon didn't think it would to be difficult to get a chance to speak with him. It was a little more difficult to disentangle Sailor from Darius Simonides, but Rhiannon feigned a total fascination with magic and finally drew her cousin away.

Sailor made her unhappiness known, though. "Rhiannon, I know this means nothing to you, but I want a life beyond this Keeper thing, and Darius can help me with that."

"Yes, and your future looks just peachy. But you *are* a Keeper. That's the way it is. The Elven Keeper. I don't even want to live in L.A., Sailor, but here I am." Rhiannon stared into her cousin's eyes. "And right now I need you."

Instantly Sailor looked contrite. "I'm sorry. Let's go see your magician."

Backstage, the magician—who billed himself as the Count de Soir—was happy to greet them. He thanked Rhiannon for participating in the show, and he held Sailor's hands and kissed her cheeks, telling her that the Elven were extremely lucky that their new Keeper was so young and beautiful.

Rhiannon let them flatter each other for a few minutes and then stepped in. "Count, can you tell me, please, where the answers were coming from? I didn't see a ringer out in the audience who could have been sending them to me."

"Ah, the answers," the count said, drumming his fingers on his dressing table. Then he looked at her and said, "You live with my old mentor."

Rhiannon frowned, and then arched her brows. "You mean...Merlin?"

He nodded. "I saw him in a dream, and he said that I was to help you."

"You saw him in a dream?" Rhiannon repeated. That sly old dog. He was haunting the magician, and the man didn't even know it.

"He told me to use my magic for good. I don't have all the answers, of course, but I read the newspapers. Not online, either. The real thing, front to back, and I've been waiting for someone to ask about a friend or family member who's gone missing here in L.A. There is no such thing as a John

Doe. Not really. Everyone is someone. I listen and I learn. I knew that you'd be working here." He lowered his voice, looking around his small dressing room. "I know that the man you were sitting with is Brodie McKay, a cop, not an actor named Mac Brodie."

"But how did you know that someone looking for a dead man would come to the Snake Pit and ask you about him?" Rhiannon asked.

"That's easy," the Count told her. "Everyone who wants to see or be seen comes to the Snake Pit."

Rhiannon thanked him and said goodbye. Before they left, the count kissed Sailor's hand and told her that he would see her the next night at the council meeting.

When they left, Rhiannon took Sailor's keys from her. "I'm driving," she said.

"I'm perfectly sober," Sailor told her.

"I'm sure you are, but I'm more sober, since I never even got my beer," Rhiannon said.

Traffic was comparatively light, and the drive home was quick.

When Rhiannon parked, Sailor looked over at her. "I know you think my whole life is all about

me—me, me, me—but I really am here to help
you. And I'll be a good Keeper, you know. Luckily
I have the Elven, mostly law-abiding citizens who
prefer mind games and getting along in life to fighting. You and Barrie are cut from tougher cloth, so
it makes sense you inherited the vampires and the
shifters. But whatever you think, I *am* here for you."

Rhiannon immediately felt guilty. She gave
Sailor a hug. "Good night—and I'll count on that."

Sailor nodded. "By the way, watch out."

"Of course."

"No, I mean, watch out for your heart—and your
sanity. With Brodie."

"I'll be fine," Rhiannon said. "He's a cop and
I'm the vampire Keeper. We're working together,
that's all."

"No, you're playing the part of lovers. And you're
going to want it to be real," Sailor warned her.

"Don't worry, I know what I'm doing," Rhiannon
assured her, then watched Sailor go into the main
house before letting herself into Pandora's Box. She
was exhausted, and she quickly prepared for bed,
dully wondering if anything she'd learned tonight
would help them in their investigation. Brodie, she
knew, was just as frustrated.

Brodie.

Watch out!

Lying in bed, she found that she was thinking about the Elven detective, and that she was thinking about him in the very way Sailor had just warned her that she shouldn't. She was a sucker for tall men to begin with, probably because of her own height. And there was no way out of the fact that Elven males were…

Beautiful. Gorgeous. Men probably didn't want to be thought of as beautiful and gorgeous, she told herself drily. Too bad.

Elven males were also athletic, well-muscled, agile….

But it wasn't Brodie's physique that drew her, she thought. Or not only that. It was his eyes; it was his intensity. It was the way he looked at her, and the way she felt when he touched her.

She tossed, pounding her pillow, a blush rising to her cheeks. That afternoon, when she'd been in the shower, she'd had the most absurd fantasy of stepping out of the shower, grabbing a towel and walking downstairs. His flesh was almost as golden as his hair, and she longed to touch it. She'd imagined stepping up to him and letting the towel drop, telling him that too much work would leave them exhausted and incapable of logical thought, and that surrendering to the desires of the flesh could leave them ready to tackle the world again.

Pride was a great savior, though, and she'd done no such thing.

And yet...

She was imagining him again now, tall and imposing, seductive in his chinos and tailored shirt and black leather jacket.

A sound broke into her fantasy, something high-pitched and continuous. The sound of...

The alarm. One of her cousins had hit the little red button.

The House of the Rising Sun was under attack.

Chapter 7

The worst part about his job wasn't the dead, Brodie thought. It was the living.

He watched Nick Cassidy as he waited anxiously in the family "viewing" room at the morgue. Tony Brandt had no intention of walking the young man into the back and right up to the corpse of his partner. He was showing the face—cleaned up and as human as it was going to be without the talents of an expert mortician—on a monitor.

There was no doubt that Nick Cassidy had loved the man he saw on the screen. Brodie saw what he had expected and dreaded. First the look of denial, followed by the dawning of realization—and then the horror that what he saw couldn't be denied.

And last of all the tears.

Nick Cassidy convulsed and sank to the floor, shoulders shaking, hands to his face, tears streaming through his fingers.

Brodie let him cry, because there were no words to say. It wasn't going to "be all right," and nothing would make this moment better.

"Do you have family in the area?" he asked at last.

Nick shook his head. "Our families disowned us. We haven't seen or talked to any of them in...a decade. Not that I really had any family. My dad took off when I was two...my mother remarried some macho jock and I...I left at sixteen. Never looked back." He shook his head. "I'm not going back to my family now."

"Family doesn't always have to do with an accident of birth," Brodie told Nick. "Do you know anyone at all in the L.A. area?"

"Acquaintances, that's all," Nick said as he stood up slowly. He was suddenly angry. "Who did this? Why Jordan? He was the nicest guy in the world, never hurt anyone, loved the world, even when the world kicked him in the teeth."

"I don't know," Brodie said. "But I intend to find out. And you can help me with that. I need any emails you got from Jordan, and I need you to try to remember every conversation you had with him after he came down here." He paused, shaking his head. "Why didn't you file a missing person report?"

"Because last time I talked to Jordan he was all excited. He'd auditioned for the road show, and if he could travel, he was basically guaranteed the part. I just thought he was traveling at first, and when I started getting worried, I guess I was too upset to think of anything but coming down here to look for him myself."

"Nick, does the title *Vampire Rampage* mean anything to you?"

Nick stared back at him blankly. "It was a vampire play. I don't know if he ever said the name."

Tony showed up in the viewing room just then. He looked at Brodie, and Brodie nodded.

"I'm going to need you to help me," he said gently to Nick. Can you help me fill out some papers so the detectives can find out who did this to your friend? He really needs you to be strong right now."

"I—I…yes. Jordan…oh, Jordan!" Nick started to sob again.

Tony got him seated and looked at Brodie. "I've got this," he said. "You look like hell. Can't burn the candle at both ends forever, you know. Get out of here. Go home and get some sleep."

"I drove Mr. Cassidy here," Brodie said.

"I only came in to meet you," Tony said. "When he and I are finished, I'll see that he gets back to his car or his hotel."

"I'm going to need to interview him tomorrow," Brodie said.

"Of course. I'll make sure to get an address where you can reach him."

Brodie still stood there. He would never get used to having to tell people that their loved ones were dead.

"I've got this," Tony assured him.

"Thanks," Brodie said gruffly.

He was on the freeway when his phone started ringing.

He answered it quickly. "Brodie."

It was Rhiannon. "I need you. Can you get over here? Now? *Please!*"

Never in a thousand years had Rhiannon expected that the compound alarm would ever actually go off.

She was out of bed in two seconds and racing downstairs. A cabinet in the living room held an array of weapons. She opened it and hastily decided on a small crossbow that shot silver-tipped arrows—an effective choice against both werewolves and vampires.

She started to race for the door and then realized she wasn't even sure where she was going, because only the signal system at the tunnel entry would tell her whether it was coming from the main house or Gwydion's Cave. She grabbed her phone off the desk and stilled her shaking fingers long enough to dial Brodie's number, and then she dropped the phone, racing toward the kitchen. As she ran to the basement and reached the tunnel, she saw that the alarm had come from Sailor.

Rhiannon knew that it was her fault if Sailor had

been targeted—she had involved her cousin in everything that was going on.

The tunnels were equipped with emergency lightning, so she had no problem finding her way. She took the turn to the left, toward the main house, and nearly collided with Barrie, who was racing from Gwydion's Cave.

"What's happening?" Barrie asked anxiously.

"I don't know!"

They burst into the basement of the main house and ran for the stairs that led up to the kitchen. They found Merlin waiting for them at the top.

"What is it?" Rhiannon demanded.

"Shadows, dark shadows, swirling around Sailor. And there was a raven—a *real* raven—sitting on her bedpost. And I can't wake her up!" Merlin said.

With Rhiannon a step ahead of Barrie, they raced through the house and upstairs, then into Sailor's room.

Merlin had told the truth. A massive raven was now sitting on Sailor's chest.

Right on her chest!

Rhiannon couldn't use her weapon without skewering her cousin, so she tossed it down and made a dive for the bird. It flapped its giant wings and rose from Sailor's chest, then flew at Rhiannon with talons extended toward her. But Rhiannon felt the adrenaline pumping through her and ducked back down for the weapon. She didn't have time to discharge it, but she swiped with all her strength at the raging black creature throwing itself at her.

Barrie made a dive for Sailor, shaking her. "Sailor, wake up!"

Rhiannon managed to slam the crossbow right into the raven. It let out a terrible screech of wrath and began to flap wildly toward the ceiling; then it wheeled and headed for the stairs, flying down toward the first floor.

Rhiannon heard a furious oath explode from the stairway, and she realized that Brodie was there, running up the stairs as the *thing* raced down them. He slammed a fist into the massive bird and it fell to the floor, but when he reached down to grab it, it surged to life again and flew toward the living room.

"Catch it! I think it got her—I think it did something to Sailor!" Barrie shouted.

Rhiannon joined Brodie in the living room, where the raven was flying in frantic circles, searching for a way out. But as fast as it moved,

Brodie moved faster. He caught it with his fist again, and again it fell to the floor.

Rhiannon took aim and caught it with a silver-tipped arrow.

What happened next seemed like a scene in a movie built on digital special effects. The raven disintegrated into a cloud of black ash that first seemed to take the form of a man and then a skeleton, before raining down in a haze of black particles.

At the end something bounced down to the floor.

A skull, quickly followed by fragments of bone.

Rhiannon stared at Brodie, shell-shocked and speechless.

He looked back at her and walked over to the pile of ash. He bent low, taking a pen from his pocket to poke at the skull so he could study it. The lower jaw was missing—it had landed across the room.

He looked at Rhiannon. "Old vampire," he said. "Very old. They only crumble to dust like this when they're old. The new ones can be...messy."

Barrie came rushing down the stairs, accompanied by Sailor, who looked as if she didn't quite know where she was, much less what had happened.

"What's going on?" Sailor asked.

Rhiannon spun around to look at her cousin. "You don't know?"

"I was dreaming. A nice dream," Sailor said.

"A *sexual* dream?" Brodie asked her.

Sailor flushed scarlet. "Yes...and then I felt Barrie shaking me...and then I woke up. I—what happened? Why are you all in my house—and why is there a giant pile of dirt on my floor?"

Brodie strode over to Sailor and inspected her throat. "Clean, thank God...." He looked thoughtful as he said, "It's a good thing that we got him. Whoever the hell he was. Whatever poison he put into Sailor died with him."

"Poison?" Sailor gasped.

"It's all right—it's gone," Brodie said wearily. He looked at Rhiannon. She thought that she saw the slightest sparkle of respect in his eyes.

"A vampire dared to enter the home of a Keeper?" Sailor asked incredulously.

"And it went after Sailor, not Rhiannon," Barrie pointed out.

"Rhiannon can access the power of her charges," Brodie said. "And vampires can sicken and die from attacking other vampires. What I want to figure out right now is how the hell the damned thing got in," Brodie mused aloud.

"The window," Sailor said. "I was...warm, so I got up and opened the window, then fell asleep again."

"I guess it was that kind of a dream," Barrie said.

"Let's make sure all the windows are closed, because eventually we're going to have to get some sleep," Rhiannon said.

Rhiannon had forgotten Merlin, who had appeared at some point and was now standing near the sofa, looking thoughtful.

"Whoever it was, one of us had to know him," Merlin said.

"What?" Sailor asked.

Merlin looked at them in exasperation. "Whoever he was—"

"Or she," Brodie interjected.

"Or she," Merlin agreed. "One of us had to know them. A vampire can't come in without being invited. There are a lot of silly rumors about vampires, invented by everyone from Stoker to Hollywood, but that one thing is quite true. Whoever you just killed was someone who'd been invited into the House of the Rising Sun. Might have been yesterday, might have been decades ago—but somewhere along the way, it happened."

"And they were old, very old," Rhiannon murmured.

"We'll find out who it was—and why," Brodie said. "For now, though, let's search the house and close it up tight."

"It had to be *her!*" Sailor said suddenly.

"Her?" Rhiannon asked.

Sailor looked at Brodie. "You know. Audrey Fleur. She's angry at me because she wants to be in the movie and I got the part instead of her."

"Sailor, I just can't see any vampire taking a chance on entering the home of a *Keeper* over a role in a movie," Rhiannon said.

"We'll worry about who it was later," Brodie said. "For now, Barrie, go upstairs with Sailor and keep an eye on her. Rhiannon and Merlin and I will check out the house. And when we're done, well, we're all staying here tonight. That's a nice big couch over there, and it will do me just fine."

"All right," Barrie said. "Sailor, let's go. I have to be at the paper early tomorrow, so I need to get some sleep."

"Are you nuts? I couldn't possibly sleep right now," Sailor said.

"Well, then, you can watch me sleep," Barrie said. "Let's go."

They went up the stairs, and Merlin followed them, saying, "I'll holler if I find another open window."

"Thanks, Merlin," Rhiannon called to him.

She was suddenly acutely aware of the fact that she was alone with Brodie and wearing nothing but an oversize T-shirt and a pair of lacy panties.

Luckily he seemed focused on the possibility of renewed danger at that moment. And he could have no clue whatsoever that she'd been fantasizing about him when the alarm had gone off.

"How many rooms?" he asked her.

"Living room, dining room, kitchen and a family room out back on this floor. And a few closets," she added quickly.

"Start from the back, and I'll start from the front, and we'll meet in the middle," he told her.

Rhiannon was thorough; she even looked into cabinets when she hit the kitchen. Brodie met her there. "Merlin says Sailor closed her bedroom window and there's nothing else open upstairs."

"Thanks," she said. "Brodie, how did you get onto the property?"

"I'm Elven," he reminded her. "I parked at the top of the drive and cleared the wall in a single bound, just like Superman," he said lightly.

She laughed and realized that whatever might come of it, she was suddenly glad that he was in her life.

"Thank you," she said. "Thank you for getting here so quickly."

He nodded. "It's my job. It's what I do," he said. There was a husky tone to his voice, and he added quickly, "We might want to sweep up our uninvited guest."

"Good idea," she said, going for a broom.

"Are there two of those?" he asked her.

"You don't have to—"

"Yeah, I do," he said as she handed him a second broom.

He went back to the living room with her, and they began sweeping up the piles of ash. "The place is definitely going to need a good dusting tomorrow," she said.

Brodie hunkered down by the skull, then retrieved the jaw. "I'm going to take these to Tony

Brandt. It's a long shot, given his age, but maybe we can trace our vampire through his dental work."

"Can you tell from the skull what sex our visitor was?" she asked him.

Brodie shook his head. "I can't. Maybe Tony can. You have some kind of a tote here? Something I can carry this in?"

"Sure." She went into the kitchen and delved into the broom closet. She found a reusable fabric grocery bag and took it to him.

"Perfect," he told her as he put the skull and disarticulated jawbone into the bag.

They stood there awkwardly for a moment. Then Rhiannon swung into hostess mode. "There are four extra rooms upstairs—you're welcome to a real bed."

"I think I'll just stay down here," he said. "Maybe not awake and aware, but ready to be up, awake and aware if I need to."

"Okay. You know, you don't have to stay. I can…I can keep watch 'til morning."

"I'd be happier staying the night."

"Okay. But at least let me get you a pillow and a blanket."

"That would be great."

She ran upstairs to the linen closet, then hurried back bearing a pillow and bedding. "The couch opens up into a bed," she told him.

"I'll be just fine the way it is," he assured her.

"Okay. Well, then, I'll leave you," she told him. "If you're the first one up, there's coffee in the pot already—a tradition in the main house—and there are tea bags and hot chocolate and cereal... Help yourself."

"I'll do that."

"Good night, then."

"Good night."

He smiled and nodded but didn't turn away. For a moment she envisioned a strange fantasy in which he stepped forward and took her into his arms. She pictured herself touching his face, fascinated by the lines and strength of it. Then his lips touched hers, and she was infused with the fire his gaze ignited when she least expected it.

She blinked quickly, offered him a brief nod of acknowledgment and turned away.

Rhiannon hurried up the stairs and looked into Sailor's room. Despite Sailor's earlier protest that she was wide awake, she was sound asleep, just as Barrie seemed to be at her side. Rhiannon smiled, surprised to realize that she felt like a mother hen looking in on them. She *was* the oldest; she had Barrie by a year, and Sailor a year and a half.

And now, here in the Canyon, it was down to the three of them to keep order.

They'd done all right tonight, she thought. Yes, Brodie had helped, but most people in the world got by with a little help, and she realized that to be the best she could be, she had to be open to help when it was available.

She walked down to the guest room where she had always slept when she came out to California to visit. There were still posters of her favorite rock bands on the walls. No one had ever taken them down. The room had been hers, and if things hadn't worked out the way they had she wouldn't even be in L.A. No, the main house was Sailor's, and she didn't begrudge her cousin in the least.

She walked over to the dresser. The years of her youth seemed combined there. Ticket stubs from plays, concerts and movies had gone into a cup. She opened the little jewelry box. A tiny statue of Judy Garland popped up, and "Over the Rainbow" began to play.

She needed to clean out the room, she thought drily. It was wonderful, but it was hers no more. The old Keepers were not coming back.

But for tonight...

She turned off the overhead light and lay down, but unlike her cousins, she really was wide awake. Her heart was still pounding too quickly.

Sleep, she needed sleep.

It would be nice to slip back into that fantasy she'd been having when she was so abruptly awakened by the alarm.

No, not a good idea, not when the object of her fantasy was lying on a couch just below. Flesh and blood. So close she felt she could still feel the leather of his jacket, the touch of his hand, and hear his voice.

No, no, no, no.

Dear God, he was Elven! She had to stop thinking about his eyes, his face, his body and his touch! He would read her mind if she didn't keep her guard up, and then she would die of humiliation. She barely knew him, and she was having hot, sweaty, imaginative dreams about what she'd seen of him and wondering about the parts she hadn't.

To distract herself she started thinking about to-morrow night and the council meeting. Her first...

They probably assumed that she would just listen.

If so, they were assuming wrong.

It wasn't mandatory that every Other attend every council meeting, much less the informal multi-race get-togethers afterward, but most liked to enjoy an evening where there was no need for pretense. It was wonderful to live in a mixed world, but there was a real relief in escaping pretense for a place where everyone was different and the various races could mingle. Sure, throughout the years and across the globe prejudice had reared its ugly head, even between the other races. Shapeshifters who hated werewolves. Werewolves who thought they were better than the vampires. Vampires who looked down on the Elven. Most of the time that prejudice came from the same sources as in the human world: fear or poverty or envy. But with the Others' supernatural abilities, the consequences could be much worse, and that was why the Keepers existed. They were the hand of tolerance and balance in a world where, even taken all together, the Others were still just a fraction of the population, always in danger of discovery and extinction. Dissension and malicious behavior could endanger them all.

She rolled over in misery.

And the vampires were at it right now—when she had barely arrived.

She felt her anger begin to burn again. There was no doubt that a vampire had invaded Sailor's home tonight, no doubt that somewhere out there, at least one vampires was pursuing evil.

She would never fall asleep if she stayed this angry.

She forced herself to go over song lyrics, and eventually she dozed off. When she opened her eyes again, the sun was sending delicate patterns of gold through the curtains.

Brodie woke at seven, and he could smell coffee brewing. When he opened his eyes, he saw that one of the Gryffald cousins was standing by the couch, holding a cup of coffee and staring down at him. It was Barrie. Disappointment filled him.

"Good morning, Detective, and thank you for staying the night. Coffee?"

"Sure. Thank you."

Barrie handed him the cup. As he sat up, she perched next to him, staring at him. "Are the police going to give any kind of a press conference about the murders? I've been doing my best to get information out of my sources on the street, but no one seems to know anything about a vampire on a killing spree. I was thinking that some press coverage might make someone remember something, maybe lead to ID'ing the victims."

"And it could make a killer hungrier," Brodie said.

"Hungrier?" That was Rhiannon. Freshly showered and dressed for the day, she was coming down the stairs. "A vampire broke into this house last night. Sailor could have died. I think we might as well go for broke and give Barrie a chance at a big story."

Rhiannon was angry, he thought. He didn't need to read her mind to know that.

She was taking last night's attack personally, which, he supposed, was natural. She was the vampire Keeper, and her cousin might have been killed by one of her out-of-control charges.

"All right, slow down and let's think about this," he said. "The attack last night might have been intended purely to enrage you, Rhiannon, and make you react rashly. It was meant personally, yes, but you can't let yourself take it that way. You're a Keeper. You have to remain in control at all times." He turned to her cousin. "Barrie, I'll talk to my captain about your idea for a press conference. I have an identity now on one of the victims, and I have a tech working on trying to figure out who the others were, but you're right that getting the public involved might help. I'll see that a police spokesman calls you about any press conference, all right?" He looked back at Rhiannon, who nodded curtly and walked into the kitchen, presumably in search of coffee.

"Thanks," Barrie said, rising. "I have to get to work." She paused, though, and asked, "Do you think that attack was specifically directed at Sailor? Or are we all in danger now?"

Brodie looked at Barrie. "I don't know. I think you all need to be careful until we figure this out. Maybe I should drop you at work."

"I'm game," she told him.

"Rhiannon? How about you?" he asked as she came back into the living room.

"I don't have to be anywhere until this evening, so

I think I'll stay here with Sailor, who's still asleep. I'm still a little worried, though. Will you give me a call and let me know whatever you find out?"

He nodded, finished his coffee and carried the cup to the kitchen.

Rhiannon followed him and leaned against the sink, looking serious. "Should we...meet tonight? After the council meetings?"

He wished she hadn't followed him into the kitchen. They were too close.

"Absolutely. Go to the Snake Pit. Barrie will already be there, because that's where the shifters meet. I'll bring Sailor, since we'll be at the same meeting, and meet you there."

Yes, being this close to her was definitely a mistake. He was dying to reach out and touch her. He could smell the shower-fresh dampness of her skin, and he could almost feel the touch of her hair against him.

This wasn't going to work. He had to get out of here. "I need to get home for a quick shower, and then to the station and the morgue," he told her. "I'll drop Barrie, make sure she's safely at the paper. Can you take Sailor to the café with you this afternoon, then drop her at the old church for her council meeting before you head to your own?" His voice sounded like a growl. Hell, at that moment, he might as well have been a werewolf. He offered her a forced smile before he collected the tote bag and headed back to the living room to collect Barrie.

It was an easy ride to the newspaper office, and from there he went back to his own place to shower and change, before making his way to the station.

Adam was grinning when Brodie approached his desk. "You should kiss me!" Adam told him. "I mean, don't, but you should."

"You've found something?"

Adam nodded. "Five names. One was Jordan Bellow—but I understand that he was identified last night. There are four more—two are women, though, so they aren't your corpses. The two remaining men are Oscar Garcia and Deacon Steitz. Oscar grew up in foster homes, but he'd been at a halfway house in Oregon before going to Hollywood—to audition for a play. The guy running the halfway house said that he'd been a good guy, but he kept slipping in and out of AA. Kept having relapses. When he never came back to the halfway house, the guy just figured he'd gotten the part.

Deacon Steitz was a loner. Both parents died in a car crash when he was twenty-two. He spent time in Chicago working the comedy clubs, then told a friend he was heading to California to try for the big time. The two women—Lila Mill and Rose Gillespie—were two more acting wannabes. Lila was a Southern California girl, twenty-three, tried three different colleges, always shopping around for scholarships, and then told a friend that she was going to audition for the 'perfect' play and not to expect to hear from her until she'd made it big. Similar story for the other woman. She was excited, heading out to audition for a play that was going to be her big break. She was being very secretive about it, though, so no one actually knew where she'd gone. Still don't, since we don't have two dead women."

Brodie felt as if a rock had slipped down his throat to his stomach. "We don't have them yet," he said wearily. "All five of them auditioned for *Vampire Rampage?*"

"Yep—I went off the lists you gave me. Four of them made the callbacks. I found the fifth when I checked the initial audition lists."

"Good work. Thanks, Adam," Brodie said, but

the words felt dry in his mouth. "Pull up a map of the Canyon area for me, will you? Find me something that shows me all lakes and waterways."

Adam groaned. "You'll have to give me a few minutes."

"You've got it."

"So, why are you still standing there?" Adam asked him.

"I can stand for a few minutes."

Adam turned back to his computer.

Brodie waited.

There were two more bodies out there. Two women. He had to find them.

While Adam worked at the computer, Brodie drew out his cell and gave Tony the names he had just gotten from Adam; he was certain that they could officially ID their John Does now that he had the names.

Five people had disappeared, unnoticed because of the lives they had led, until finally one's lover had come looking for him.

"You're sure?" Tony asked.

"Nothing is sure until you do the forensic testing."

"I'll get right on it."

"I'm ninety-nine percent sure there are two dead women out there, too. I'm going to find them."

Tony sighed. "I'll be waiting," he said.

Adam was still on his computer when Brodie hung up. "By the way, have you seen the paper today?" the younger man asked.

Brodie tensed, remembering that picture Jake Reynolds had snapped last night.

"No. Why?"

Adam glanced up for a minute. "You look good. Hot Hollywood star all the way. And your date— she's even hotter. Up and coming singer, huh?"

"Adam, where's the paper?" Brodie asked, trying to keep his temper in check.

"Right there, other side of my desk. I know I can get the news on the computer, but I still get a paper every day. I like turning the pages, doing the crossword puzzle."

Brodie wasn't listening as Adam droned on, telling him the advantages of real paper over a computer screen. He picked up the newspaper and began riffling through it—the picture was on the nightlife page.

It was a good picture, actually. He and Rhiannon were looking into each other's eyes. He had to admit that if he'd seen that picture of two others, he would be convinced they were a real couple.

He hurriedly read the caption underneath the photo, which didn't say much. *Actor Mac Brodie from the play Vampire Rampage, out with the Mystic Café's trending new singer, Rhiannon Gryffald. Could she be the girl of his dreams?*

And that was it.

Brodie let out a sigh. He decided that gnomes weren't really such nasty little beasts.

"I've got your maps," Adam said. "You've got a lot of water to cover."

"Then I'd better get started," Brodie said, taking the maps from Adam with a terrible sense of foreboding. The minute he looked at the first map, he knew exactly where he was going to find the next body.

Chapter 8

Rhiannon took Sailor with her to work at the Mystic Café, where she had an evening set scheduled, since the council meetings didn't start 'til late, when most of L.A. was safely tucked into bed.

She was surprised to see that the café was full when she arrived, and that most of the clientele seemed to have coffee and pastries already, and were actually waiting—for her.

"Hey, it's a crowd!" Sailor told her happily.

"I wonder why."

"I don't," Sailor said, pointing to a little table next to the small stage. "Look."

Sailor looked. The newspaper was lying on the table, folded open to the nightlife page. And there she was, staring into Brodie's eyes. Jake Reynolds had done everything she had asked him.

"Oh, my God, I am so jealous," Sailor said. "And look at all the people in here. Hugh is going to be thrilled."

"Yes…but…"

"Oh, come on, Rhiannon. You were irritated about coming to California, sure your career was over. Now you have a real audience," Sailor said.

"Yes, but…"

Yes, she had an audience. But what did that mean next to the fact that people were dead? And most likely at the hands—or fangs—of a vampire, maybe even one of *her* vampires. She realized now that she wanted to be a good Keeper—a respected Keeper, like her father before her.

Hugh made an appearance just then, a huge smile on his face. He actually paused to hug them both. "I've made a fortune already tonight, so don't mess up. None of that 'I Hate Hollywood' crap tonight, Rhiannon. No more 'I hate actors.'"

Sailor looked at her. "You hate actors?" she asked.

"Of course not. I was just angry about the interruption from—oh, never mind." She turned away to get her guitar out of the case. She should have known that impromptu song was going to come back to haunt her.

The night went well, so well that at one point the place was standing room only.

"I can't believe it's council meeting night. I wouldn't close! I'd stay open 'til dawn," Hugh said to her during a break. "Here's hoping tomorrow will be just as good."

"I don't work here tomorrow," she reminded him. "I'm at the Snake Pit tomorrow, remember?"

"Tell that slimy shapeshifter you can't make it," he said.

"I can't do that and you know it. But we've still got an hour 'til closing, so let's make some money, okay?"

Hugh was unhappy, but when 10:00 p.m. rolled around he made the announcement that they were closing and people began filing out. When the last customers were gone, and Rhiannon had her guitar and equipment ready to go, Sailor let out a soft whistle.

"Rhiannon!"

"What?"

"You made money—a lot of money. You have a few hundred bucks here."

"Good. The way things are going, I'm going to need it," Rhiannon said. "Come on, we have to get moving. I have to drop you at the church and get to the House of Illusion before eleven."

"Hey, aren't you going to take the paper?" Sailor asked her.

"No, why?"

"Because that picture is hot, that's why. Do you two have a real thing going on?"

"We just met."

Sailor laughed. "That doesn't mean anything. You either have chemistry or you don't. And you two seem to sizzle."

"There's a serious situation going on," Rhiannon said primly.

"You *are* attracted to him. Natural, I suppose. He *is* Elven, after all."

"I've known dozens of Elven," Rhiannon said, "and I assure you, I didn't want to jump in bed with them."

"Just Brodie."

"Sailor!"

"Hey, you know what they say? Once you go Elven, you know you've been to heaven."

"It's taboo," Rhiannon murmured. "We're not supposed to...mix."

"Why?" Sailor said.

"I don't know. That's just what they say," Rhiannon told her.

"I've heard of a vampire Keeper down in New Orleans who fell in love with a vampire cop," Sailor said.

"I think there could be repercussions."

Sailor laughed. "Then just give in and sleep with him."

"Sailor..."

"Hey, I wish *I* could stumble on to a Mr. Right."

"Come on, we're wasting time," Rhiannon said.

The freeway was moving smoothly enough, but Rhiannon swore at every driver who slowed her down for two seconds. Sailor just rolled her eyes and told her, "Calm down."

"It's our first time attending council meetings as Keepers," Rhiannon reminded her.

"That's right, and they'll wait for us if we're late," Sailor said, grinning.

Rhiannon looked at her and smiled slowly in return. There was something in her cousin's tone—a touch of steel—that said she was going to do just fine.

She dropped Sailor at the deconsecrated 1890s church on Vine—by day it was a very trendy boutique carrying very trendy clothing. She saw the magician from the night before—the Count de Soir—and several other Elven at the entry. Sailor would be in good hands, but still Rhiannon was afraid to leave her. Then she saw that Brodie was there. He saw her, too, and came walking over to the car. He looked grim.

"What's wrong?" she asked him.

He waved a hand in the air. "We'll talk later. Come on, Sailor, I'll walk you in."

"Wish me luck," Sailor whispered to her.

Rhiannon nodded, but she was looking at Brodie. "Keep her safe. Please."

"Count on it. We'll see you at the Snake Pit after this," Brodie promised her.

Then he and Sailor turned away, and Rhiannon quickly drove on to her own destination.

Because the House of Illusion was owned by a vampire magician, Jerry Oglethorpe, the vampire council was held there. Jerry knew all the traditional magician's moves, but he also liked to do a little cheating that left his audience—and his peers—awed. As a vampire, he could perform illusions that the others couldn't begin to match. Some young magicians were counting on the hope that when he died, his secrets would be revealed. Rhiannon often felt sorry for them; they had no idea that Jerry would probably outlive them, and his secrets would never be known.

Rhiannon hadn't been to the House of Illusion often. The majestic castle hidden away in the Canyon was really a social club for magicians, but on Friday and Saturday nights it functioned as a magicians' showcase. They sold tickets, but you had to be invited to buy one. That kept the House of Illusion a fantasy—and made attendance there a must-manage-to-do for many of the tourists who came to Hollywood. And it made the Count's invitation to the audience at the Snake Pit a real coup.

But once every two months, on the second Thursday night, the vampire council was held. There was an elected president who presided over the meeting, but the Keeper was the real power.

Rhiannon was already in her seat, in the first row in front of the stage, when Darius Simonides rose to preside over the council. He knocked his gavel on the podium twice, calling the room to order. Rhiannon looked around as conversation died down to whispers and then disappeared altogether.

The room was filled with vampires from every walk of life. Many were in film and TV in one way or another: producers, directors, actors, agents, sound men, electricians, costume designers, set designers, script writers, musicians and more. There were also bankers, ad execs, waiters and waitresses, shop owners and other businessmen and women. In a way, she mused, it almost looked like a PTA meeting, except that some in attendance were very young and some were very old.

"Welcome to this convention of our people," Darius said. "First, may I please have the minutes from our last meeting?"

The minutes were read. The last meeting—the last one her father had attended—had apparently been very dull. They had talked about sources for blood, most of which were slaughterhouses, and employment opportunities. A party was being planned for Halloween, and the discussion had centered on the date, since many vampires had previous commitments on the holiday itself.

Darius asked for old business, which was equally boring.

New business came next. A banker had ordered blood from a new venue and found it to be very high quality. A woman stood up and announced that she was purchasing land on the outskirts of Santa Barbara, and planned on cattle ranching. Someone else suggested a summer party.

Seriously, a PTA meeting would have been exciting in comparison, Rhiannon thought.

Except that it was very likely one of the seemingly normal vampires in attendance was a killer.

At last Darius brought up the most pressing piece of new business. "You all know that we've had to say goodbye to Piers Gryffald," he said, and his words were greeted with a groan. "But I'm happy to say that the new Keeper of the Canyon vampire society is here with us tonight, fresh, young, beautiful—and ready to take on her duties and become an integral part of our brother and sisterhood. I present Miss Rhiannon Gryffald."

She was greeted with hearty applause, but since it would have been rude of them to welcome her in any other way, she didn't read too much into that.

Rhiannon left her seat. Darius met her at the stairs and politely escorted her up.

"Thank you all for that cordial welcome, and thank you all as well for your show of warmth for my father. I know we'll all miss him while he serves the Otherworld in his new capacity."

Those words were followed by more applause. She lifted a hand.

"There is a grave matter facing our membership at this very moment," she announced, making sure that her voice rang loud and clear. "The police have found three bodies that show signs of vampire attack. We're lucky that, so far, the medical examiner who has handled all three autopsies is Dr. Anthony Brandt, a fellow member of the Otherworld. So far the press has taken very little interest in the case, though that may change soon, so we need to be prepared for rumors of a murderer imitating a vampire when he kills."

A man in a typical banker's suit stood. "Why haven't we heard anything about this before?" he demanded. "Why has there been no report of the murders at all?"

"There have been reports. But the dead were John Does, and their deaths were relegated to the back of the paper. Additionally, some details of the crimes have been withheld by the police," Rhiannon said. A discontented murmuring started, and she knew she had to nip it in the bud.

"So," she announced loudly, her voice ringing with authority, "as we all know, there are members of the human race who believe that vampires exist, and others who *know* they do, so it is certainly possible that a human being is using this method of murder to make the killings appear to be the work of a vampire. I want you to know that I'm your greatest champion. I know that you and the other members of the vampire community just want to survive and pursue your dreams. And I want you all to be aware that I *will* find out the truth of these murders in conjunction with other members of the greater Otherworld. If a vampire *is* guilty of these attacks—attacks that put the entire community in danger—that vampire will face the greatest punishment we are authorized to mete out." She paused and looked around the room. "Total extinction. Don't believe for a moment that I will not fulfill my duties to the letter of our mutual law, or that I will shirk in any way when it comes to protecting those who are innocent. I strongly suggest that anyone who knows anything tells me what they know, so they won't suffer along with the murderer."

She stood for a moment, staring out over the now silent crowd.

"It has to be a human!" someone in the audience said. "We're happy here. Why would we kill anyone?"

"As I said, it *is* possible that a human being is the killer," Rhiannon said. "And that possibility will be investigated. But a *vampire* attempted to attack my cousin at the House of the Rising Sun last night," she said. "That vampire is now ash. Be assured that I will not tolerate any attack on myself, my home or my family, and that transgressors *will* die without benefit of interrogation. If anyone knows anything about this attack, I need to know what you know. At the same time, if there is any threat to this community, I will just as aggressively seek to protect those of you who are innocent. But I will not forget what happened last night, and I won't stop until I have an answer." She paused again, looking around the room. "I am my father's daughter. Please don't believe that my justice will be any less swift. In the meantime, I am available whenever I'm needed by any one of you, just as my father was before me. In closing—if you find that you're missing a friend or acquaintance, please come to me. Because there is a pile of ash at my house that was once one of you."

She turned to Darius, who was staring at her, as stunned as the others. She smiled and said, "Thank you, Darius. I look forward to a long and mutually beneficial relationship with all of you—again, just as my father enjoyed before me."

Darius didn't offer her a hand back to her seat. It didn't matter. She was perfectly capable of walking down a few steps on her own.

She was sure that Darius had originally planned to say more, but he seemed tongue-tied. Finally he banged the gavel on the podium. "This meeting of the Canyon vampire community is hereby dismissed!"

He came down the steps in a hurry. Rhiannon was certain he had a lot to say to her—no doubt he intended to chastise her for alienating the community from the get-go.

But she certainly hadn't alienated them all, because a lot of people came up to her to shake her hand and say they were glad she was going to take a firm stand. Others remembered her from when she was younger and spoke to her about her family, while some just wanted to welcome her.

Jerry Oglethorpe came over, studying her gravely. "Good start, Miss Gryffald."

"Thank you, Jerry. And while I have you, a magician who bills himself as the Count de Soir was performing at the Snake Pit the other night. He invited his entire audience here on Sunday night. Does that have any bearing on my case?"

"The Count de Soir—he's Elven," Jerry said.

"I know that. He told me that he saw Merlin—remember, Ivan Schwartz, the magician who owned the House of the Rising Sun—in a dream. And that Merlin told him to help me," Rhiannon said.

"Of course I remember Merlin," Oglethorpe said. "He was one of the finest magicians—and men—I ever knew. I don't know whether the count's invitation has anything to do with your case, though. He *is* performing Sunday night. I'll reserve a table for you."

"Thank you, Jerry. We'll be here   my cousins and I. And probably a friend," Rhiannon said.

Darius came up to her then. "My, my, Miss Gryffald. That was rather…hostile."

She shook her head. "I'm not being hostile, Darius. I am here to fight for the rights of the vampires, but someone out there is putting the entire vampire race at risk with these killings. If I don't find the truth, his actions will eventually bring down our entire house of cards. That's why it's so important that this community understand that I'm not a figurehead."

"You've certainly created a stir."

"Across all species in the Otherworld," she said. "The matter is being brought up at two other council meetings tonight, perhaps more." She paused. "Darius, my cousin was attacked last night in her own home. And it wasn't by any wannabe vampire. This was the real thing."

"Male or female?"

"I don't know—it was a very old vampire. No messy organ tissue left at all—except for a few bones, the intruder turned entirely to ash."

"Male, then, for the sake of conversation," Darius said. "Which of your cousins did he come after?"

"He attacked Sailor when she was sleeping."

"Sailor?" Darius said, sounding surprised.

He knows something! Rhiannon thought.

"Yes. Darius, if you know anything—"

"Don't you use that tone with me, young lady!"

he said. "If I could prevent danger to anyone, I would. Especially Sailor. She is my godchild."

He turned and walked away from her. Jerry Oglethorpe looked at her and shrugged. "Rhiannon, Darius is old guard. He's not just powerful in our community. He's extremely powerful in Hollywood and the entire film business. He's just huffy because you wounded his pride, saying what you did without consulting him first."

"Thanks, Jerry. Well, I guess I'm headed to the Snake Pit," she said.

He grinned. "I'll be there eventually myself. This is a big night for all of us Others. There's been a lot of anticipation and excitement about you and your cousins taking over as Keepers, you know. Anyway—" he smiled "—I'll see you there. Be careful on the drive over, okay?"

"Why?" she asked sharply.

"Okay, Rhiannon, now you're sounding paranoid. Be careful on the drive because it's late and this is L.A., where way too many people drive drunk, and drunk or sober, everyone drives at eighty and changes lanes without signaling. Okay?"

She smiled. "Yes, Jerry, okay. And thank you."

She left the House of Illusion and was approaching her car when she heard someone behind her. Instinct sent shivers up her spine, and she spun quickly to assess the threat.

It was the actress Audrey Fleur. She clapped as Rhiannon turned. "Bravo, Miss Gryffald. Wonderful speech."

"Thank you," Rhiannon said, even though she was well aware that the other woman was being sarcastic.

"Terribly distressing, of course," Audrey said. She walked over and leaned against Rhiannon's Volvo. "It was so upsetting last night when that poor man started asking about his lover. I'm assuming he's one of the dead?"

"Yes."

"Do you think that a rogue vampire would really defy your authority?" Audrey asked, her eyes wide, her voice scared—but a smile was playing over her lips.

"I don't actually *know* much of anything yet, Audrey. When I do, everyone will learn what *I* learn. I'll call a special session of the council if necessary."

"Wow! You really think you're that good?"

"I intend to be."

"Well, bravo once again. See you at the Snake Pit," Audrey said, pushing away from the Volvo and starting toward her own car. She turned back. "Oh, by the way, do be careful. Keepers have been killed in the past, and we would never want anything so horrible happening to you."

Rhiannon stared after Audrey and wondered if the woman really did hate Sailor for "stealing" her role. Because if she hated Sailor, she might hate them all.

But they'd killed the vampire who attacked Sailor last night.

And it obviously hadn't been Audrey, since she was definitely alive—or rather, undead—and kicking.

She got into her Volvo and looked at the clock in the dash. 1:00 a.m. The meeting had lasted nearly two hours, she noted. As she drove, she replayed events in her mind.

Last night they had killed a vampire. Maybe that had been *the* vampire, the one killing human beings and draining their blood. She needed to ask Brodie about that theory, see if maybe he thought they had come to the end of it. Of course, they didn't know who the dead vampire had been....

Or if he'd been working with anyone else.

She pulled onto the freeway. This being L.A., there were plenty of other cars; some sped by her, and some she passed. No big deal either way, since the Snake Pit was only a few exits away.

She had just taken the exit ramp when she felt a huge jolt on the roof, as if a pterodactyl had landed.

She fought with the steering wheel to keep the car under control, almost veering into the steel guardrail but managing to straighten the wheels just before she swerved into it.

She reached the end of the ramp and turned onto the street. Luckily the Snake Pit was just a few blocks ahead.

The thing slammed onto the top of the car again, sending her careening onto the sidewalk. She heard the undercarriage of the Volvo rip over the curb and managed to steer back onto the street just before crashing into a boutique.

Shaking, terrified, she delved desperately into her mind for some idea as to what to do, and then she knew. She had only one choice, and it was a choice she'd never imagined she would have to make.

She should have practiced more often, should have listened to her father.

Oh, Lord, she should have started as soon as this case began.

She slammed to a halt and sat there for a long moment. It would come again, she knew.

It could be anything, an Elven, a werewolf, a vampire, or, a shapeshifter, with its ability to become anything at all....

Shapeshifters lost strength when they shifted. Werewolves could only rip and tear when they changed into the beast they were at heart. Elven might be powerful, but they would always be Elven, the least aggressive of the races. And vampires... well, she could be a vampire, too.

And so she straightened and willed herself to change. She felt her fangs growing, her canine teeth elongating, and she felt the strength growing in her limbs.

She got out of the car and looked around, saw nothing.

A Buick drove by. The young couple in it stared at her, and the man hit the gas.

"I know you're out there!" Rhiannon cried. "You're out there, and you're a coward, attacking by night. Well, you won't get me. You won't get me, and you won't get my cousins. I will destroy you first, do you hear me? Your reign of terror is over!"

There was no sound at all then. Not even a car drove by.

Shaking, she got back into the driver's seat.

Had it been Audrey Fleur? Had Audrey been truly threatening her outside the House of Illusion?

She turned the key in the ignition and winced at the sound the car made as she started driving again, then cursed softly. Her car was going to need work.

For a moment it occurred to her that maybe her attacker was trying to frighten her into leaving L.A. or just cowering in her house, too afraid to perform her duties. And then...

Then, when she was weak and beaten, strike again and...

Take over the city? Could it be that simple?

She made her way the last few blocks to the Snake Pit, left her car with the valet and hurried inside.

She saw Brodie sitting in a booth with Sailor and Barrie the minute she arrived. The club was full; it seemed as if everyone from every race had shown up. Of course, since the shifters held their meeting there, they outnumbered everyone else. Piped-in music was playing in the background.

Brodie stood, frowning as she arrived. "What's wrong?" he asked her quickly.

"I'm fine," she said, feeling too shaken to talk about it. She slid into the booth next to Barrie. "How were your meetings?" she asked them.

"Mine was lovely," Sailor said.

"Everything went very well," Barrie said gravely. "And by the way, nice picture of you and Brodie in the paper today."

"Yes, the gnome came through," Rhiannon said.

"How was *your* meeting?" Barrie asked Rhiannon.

"Lovely," she said sarcastically. "I told them one of them might be a murderer. I went over really well. Although," she added, "some of them did seem to genuinely appreciate my honesty."

Barrie smiled. "I brought the situation up with the shapeshifters. They all swore they'd keep their eyes open."

"I spoke to Hugh on my way in," Brodie said. "He said that he talked to the werewolves, but they assured him that a wolf wasn't guilty—you wouldn't be looking at a few pinprick marks if a werewolf had gone rogue, you'd be looking at victims that had been torn apart."

"True," Rhiannon admitted.

"Did you tell them about last night?" Sailor asked her.

Rhiannon nodded.

"Wait, wait!" Barrie said, raising her hand. "Are we really supposed to be discussing our meetings? I thought we were supposed to keep some confidentiality going."

"Between *us?*" Rhiannon asked her.

"Yes, even between us," Barrie said.

"There are times when we're going to have to be open and brutally honest—especially with each other. When a situation might not involve the entire community, that's one thing. When what happens may have repercussions for everybody, that's different," Rhiannon said. "We're still learning here, of course. We were thrown into this situation. But that's the way I see it, and I think my view is logical."

"I don't really see—" Sailor began, but then she broke off. "There's Darius. And he's looking for me. He looks concerned. Excuse me, please, I'm going to go talk to him."

Rhiannon watched her cousin walk away, and then turned to Brodie and Barrie. "She doesn't seem to realize that she was attacked by a vampire last night, and if Merlin hadn't hit the alarm, we couldn't have stopped it."

"Do you think the attack last night was directed against *her*—or against her because of *you?*" Barrie asked.

"I don't know. I just don't know." Rhiannon looked at Brodie. "I had a wonderful moment tonight thinking that although we might never know his identity, we might have killed the killer last night. But now I don't think that's the case."

"What happened?" he asked sharply.

"Something kept attacking my car when I was on my way here. And I'm pretty sure that Audrey Fleur threatened me," she told him.

He frowned. "Audrey?"

"You suspect her, too?"

"I wish to hell I knew—but she's the only vampire in the play," he reminded her. "Do you know if she's here?" he asked, looking around.

She set a hand on his and said quickly, "I don't know. But she was getting into her own car. If she drove here, then it certainly wasn't her."

"She could have parked somewhere and come after you," he told her.

Her hand still rested on his, and suddenly she wasn't thinking about being attacked anymore. She was far more afraid of something that Sailor had said earlier. *Once you go Elven...*

She drew her hand back. "I want to act as if nothing disturbing happened at all. Whoever is behind this, I want them to believe that I can handle whatever they throw at me."

"There's a story in this somewhere," Barrie said, and then her attention was caught by something across the room. "Your nasty little costar is here," she told Brodie. "She's right over there with Sailor and Darius. And look who's joining them. That shapeshifter doorman from the theater—what was his name? Bobby something? He looks as if he's hungering for Audrey, who's fawning all over Darius."

"Bobby Conche," Brodie said. "And see how he's watching Sailor, too? He just loves actresses. All the pretty ones, anyway."

Brodie looked as if he was about to walk over and confront Audrey.

"Wait," Rhiannon said. "Let's watch and see what she does."

They watched, but Audrey didn't do anything interesting. She just sat there chatting.

"I'll go join them," Barrie said. "And I'll watch out for Sailor. No one is going to try anything in here tonight, that's for certain."

"All right," Rhiannon said.

When Barrie had gone, Brodie looked at Rhiannon and said, "I don't like it. You're in serious danger."

She smiled at him. "Brodie, we Keepers are well able to defend ourselves and keep the law."

He caught both her hands, and his eyes met hers. "Rhiannon, someone else is dead," he told her.

She swallowed, lowering her head. Her guilt was choking her.

This was happening on her watch.

"Today? Someone was killed today?" she whispered.

He shook his head. "I had my tech go through the casting lists, and so far four of the five people he researched and couldn't find are dead. I found a woman today at the bottom of a pond in the back of an estate not far from the theater. So far Tony

Brandt can't get a handle on when she was killed—could have been a week ago, could have been two. She was completely submerged and...well, you know what nature does to a body," he said quietly.

"Brodie, what do I do?" she asked miserably.

"We'll find the truth."

"But—it's my responsibility."

"No one works without help, Rhiannon," he told her. "And the thing is, now you know you're in danger, so now you know to protect yourself from it. And chances are your attacker is connected to our killer—if it's not the same person—and now we know for sure that our killer is connected to the play."

"I'm sorry to say it, but if we really are looking for a vampire, then we need to look at Audrey."

"And Darius," he added quietly.

"Why would Darius risk everything he has in order to gain...nothing?"

"I don't know, but we need to investigate them both. It's hard. We can't pin them down with a 'where were you on the night of whenever,' because we don't have a time of death." He was quiet for a moment. "I don't want you alone, all right? Tomorrow...during the day..."

"What?"

He sighed. "I'll keep you with me."

She grimaced. "You don't sound terribly happy about that. And frankly, I'm more concerned about Sailor. She could have been killed last night."

"And you could have been killed tonight. Anyway, Sailor told me she's having a costume fitting tomorrow. She'll be surrounded by people," Brodie said.

"That doesn't explain why you don't sound happy about having me with you."

He drew a deep breath. "Because I'm going to be searching for a fifth body."

Chapter 9

They stayed for another hour. At one point Rhiannon ended up in conversation with Audrey, but she didn't say a word about being attacked on the way in, and if Audrey was expecting her to be upset or afraid, she didn't show it.

Brodie spent some time off in a corner with Tony Brandt, and she knew by watching his face that they were discussing the case.

Finally even the denizens of the night began to head home.

Rhiannon joined up with her cousins and Brodie, and they walked together out to the valet stand.

"We're good to go," Rhiannon told him. "The three of us can take my car. We'll be all right getting home."

He stared at her incredulously. "Rhiannon, I respect you, and I know how competent you are. Whatever you said tonight, all the vampires are watching you now, and they look as if they've had a good slap in the face, a wake-up call, like they realize suddenly that someone *is* watching. But come on. Last night there was a vampire attack basically in your *own home*. Tonight— *as you were leaving the vampire council*—you were attacked. Try to shake me all you like, but I'm following you home."

She stared at him silently, then turned to hand over the slip for her car.

"Rhiannon?"

"You just said that you're going to follow me no matter what. Is there something I should say?"

He grinned, that slow, lazy Elven grin that made her go a little crazy every time she saw it, and the blood surged warm and hot through her veins, making her fingers tremble, as warning bells went off in her mind.

"I guess not," he said.

An attendant brought Rhiannon's car around.

She slipped into the driver's seat, and Sailor got in next to her. "I'll go with Brodie so he isn't driving alone," Barrie told her.

"Whatever you want," Rhiannon responded, giving in to the inevitable. Her tone, however, was sharp.

A few minutes later, with Brodie's car visible in her rearview mirror, she waited for the sound of something huge landing on top of her car. She was tense, but Sailor didn't seem to notice.

"This has been such a great night," Sailor said. "I think Elven are the wise men of the Others. They're so intelligent and…rational. They were so nice to me, too."

"I'm so glad," Rhiannon murmured. "Barrie sure clammed up earlier."

"She feels that her duty is to the shifters, that our first duty is to our Others, rather than ourselves. You know Barrie. Not happy unless she's crusading for something."

Finally they arrived at the compound—and with no further incidents, which left Rhiannon feeling both grateful and relieved.

She opened the gate and she drove through. Brodie was right behind her, and despite the fact that she wasn't looking at him and certainly wasn't touching him, she could somehow *feel* him.

They parked and got out of their cars. Sailor immediately spoke up. "Look, I know you all feel like you have to guard me like a pack of Dobermans, but I won't have it. We've got the tunnels connecting the houses, and we know from last night that the alarm system is working perfectly. I'm not saying we should take stupid chances, but what we *are* doesn't last a week, it's a lifetime commitment. I say we go through the houses, make sure everything's locked up tight and then we all stay in our own places. I'll ask Merlin to stay with me. Of course, if *you're* frightened…"

"I'm not frightened," Barrie said quickly. "But I do think we should check out all three houses together."

"And everyone sleeps with a cross on," Rhiannon said.

"Does that really work?" Sailor asked.

"My father said it's not the cross per se," Rhiannon said. "If you were Jewish, it would be a Star of David, and if you were Muslim, it would be the crescent. The point is that you wear a symbol of faith in a power greater than yourself. Oh, and put up some garlic. Vampires really don't like garlic—it makes them sneeze. So let's get started."

Rhiannon glanced at Brodie, who had been silent. He smiled at her and nodded. She realized that he was being intentionally silent, letting her take the lead. She felt a surge of gratitude for his sense of faith in her.

With Brodie in tow, they went to work. Luckily Sailor was a vegetarian who made a lot of Italian dishes, so her kitchen was well stocked with garlic. They left cloves around the windows and doors of each house.

Brodie checked closets, cabinets—and the tunnels. Merlin stuck to the main house, and followed them around. "I don't need to sleep, so I'll stand guard," he said gravely. "I'll watch over Sailor."

"I'll stay on the couch at Rhiannon's," Brodie said. He looked at Barrie. "Maybe you should stay with one of your cousins."

She shook her head. "I have work I've got to do before I go in to work. I'll be fine." They all stared at her. "Look, it's almost daylight. Vampires don't have the same strength in daylight that they do in darkness. Plus I've been practicing my shifting. If anyone gets in, I'll turn into a dust mite and hide until one of you comes." She grinned.

"It really might be better if you all stayed together," Brodie said.

"No!" Sailor protested.

"We are *Keepers*. We'll always face danger, Brodie," Rhiannon said. "We need to live our own lives despite that."

He nodded, not happy, but resigned.

As he turned and they headed for Pandora's Box together, Rhiannon thought she heard her cousins giggling. She turned quickly and saw them staring at her like a pair of doting old nanas. She shook her head slightly and hurried toward home, trying to ignore them. Brodie was staying with her for safety's sake. This was business, not pleasure.

Right?

"I think your cousins want us to sleep together," Brodie said.

Startled, her face turning a half dozen shades of red, she looked at him. "They, um, can be a bit juvenile."

He lowered his head, hiding a half smile as they stepped into her house. She locked the door behind them, turned…and found that he was ridiculously close to her. She looked up at him. The breath seemed to rush from her lungs.

"It doesn't matter what your cousins think," he told her. "It *does* matter what *you* think."

"What *I* think?"

"About us sleeping together."

There was so much she could say, and even more that she *should* say.

But she was speechless.

He reached out, lifting a strand of her hair. "It seemed like such a wonderful strategy to explain your presence at the theater so you could watch what was going on there. But right after it started— I mean *right* after it started—I wanted it to be true."

"You did?" she whispered, then shook her head. "No, no, that can't be true. You didn't have any faith in me."

"Oh, it was worse than that! I thought you were an ineffectual, self-centered pain in the ass."

"How…rude," she told him. They were face-to-face, so close they were practically touching. His Elven magic seemed to wash over her in a tidal wave of staggering warmth and sensuality, and golden seduction.

She set her fingers on his chest, straightening the

collar of his tailored shirt. "That's okay—I don't think I could even begin to describe my first impression of you."

He caught her hands. "But it's changed?" he asked softly.

"The jury is still out," she said. It wasn't, though. Not really. He was dedicated. He was...noble, even, she thought. He was Elven; she was a Keeper. Elven could be anything in life, and he had chosen, like her, to protect and serve.

There were a million reasons why she should back away. They were embroiled in a horrible situation together, surrounded by death and tragedy, by a threat to everyone and everything they knew, to the entire world of the Others and the city where they all hid in plain sight.

And yet the worst of it was that she was worried not for her world but for her heart and soul.

And not a drop of the fear tearing through her could save her.

Maybe it was everything in her life coming together in this one moment that aroused her need for him in that moment.

Or maybe it was because he was Elven, and as

everyone knew, Elven radiated sensuality...sexuality.

Or maybe it was just that strangely ineffable something that was an innate part of existence, the unique chemistry that made one person more attractive and seductive than anyone else.

All she knew was that she'd never imagined wanting anyone the way she wanted Brodie McKay at that moment.

Alarms went off in her mind, her instinct for self-preservation screaming a warning somewhere deep inside.

A warning that went unheard.

She moved closer to him, until her body was pressed against his. She placed her hand on his cheek and marveled at the strongly sculpted line of his jaw as she looked into his eyes, entranced by the blue that seemed to hold the ocean, the sky, the world.

"Right or wrong," she said huskily, "I say, let's do it."

He smiled, slowly, sensually, and heat suffused her body. At last she felt his lips on hers, his tongue teasing along her lips and then sliding into the depths of her mouth. Her knees threatened to give out, yet she felt ridiculously strong at the same time.

When her knees finally did give way, he picked her up. His eyes were fixed on hers as he walked toward the stairs, so focused that he bumped into Mr. Magician as he passed. Mr. Magician moved his gloved hand and dropped a fortune into the receptacle. Brodie balanced Rhiannon against his chest and reached for the card.

"What does it say?" she asked.

He grinned. "'Do it.'"

"You're kidding."

"I am not," he assured her.

"Then we've been blessed," she said softly. "So let's do it."

Laughing, he carried her up the stairs, then paused at the top.

"To the right," she whispered.

He used his shoulder to push open the bedroom door. The light from the hall drifted in, spotlighting the bed with its red and black cover. He fell to the mattress with her still in his arms, then paused, looking down at her for a long moment before he kissed her again.

Is this Elven magic? she wondered.

Or something more?

No kiss had ever been so deep, so erotic, such an irresistible promise of what was to come. So intimate—and becoming more so with every sweep and thrust of his tongue. When they broke apart, they were both breathless. He struggled out of his jacket; she worked at the buttons of his shirt. Her sweater hit the floor, and their shoes flew in several directions. It seemed to take forever to strip off their clothing, but each second felt precious and seductive. Finally he lay naked beside her, and she saw that his skin was golden everywhere, the heat from his body like liquid gold that rushed through her with the irresistible force of lava. Again they kissed, and then his kiss left her mouth, moving, sweeping golden fire along her skin. She clutched his shoulders, pressed her lips to them. And as he moved against her, she was compelled to move, as well, responding to every slight caress, every breathless touch of his lips.

His hands were large, his fingers long and his touch exquisite. She felt his caress and then his kiss, followed by the weight of his body as he moved lower. She arched against him until she had enough leverage to flip him over so he was lying beneath her, and then she leaned over him, her hair brushing along his flesh as she kissed her way lower, until he caught her in his arms again and they rolled together, entangled in each other's limbs. And then he was above her again and finally, *finally,* inside her. The room itself seemed to shimmer with each golden thrust of his body.

She was heedless of anything beyond the bed, yet acutely aware of every sensual moment between them: the feel of the satin coverlet beneath them; the vibrancy of the hall light as it streamed across his skin; the very air between them, which seemed visibly charged with electric ions. But most of all she was aware of the way his muscles rippled with his slightest movement, and the way his body seemed to be a part of hers. The rhythm between them grew frantic and strong, accompanied by the beating of their hearts, the rasp of their breath and the sweet, driving, near-desperate sensation growing at her core. She arched, she writhed, she rose to meet his every movement, their passion explosive and golden, rising to a burst of searing fire that broke into a climax as molten as the sun, as the power of their very existence. Finally she lay there feeling the sleek beauty of his damp skin, feeling *him,* his heartbeat, his breathing, the touch of his flesh hot against her.

It was the most physically amazing thing she had ever experienced, carnal and erotic. And then he was above her again. He kissed her mouth with the greatest tenderness and reverence, and she realized that as ridiculous as it might sound, as foolish as it might be, she was in love...not lust, but love.

But whether it was the kind that could defy the world and the ages, the kind her parents had shared, she didn't know.

She did know that she would fight to hold on to what she had...

Lest the world take it away.

He lay at her side, and she curled against him. She worried that she might feel awkward after her climax burned out and the flames of their lovemaking died down to embers, but she felt as if she was right where she should be. And her fascination with every inch of his flesh lingered. Would always linger, she was sure. Somewhere up in the hills a pack of coyotes started to howl, and she even heard the cry of an owl on the wind, the night itself beautiful and wild.

His hand was resting on her back, holding her

gently near, and she winced at the thought that they had met only because people had died.

"Don't," he said softly.

She lifted her head, seeking his eyes, and realized that he had slipped past her guard and read her mind. For some reason that didn't even bother her the way it would have just a few days ago.

"We will find the killer," he said softly. "And neither of us can change what happened before we came on to the case." He moved, shifting to look more directly into her eyes. "Everyone, no matter what responsibilities they have to live up to, gets their time to live and their chance to enjoy that time. If we don't take that, then there's no sense to any of it."

She nodded. "I just… I was just thinking that it seems wrong to be so happy when…"

"I know. But you can't let yourself think that way," he whispered.

"But—"

"No."

He kissed her lips again.

Making love this time was slow. Deliciously slow, almost agonizing. The first time had been filled with desperation, while the second was filled with intimate foreplay and long moments in which desire spilled slowly into ecstasy, until finally the world filled with explosive golden fire again. Finally, when she lay panting in his arms once more, she realized that the world *was* golden. Morning had come, and a new day was beginning.

Brodie opted not to go in to the station that day. Rhiannon slept late, but when she finally came down the stairs, he was immediately aware of her, the sweet scent of her like a beacon in the air.

She walked over carrying an oversize cup of tea and sat on the corner of the desk in the corner of the living room, where he was using her computer.

"What've you been doing?" she asked him.

He leaned back. "I talked to the kid we met the other night—Nick Cassidy. He's sending Jordan Bellow's toothbrush and hairbrush to Tony Brandt, and making arrangements for his dental records to get to the morgue to confirm his ID." He was quiet for a minute. "I tracked down acquaintances of the other probable victims, looking for items for a DNA comparison, hunted for dental records. I'm checking their banking and credit card information, putting together a history of their last known movements."

"Do you still want to check out the lakes and stuff? I can be ready in about ten minutes," she said.

He nodded. "Yes, I have to. We're still missing one probable victim. I want to see if we can find her."

"Did you find any places they all frequented?" she asked.

"Yes. They all used the same gas station on Vine. Three of the five went to the same donut shop. All five used two places whose names are a bunch of letters and numbers. I was about to call the credit card company to find out what they are."

"Let me see," Rhiannon said.

He beckoned her closer, so she could see the computer screen. It was a mistake. Her hair fell and brushed his shoulder, and he was suddenly overwhelmed by the scent of her.

To his relief, she straightened suddenly.

"What?" he demanded, spinning the chair to face her.

"I know what they are!" she told him. "MC1888—

that's the Magic Café. MC for Magic Café, and 1888—the year Hugh Hammond was born."

Brodie was suddenly deeply scared—for Rhiannon.

"What's the other one?" he managed to ask, but he already knew.

"MGHOI stands for Magic, House of Illusion."

Brodie turned and started reading through the credit card reports. "Add that to Nick Cassidy... three visits to the Snake Pit. Lila Mill, two visits the Snake Pit. Rose Gillespie, one visit." He looked over at Rhiannon. "Whoever the killer is, I have a feeling it's someone we see every day of our lives."

He heard a sudden whir.

Mr. Magician was doing his thing again.

He walked over to the machine and picked up the little card. He read it, then turned to Rhiannon, stunned. "It says 'Bingo,'" he told her after a long moment.

"I'll get ready. We'll go and search for the last victim."

He nodded glumly. "I'm going to get some patrolmen working on it, too. Even narrowing the search sites down to the general area of the theater, there's too much water to cover," he said quietly.

He looked up at her, worried. "I shouldn't do the play tonight. I should go with you to the Snake Pit."

She smiled. "Thank you for worrying, Brodie, but we can't be together if being together means we can't do our jobs. I'll be fine at the club. You have to do the show tonight. When you're done, you can come and find me at the Snake Pit."

He sat back down at the computer and began typing hurriedly.

She stepped up behind him. "What are you writing in such a frenzy?" she asked him.

"I'm going to give your cousin a story to run in the paper. And then we'll see who—and what—comes out of the woodwork."

By four o'clock Rhiannon was exhausted. They'd checked out five bodies of water, two that were on private property and three that bordered various roads.

"Where now?" she asked Brodie as he slid back into the driver's seat.

He drew out his map, pointed north and said, "I have uniforms working up there, so...let's head over here, along Mulholland. There's a little man-made lake right in there, off a hairpin curve."

A hairpin curve? On Mulholland, that could mean anywhere.

Rhiannon nodded. "Wherever you want. I'm going to check on Sailor and Barrie," she said as she pulled out her cell. It didn't matter where they went. She was just along for the ride.

Barrie, who was at work, answered right away. "I'm working on an article using everything Brodie gave me. Don't worry, though. I'll be careful how I word things so I don't give away too much but I still draw out the killer."

They chatted for another minute or two, and then Rhiannon tried Sailor's number. It went straight to voice mail.

"I told her to listen for her phone," Rhiannon said crossly.

"It's Sailor, Rhiannon. You know how she is. She starts reading a script and loses track of the world," Brodie said.

Rhiannon left a message, trying to keep her voice level as she told her cousin to call her ASAP.

A few minutes later Brodie pulled off the road beside an empty lot. She looked at him. "I don't see any water," she said.

"It's over that little rise."

Brodie walked ahead of her, and she followed, not really giving him her attention. She was worried, and she needed to find Sailor. Brodie was right, of course. No matter what she said, Sailor would get involved in something and forget about her phone. In fact, she probably hadn't even heard it, because she was still at the costume designer's office. Barrie would be picking her up at the studio, and Barrie was still at work. Sailor was undoubtedly in the midst of a fitting, standing there all pinned together, unable to move.

In which case she was bound to call back soon.

They walked up the little hillock and then down. There was a small pond before them, longer than it was broad. It stretched toward several mansions on the right, a couple of which had docks extending into the water, and down toward a private road on the left. She wondered why Brodie had elected to park on the far side of the hill, then realized if he'd come in via the guarded entrance to the community, people would have started talking, and this was the kind of case he would want to keep quiet until he knew what he was dealing with.

Brodie started walking toward the houses, but she headed directly toward the water, her phone in her hand again. She hated to do it, but she put a call through to Darius. He would know how to reach the costumer, and even if she was being ridiculous, Rhiannon was desperate now to know that Sailor was all right.

Darius didn't answer his own phone, of course. Instead she got Mary.

"Hello, dear," the older woman said when Rhiannon introduced herself. "He's with a client, but you just hang on and I'll go see if I can get him for you."

Rhiannon walked along the shoreline, waiting.

Then she stopped, frozen.

About fifteen feet out she could see something that definitely didn't belong there. It looked like a cross between a blob and a mannequin, but she had a terrible feeling she knew exactly what it really was.

Brodie was quite a distance away at that point, so she waded into the water. It was shallow at first. Then she cursed as the bottom sloped abruptly away and she found herself in water up to her waist. She held her phone over her head and kept walking, seeing as she was already wet.

She reached for a piece of fabric, hoping to draw it nearer.

And an arm came free in her grasp.

She began to scream.

Chapter 10

They'd found her, Brodie thought dully.

The last of the victims. Or the last of the victims they knew about, anyway.

God help them. They had to stop the killer before he struck again.

The corpse belonged to a woman, though that wasn't easy to discern.

She'd been in the water for several weeks at least. She'd been weighted down with a cinder block—undoubtedly obtained from a pile in the vacant lot—until she grew too bloated with gas for it to hold her. The rope was a typical brand, found at any local hardware store. And after so much time, there was no evidence of any other sort left at the crime scene.

Tony Brandt had come out to the scene to inspect the corpse—the pieces of the corpse, at any rate. Fish had eaten away at the soft tissue, and once it had made its way to the surface, birds had been at it, as well.

"Fingers are missing again," Tony Brandt said.

"How are you doing with identifying the others?" Brodie asked him.

"Two out of four, and since one was Lila Mill, I'm assuming this is Rose Gillespie. I had her head shots sent over. She was a pretty girl when she was alive," Tony said. "Did you ever meet her, by any chance?"

Brodie shook his head. "I wasn't at the original auditions or the callbacks. I got the part when the original actor took off for home."

"Ah, yes, that's right. Well, I'll do my best with what I have. I'm taking her to the morgue now, but…" Tony's voice trailed off.

But…

But the body had been in the water awhile, plus it had rained in the past few weeks, washing away any evidence from the shore—even the damned weather seemed to be against them.

"Anyway, you know where to find me when you need me," Tony said.

Brodie motioned to Adam Lansky, who had come out with the crime scene team.

Adam wasn't used to being away from his computer, much less coming face-to-face with a rotting corpse. He looked ill.

"You all right? You're green," Brodie said.

"I'm okay. Hey, if I'm ever going to get into the field, I've gotta learn, right?"

Brodie nodded. "I'm going to leave you here, because Rhiannon and I have to get ready for work. Just keep an eye on what's going on, and when they're done here, so are you. You've done good work, Adam."

"Thanks," the younger man said.

Brodie turned and stared halfway up the rise, where Rhiannon was standing with a police blanket around her shoulders. She was drenched from the lake, but she was calm now. In fact, she had composed herself quickly after discovering the corpse, which was tough. Even a seasoned detective might have screamed at finding himself at the business end of a decomposing arm.

Adam followed the direction of Brodie's gaze. "You're lucky. How many women look that pretty soaked in slime? And she's so talented."

"You've seen her play?" Brodie asked.

"Yeah," Adam said. "I went to the Mystic Café." He flushed. "I saw her last night. I was curious after I saw that picture of you and her. She's good."

"Yeah, she is," Brodie murmured. "All right, we're going. Call me if anything major turns up."

"Hey, Brodie!" Adam said. Brodie looked back, and Adam pointed toward the hill. "You might want to watch it. There are two news teams up there. The uniforms are keeping them out of the immediate area, but when you're leaving… And if you show up on the news, everyone at the theater is going to know you're a cop."

"Thanks," Brodie said. He looked up the hill. Rhiannon was still standing there in her blanket. There really was no way to get to his car without going by the news crews. He turned back to Adam. "I need you to get my car. Send Rhiannon down to me. We'll walk out by the road and meet you at the corner."

Adam grinned. "Pleasure, Brodie."

Adam watched as Brodie climbed the hill and talked to Rhiannon, who quickly started down toward him. He had no idea what he should say to her. It was one thing to view a body on a coldly clinical autopsy table.

It was quite another to find one decomposing in a pool of algae-coated water and muck.

"You all right?" he asked her when she got there.

She nodded. "I'm fine now. Darius got hold of Sailor, and she just called me back. Brodie, this is all so horrible. The attack on Sailor, the dead woman—none of it seems real. And Sailor…she just doesn't realize her own danger."

"She's stronger than she looks," Brodie said. "Now come on. We have to walk around to where Adam is meeting us with the car. I really don't want to get caught on camera."

She nodded, but she still seemed lost in her own thoughts as they started walking.

"Rhiannon, Sailor is going to be all right."

"I hope so. She's the Elven Keeper, and the Elven—" she began, and then broke off, looking at him.

"You think the Elven are the weakest among

the Others?" he asked her. "Let me tell you something. Elven have brought down vampires and werewolves—and more than once. We may not have fangs or claws, but we know all about stakes and silver bullets. And we have one asset that the rest of the Others tend to forget about when they're in full attack mode."

"What's that?"

"Brains—and the ability to think before we plunge in."

"Oh, Brodie! I didn't mean to offend you, it's just that I'm not sure Sailor has ever even tried to access her Elven qualities, other than teleporting."

"And you've had a lot of practice accessing your inner vampire?" he asked her sharply.

"No," she admitted. "But I'm going to get a lot of practice now."

They skirted close to the water at that point. He must have made a face, because she looked at him and almost smiled.

"You really hate water, huh?" she asked.

"I don't hate it. I can swim, and I've even gone diving a few times. We just can't be away from solid earth for any length of time," he said.

Adam pulled up at that point, so they stopped

talking as they got in the car and Brodie thanked the tech for his help. They both waved as Adam walked away.

They were silent for most of the drive. Finally she asked, "Brodie, all these people were dead before you ever got the case, right?"

He nodded.

"Why would someone have targeted them? Hatred? Jealousy? Could it really be over a role in a play? It couldn't even be the *same* role, since the killer went after both men and women."

"Here's what we know. All the victims auditioned for *Vampire Rampage*. With the possible but unlikely exception of the one you found this morning, all the bodies have tiny puncture marks, but they could have been inflicted by a sharp instrument, but if that's true, the intent was to make the murders look like the work of a vampire. And Sailor was *definitely* attacked by a vampire, now deceased. You were attacked by someone or something that could have been a vampire. We don't know for sure that the attacks on you and Sailor are connected to the murders, but my gut tells me they are. One way or another, a vampire has to be in on this. The question is whether a human being is part of it or not. A human being who knows about the existence of vampires could be making use of one of them for his—or her—own purposes."

By then they had reached the compound, so she pulled her clicker out of her purse to open the gate, and they continued up the driveway.

"You can just drop me off, you know," she told him. "I know you have to be ready for your call, and I don't want to make you late."

He shook his head. "I'll wait. I'll take you to the Snake Pit and meet you there after the show."

"You don't need to do that. I was pretty shaken up before, but I'm all right now."

"I believe you. But there's not a soul out there who isn't *more* all right when someone else has their back. I don't mind *you* having *my* back," he said.

She smiled at that. "I like you having *my* back, too."

"I'm glad, but the way you just said that…probably not good for me to think about that right now."

"Or me," Rhiannon said. "Sorry, mental images and all that…" Her voice trailed off, and then she grew serious. "It's Sailor I worry about, Brodie. I mean, it is true—none of the three of us has had a lot of experience. Our dads were young—we didn't think we'd be taking over for years. But Barrie is dedicated to two things—journalism and being a Keeper. And as she pointed out to me, she can change into a dust mite and hide. Sailor…"

"Sailor is going to be all right. I don't think Sailor was the intended victim, I think *you* were. Whoever that vampire was, I sincerely doubt he intended to die in the attack. He could have killed Sailor long before you got there. He waited there for you, because his whole intent was to bring you into the fight."

"Maybe so, but all that means is that someone could use Sailor against me again," Rhiannon said, shaking her head in frustration. "I wish we knew where to start!"

"Why, Watson, that's easy," Brodie said.

"It is?" she asked. "Then why haven't we solved this already?"

"Process of elimination, my dear Miss Watson."

He was glad to see a real smile curve her lips. "Wait! I don't want to be Watson. I want to be Sherlock."

"No doubt, but I'm the detective," he reminded her.

Brodie waited in the living room while she

hurried upstairs to shower and get changed. The temptation to join her was painful, but they had to remember who they were. And he was sure she was going to be scrubbing herself rigorously—trying to wash away the scent and feel of death.

There was a rap on the door, and he answered it. This time Merlin had knocked.

"Come in," Brodie said.

"I'm not interrupting?" Merlin asked.

"Not at all. Rhiannon is getting ready for work. I'm going to drop her at the club before I go to the theater," Brodie said.

Merlin nodded. "Have you seen the news?" he asked.

Brodie arched a brow and walked over to turn on the television. An attractive reporter was on the air at the scene of the crime. He stood silently watching with Merlin by his side, wondering just how much the press had figured out so far.

Luckily, while the cops had connected the victims, the press had yet to do so. But tomorrow, after Barrie's story hit the papers, everyone would know they were searching for a serial killer. The details wouldn't be in the article, but a warning would be.

"Five," Merlin said woefully. He looked at Brodie. "How many more do you think there will be?"

"I don't know," Brodie admitted. "If we're lucky, none." He prayed that was true, and that he could keep L.A.'s newest Keepers safe.

Mr. Magician began to whir. Brodie turned just as the gloved hand dropped a card into the receptacle. "Again," he murmured in disbelief.

Merlin smiled. "Don't be so surprised. That's old Eli Wertner. He was famous for his coin-operated machines. Poor old Eli. I don't think he quite got the hang of being a ghost, but something of him remains in the machine. He was a good man. I'm sure he's only trying to help."

Brodie walked over to the machine to take the card.

"Well?" Merlin asked him.

Brodie looked over at Merlin. "Everyone has an agenda. Charity begins at home."

Merlin shook his head worriedly. "Someone is out to hurt these girls," he said. "Whatever you do, please don't leave them alone."

"I don't intend to," Brodie said grimly. "Of course, it would be helpful if your old friend would make his messages a little clearer."

* * *

Rhiannon was really enjoying performing at the Snake Pit, a realization that surprised her after the day she'd had.

No amount of soap and water had made her feel any better. Even though they were short on time, she hadn't been able to bring herself to get out of the shower, and after she'd scrubbed and shampooed for the fourth time she'd found herself wishing that Brodie had come up and joined her. She felt guilty for that, as she stood there with the stench of death still on her from a young life cut short, but she couldn't help the longing of her heart.

She knew she had to hurry, though, so she told herself it was a good thing he wasn't reading her mind at that moment. Besides, they had obligations. They were what they were, she a Keeper and Brodie Elven and a cop. They could never have a normal relationship, because their lives weren't normal. *They* weren't normal.

When she finally stepped from the shower, got dressed and went downstairs, she found that they had a visitor—Merlin—so it was a good thing Brodie had opted for responsibility over pleasure.

But now, having been at the club for a few hours,

she was actually enjoying herself. She'd decided to mix things up and do something different from what she'd done with her band and at the café, opting for a mix of the classics and show tunes she'd always loved, and the piano instead of a guitar. The audience that night included werewolves, Elven, shapeshifters, vampires—even a tall, charming leprechaun and his girlfriend, an exceptionally pretty gnome. And of course there were plenty of human beings who had no idea of the true nature of the Others surrounding them.

Best of all—almost making her forget that she had discovered a decaying corpse that afternoon—Sailor was in the room.

Rhiannon was halfway through her second set when she saw Jerry Oglethorpe come in. He always looked like a magician, she thought, whether he was performing or not. He waved to her, then joined Sailor at her table.

At ten-thirty Hugh Hammond arrived and joined them. Rhiannon saw Sailor excuse herself and rise, and she felt a moment's panic, even missing a beat, as she watched her cousin leave the room. She didn't know why she was disturbed. Sailor was probably just heading to the ladies' room.

Rhiannon told herself that even though the killer had something to do with *Vampire Rampage,* so Sailor might be in danger on her own, too, not only because of her. But the cast couldn't possibly be there yet; the show had only just ended.

But she *was* unnerved, so she excused herself the minute she finished her song, taking her break a few minutes early. She saw Declan frown and look at his watch, but she didn't care. She rose from the piano bench and headed downstairs for the restrooms.

Everything at the Snake Pit was perfect. She entered an elegant lounge the minute she stepped through the door to the ladies' room, smiled at the attendant and called out, "Sailor?"

There was no answer.

"You looking for a friend, sweetie?" the attendant asked. "There's no one in here right now."

Rhiannon gave her a swift thank-you and hurried out, her speed increasing as she ran to the main entrance. She gasped in relief when she saw Sailor, who was heading over to the nicely landscaped area Declan had set up to one side to accommodate smokers, since the law now prohibited smoking inside.

The thing was, Sailor didn't smoke.
And someone was following her.

The play went well; the ensemble had grown tight, and Brodie thought wryly that he didn't mind acting. In fact, it was fun. The only downside was that he found himself constantly looking out at the audience, wishing that he knew whether anyone there had auditioned for the play. They'd found all the dead they knew about so far, but that didn't mean there might not be more to come.

He was determined that the Gryffald cousins would not be among those at risk. Not on his watch.

As soon as the show ended, he hurried to his dressing room to change. He was eager to get to the Snake Pit as soon as possible.

He'd just finished changing when Hunter Jackson came in, beaming and clearly thrilled with the way show was going. "Hey, Mac—we're heading out to the Snake Pit in a little while. Want to join us?"

"I was planning on it already, so sure," Brodie told him.

"I can't get over how well things are going," Jackson said. "We're at capacity every night, and we haven't even officially opened yet. The internet campaign is going great, and I've got a team already working on a game we can release when the movie opens."

"You've hit the jackpot."

"Yeah," Hunter said, and paused. "People are so strange, you know? They love vampires, think they're sexy. They don't get the dead and rotting part. Plus they like to be scared. You know, if there's news about a vampire cult meeting out in the woods, they want to go out in the woods. Me, I stay as far away as I can, but I thank God that most people aren't like me, at least when they go to the movies."

There was a tap at the door. Hunter opened it to find Kate Delaney.

"You guys coming?" she asked. "I feel the need for champagne!"

Lena Ashbury, in tight jeans and a sequined top, popped up behind Kate. "Did someone say champagne?" she asked.

"You sure did," Kate said, laughing. "Where's Audrey? Is she coming, too?"

"Oh, she took off already. She said she'd meet us at the club," Kate said.

Brodie surged to his feet and headed toward the

door, feeling uneasy. Audrey was the only vampire in the cast, and she had gone on ahead.

There was no way to know for sure that the murders had taken place right after the show, but since he'd seen one of the victims in the audience, it seemed possible that the others had come to see the show as well, and been targeted on their way out of the theater.

And then there was the fact that Audrey had been talking to Rhiannon just before her car was attacked.

"See you all there," he said. A moment later he left by the stage door and looked out at the parking lot.

He saw Audrey getting into her car.

And there was someone in the passenger seat.

Because Declan Wainwright worked so hard to keep the club's atmosphere intimate, there was a particularly large amount of foliage surrounding the 'smokers' corner."

Rhiannon knew that if she didn't stop Sailor quickly, her cousin would be hidden by the ornamental trees and tubs of flowers—along with whoever was following her.

"Sailor!" she shouted as she hurried in her wake.

Sailor stopped and turned back to look, and so did the person following her.

Rhiannon frowned when she saw who it was.

"Rhiannon, hey," he said.

"Hey, Adam," she said. He seemed abashed as she approached, while Sailor just looked curiously from one of them to the other.

"Adam, what are you doing here?" Rhiannon asked.

He blushed. "I saw your cousin leave, and I was worried."

"You were sweet to worry about me," Sailor said, "but who are you and why do you care?"

"He's a cop," Rhiannon explained. "Adam Lansky, my cousin, Sailor Gryffald. Sailor, Officer Adam Lansky."

"Do you work with Brodie?" Sailor asked.

"Yeah," he said, blushing. "And I know that Brodie is seeing Rhiannon, and that he worries about her, so since you two are cousins…I thought I'd just come out and bum a smoke or whatever, so I could make sure nothing bad was happening."

Rhiannon wondered if her perceptions had been off. Was Adam a vampire?

She casually moved closer to check him out.

No, definitely not.

"I'm fine," Sailor said. "The door is twenty feet away."

"Why are you out here at all?" Rhiannon asked her. "You don't even smoke."

"I'm meeting someone," Sailor said.

"What the— Who?" Rhiannon asked sharply.

"I don't know." Sailor handed her a cocktail napkin bearing the words, *I have information that is important to the Gryffald clan. Please join me for a cigarette.*

"Sailor—you got this note and you just came out here—all by yourself?"

"Well, of course. We're right in front of the club. There are big hairy wer—um, bouncers standing at the door, watching everything that goes on."

"Who gave you the note?" she asked.

Sailor flushed. "I'm not really sure. One of the servers—I wasn't paying attention."

Rhiannon stared at her for a moment, but she wasn't going to say anything about the stupidity of answering such a summons—especially *alone,* when people were dead and Sailor herself had been attacked—in front of Adam.

Instead she hurried past her cousin and headed straight for the smokers' corner, rounding a Japanese maple only to find the area empty. Whoever had sent Sailor the note had obviously realized she wasn't alone and managed to slip away unseen. More proof that a rogue vampire was on the loose? Because a vampire could easily have taken bird or bat form and flown away into the darkness.

Rhiannon wasn't sure whether to be angry that they had missed an opportunity to gain information—assuming that there really had been any information to be gained, and that the offer hadn't simply been the bait to get Sailor alone—or just grateful that her cousin was all right. She was also forced to acknowledge the possibility that Sailor had been the real target the other night, just as she might well have been tonight.

"There's no one here," she called back to her cousin. "Let's get back in. Sailor, I don't care how safe you think the Snake Pit is—*please* don't answer a summons like that again. Not alone." She turned to Adam. All she needed was a young geeky cop who knew nothing of the Otherworld following them around.

"Adam, thanks, and I don't mean to insult you,

but please don't follow us. We're pretty tough, and we could wind up kicking your ass before we realized you were one of the good guys."

He laughed. "Okay, backing off right now."

"Rhiannon?"

At the sound of her name, she swung around to see Declan standing just outside the door and looking at her curiously.

"Everything okay?" he asked. "The audience is getting restless."

Rhiannon turned back to her sister. "I've got to get back in there. Sailor, please?"

"I'm coming. And I won't leave again, I promise."

"You should give me that napkin," Adam said. "I can get it to the forensic experts."

Rhiannon had the napkin and she wasn't letting it go. "I want to show it to Brodie first, Adam, and then he can get it to you. Now let's go," she said. "I'd like to keep working here."

Sailor nodded and headed back toward the entrance. Adam followed her, and Rhiannon brought up the rear. Declan was waiting for her at the door. "Everything all right?" he asked.

"Of course. I just ran out for some air—and to see Sailor for a minute."

Declan seemed to sense that something was wrong, because when she started to follow the others he caught her arm. "Look—I know you're worried, so let me watch Sailor," he said. "I promise, I won't let anything happen to her."

"Thanks," she said, feeling backed into a corner. Declan might not be in the play himself, but the Snake Pit was involved with the film, which meant he was involved, too.

And Declan had been there the night she and her cousins saw the show.

Declan was a Keeper for the shifters. And that meant he could be anything he wanted to be.

She prayed that Brodie would arrive soon.

Everyone was looking like a suspect to her.

Back at her piano, she no longer saw the room as being filled with charming people who loved music.

They'd all suddenly become evil.

Chapter 11

"Audrey!" Brodie called.

She paused just before sliding into the driver's seat and looked back at him. "Hey!" she called in return. "You going to the Snake Pit?"

"Yes, I heard you were going, too," he said. He walked over and bent down to check out the young woman in the passenger seat.

"This is Penny Abelard," Audrey said. "Penny, Mac Brodie. He joined the cast when we were in production, after someone had to drop out. Brodie, Penny tried out for the role of Lucy, which is when we met. She made the callbacks, and Darius

Simonides has talked to her about a role in one of the touring companies."

"Penny, it's a pleasure to meet you," Brodie said.

"Likewise," she said. She looked like so many Hollywood hopefuls: reed thin, blond and very pretty, with huge dark eyes.

He focused his mind on her. It didn't take much effort—her thoughts were wide open and easy to read. She was a little bit jealous of Audrey, but mostly she was just anxious, hopeful, focusing all her dreams on getting that role. There was nothing evil to be found in her thoughts, not that he'd expected there to be.

"I thought it would be good for her career to be seen with us at the club," Audrey said as Penny continued to stare at him, wide-eyed. Audrey gave her a little punch in the arm. "That boy is taken," she said teasingly. "He's got a girlfriend. But he's fun to hang around with anyway. Mac, we're going to get going, okay?"

"I'll follow you," Brodie said.

"Think you can keep up with me? I drive pretty fast, you know," she teased.

He tried to zero in on Audrey's thoughts. It was

hard, even painful. But all she was thinking about was the strong desire to beat his driving skills.

He stepped away from her quickly, acutely aware that he needed to preserve his strength in case something dangerous happened later.

"No drag racing," he told her. "The cops will be on us like…like flies on a corpse."

Audrey grinned. "I'll drive safely. Let's get going."

He wished he could take Penny Abelard in his car, but that would be obvious. Audrey knew the cops were looking for a killer—a vampire killer—and he didn't want her to start wondering whether he was who he said he was.

At least she wouldn't act if she knew he was right behind her. If she was even the killer. Penny's presence in her car was strongly circumstantial, but it wasn't exactly proof.

He hurried to his car. Audrey was already pulling out onto the street as he slipped his key into the ignition.

She drove fast, but safely. She even used her blinker.

She drove straight to the Snake Pit and pulled up by the valet stand.

Both women got out of the car safely.

He gave his own keys to the valet and joined the women, who had waited for him. Before they even made it to the door another car pulled up.

"Look, there's Hunter," Audrey said with a smile. "And he's got Lena and Kate with him. We're all going upstairs, I take it?" She turned to Penny. "His girlfriend is a singer here."

"Well, I'm heading upstairs," Brodie said. "I don't mean to tell the rest of the crowd where to go."

The newcomers joined them, and Brodie led the way upstairs. The room was filled, not an empty table in sight. Rhiannon was at the piano, running her fingers over the keys and singing. He took a moment just to look at her, his body responding to the mere sight of her in a way that could quickly turn embarrassing if he weren't careful.

He was startled out of his fantasy when Sailor came up behind him, greeting him with a kiss on the cheek before turning to the others. "I've got a table we can squash into," she said. "Darius is the only one with me at the moment, and I'm sure he'll be happy to see you all."

"Thanks," Brodie said.

"Hey, I met one of your coworkers tonight,"

Sailor said as she led the way to the table. "Adam Lansky. I think he's trying to be you—he was trying to keep an eye on us. Sweet, huh?"

Brodie frowned, uncomfortable with what she'd just told him. Adam had always been a desk jockey, and he was excellent at what he did. Today he'd come out to a crime scene. He'd gone to the Mystic Café. And now he was watching the Gryffalds at the Snake Pit.

No one knew more about the murders than himself, Tony Brandt—and Adam.

He looked around and saw Adam flirting with a couple of twentysomethings at another table. So long as he was leaving Rhiannon and her cousins alone... And then he felt guilty, because what if the guy's motives were totally on the up-and-up?

He slipped in next to Audrey and thought, *Hail, hail, the gang's all here.* And for some gut-level reason he was certain that, though he still didn't know the rhyme or the reason for what was going on, the killer was in the room.

Declan and Hugh were at a nearby table, and he saw Jerry Oglethorpe across the room. The other man looked at Brodie gravely and lifted his glass.

He left the table and walked toward the stage,

catching Rhiannon's eye and nodding toward the side of the room. She didn't miss a note as she smiled and nodded back. Confident that she'd read his intent, he headed back to the others.

As soon as she announced that she was taking a break, he stood and went over to the stage to meet her. She caught his hand, and for a long moment they just stood there, staring into each other's eyes. He could sense that the audience was whispering about them.

As she drew him out of the room, she slipped something into his hand. As soon as they were outside, he frowned and looked at it.

"Sailor received this tonight. I saw her leave the room and ran after her," Rhiannon said. "I asked her what was going on, and she gave it to me."

"Who wrote it?" Brodie asked.

"I don't know. I called out to her because someone was following her—which turned out to be Adam—and by the time I reached the smokers' corner no one was there."

"Who gave her the napkin?"

"She didn't know. One of the servers."

"Then I'll talk to them all," he said grimly.

He held her arm as they returned upstairs, then

watched as she made her way back to the piano. Instead of joining the others, he walked over to the bar, where Declan was standing.

Declan lifted a glass to him. "I hear you're a hit as an actor."

Brodie shrugged. "I've had worse undercover work, that's for sure."

"How many of your cast know who and what you really are?" Declan asked him.

"Well, any Other knows that I'm an Other, too, but I'm hoping no one knows that I'm a cop and I'm there investigating them. All." He stared at Declan. "Why were you at the show the same night the Gryffald girls were there?" he asked point-blank.

Declan stared back at him in surprise, then offered him a bitter smile. "You think *I'm* the murderer?"

"I didn't say that."

"Read my mind, Elven. You'll see that my actions are pure."

Brodie gave him a dry grin. "If I tried to read your mind, you'd do your best to block me, so I'd be wasting my energy. I was just asking."

Declan let out a sigh. "I wanted to keep an eye on Barrie, find a way to get to know her better. She's a brand-new Keeper, responsible for the shifters, just like I am. When you came to the Snake Pit with Hunter Jackson, I recognized you right away—I've seen you in the papers a few times—and I realized you were working undercover. I already knew something serious was going on in the Otherworld. Rumors fly—no matter how people try to contain social media these days, someone is always posting or emailing something. I figured you were on to the same thing. I knew you were in the show, so I figured there must be a reason for that—that it had to be connected to your investigation in some way—and when I heard that the Gryffald girls were going it seemed like a good chance to kill two birds with one stone. That's all there is to it."

Was he telling the truth? Brodie decided to chance a probe into Declan's mind, and he had to admit he was surprised to find out that the Keeper was being sincere.

Brodie nodded. "In that case, I need your help."

"How?" Declan asked. "I'll do anything."

"Someone sent Sailor a note on a cocktail napkin, asking to meet her outside. Rhiannon went after her, but she never saw who was waiting. The note referred to the Gryffald family, so it could have been intended for any one of them. I have to talk to your servers and find out where that note came from."

Behind him, someone cleared his throat. Brodie turned to face Jerry Oglethorpe, owner of the House of Illusion.

Vampire.

"You don't need to question people," Jerry said quietly. "I sent the note, and the server messed up. It was intended for Rhiannon."

Two hours later, after the club had closed, Rhiannon sat at a table with her cousins, Declan, Brodie and Jerry.

"I think I know the vampire killed at the House of the Rising Sun," Jerry told them. "It was Celeste Monahue. Do you remember her?"

They all looked at him blankly.

Jerry sighed. "She was the Gloria Swanson of the vampire set—an actress who was huge in the forties and fifties. We don't age, not much, anyway, but this is Hollywood. There's always someone younger coming up. She stopped getting the roles she wanted. Darius told her that she had to accept the motherly parts when they came along, and that didn't sit well with her. She wanted work in my shows, but…magicians' assistants tend to be young and leggy, as well as beautiful. Then one day she told me she was going to make a comeback. A big comeback. And now…well, now I haven't seen her in a few days. She wasn't at the council meeting the other night. I wanted to tell you my suspicions, Rhiannon, but I didn't want to be obvious, so I wrote that note and asked you to meet me." He looked at Rhiannon apologetically, and then at Sailor. "I'm so sorry. I didn't mean to create a problem."

Rhiannon set a hand on his. "It's all right, Jerry. No harm done."

"Jerry," Brodie said. "Did Celeste say anything specific about her big comeback? What the part was or who was offering it to her?"

Jerry shook his head. "Nothing, sorry. All I know is she hasn't been seen since. I don't think she would have planned anything evil herself, but she longed to be famous again—known for her talent and her beauty. I can see how she might have been easily led astray by someone promising her that if she carried out a 'mission' she'd get everything her heart desired. I think she was your vampire and now she's ash."

"Did she ever say anything—even in casual conversation—that might have indicated that she had an in anywhere?" Brodie pressed.

Jerry was thoughtful for a minute. "Well, I don't know if it means anything, but...she seemed fond of humans lately—not in a bad way, not as a food source," he amended quickly. "She said she enjoyed discovering their talents."

"Thank you, Jerry," Brodie said, and looked at Rhiannon. He was convinced now that more than one person was involved. Someone—someone human, he suspected—was pulling strings and getting vampires to work for them.

"Come to the House of Illusion on Sunday night," Jerry said. "Brodie, your show will be dark, and Rhiannon doesn't work at the Mystic Café or here on Sunday nights. We get a real variety of Others and humans in the audience. Someone is bound to talk about Celeste going missing, maybe even make the connection that she was the one who was killed at the House of the Rising Sun." He looked at each of the three Gryffald cousins in turn. "I'd like to help. You girls were just tossed into the fray. We owe your fathers, and we owe you."

"Thank you, Jerry," Rhiannon said, and her cousins echoed her words.

Declan rose, impatient. "Like it or not, you three are in it now. You're in it up to your teeth."

He was staring at Barrie as he spoke, which made sense, Brodie though. They were both shifter Keepers, Declan the Coastal Keeper and Barrie the Canyon Keeper. The Snake Pit actually fell under her jurisdiction.

Then Declan turned to Sailor. "Honestly," he said. "There's been a string of murders—possibly committed by a vampire—and you leave your window open?"

Startled, she stared at him, then shoved her chair back angrily and stood up. "I think we've done what we can do here tonight," she said. "Could we go home now, please?"

The others rose.

"My article will be in tomorrow's paper," Barrie said. "Which means a whole lot of evil may come crawling out of the woodwork."

"Good. Maybe that will help us solve this thing soon," Declan said. "All of you, out now. I need to lock this place up for the night."

* * *

When they left the Snake Pit, it was in silence. Everyone was exhausted.

Barrie drove with Brodie, and Sailor went with Rhiannon. Caught up in her own thoughts, Rhiannon didn't realize until they reached the estate that Sailor seemed to be seething.

She slammed the door when she got out of the car.

"Sailor?" Rhiannon asked.

"Sorry—I'm fine. I'm not angry with you."

"What's the matter?"

"That man is an ass!" Sailor said.

"What man?"

"Declan Wainwright."

"Ignore him," Rhiannon said. "He thinks he's all that and a bag of chips. Half the time he treats *me* like a servant, too, but I have to be decent to him. I made more money tonight than all week at the Mystic Café. And I think he really is trying to help Brodie and me."

Sailor shook her head. "He makes me so mad! He's not an Elven Keeper, he's a shapeshifter Keeper—and he lives in *Malibu,* for God's sake. I'm an Elven Keeper—if someone wants to be a jerk to me, it should be Brodie. But he's not, and do you know why? Because he's Elven. He's decent, intelligent. He doesn't prejudge people. And it's not like I can just avoid the damned Snake Pit! It's a hot spot for everyone in the industry…everyone I need to know."

"Ignore him, Sailor. Just ignore him."

Sailor nodded. "Yeah, all right." She gave Rhiannon a hug. "Thanks," she said softly. "Good night, and don't worry—I won't leave any windows open."

Rhiannon saw Brodie watching them as Barrie waved and went off toward Gwydion's Cave. Rhiannon was touched when Brodie came over to join them and gave Sailor a fierce hug. "Get in your house and lock up," he told her. "You'll be fine."

"I will. And if you see our ghost-pa, Merlin, send him over to me, okay? He's a great watchdog." Her brows rose. "Hey, that's what we need. A watchdog."

"I'd like a dog," Rhiannon agreed.

"Well, good night," Sailor said.

Rhiannon and Brodie watched until she was safely inside the main house. Then he slipped his arm around Rhiannon. "Night. Time to rest," he murmured.

"Rest," she echoed. "And wind down…"

"Wind down," he repeated, grinning. "Nice euphemism."

Rhiannon laughed, fitting her key into the door lock. Brodie was leaning against her, and she started to laugh, ready to swing into his arms the minute they got inside. Then she saw that they weren't alone.

Merlin was standing there looking impatient, as if he'd been waiting for them forever. "Well?" he demanded.

"Just the man I wanted to see," Brodie said, and Rhiannon stared at him.

Just the man he wanted to see? *Now?*

"Why, what's happened? Have you found the killer?" Merlin asked.

"No, but we know who attacked Sailor, or at least we're pretty sure we know. Celeste Monahue," Brodie said.

"Celeste?" Merlin was clearly surprised.

"You knew her? And she's been in the House of the Rising Sun before?" Brodie asked.

"Of course I knew her. Years ago she was quite the femme fatale. She was certain she could compete with the young crop that appears yearly forever. She was a real vixen in her day, and she'd attended many a party at the House of the Rising Sun."

"So she *had* been invited in," Brodie said.

"Yes. But…why would Celeste attack Sailor, much less kill a bunch of actors who hadn't even gotten a part?" Merlin asked.

"I think," Brodie said, "that we're looking for more than one person, and the person we're looking for—who may or may not be human—is getting vampires who want to get into, or back into, the business to—"

"—to commit murder," Rhiannon said, then grimaced. "These killings took place before my father left, but I'm sure whoever's behind this isn't worried that the bodies have come to light. He thinks that I'm too young and inexperienced to catch him. But he's wrong."

Merlin stared at her. "Then you'd better find him quickly. Because he might just get away clean, because the actual killers will have vanished—into ash."

"Barrie's article will hit the street tomorrow," Brodie said. "With luck we'll force our puppet master out into the open."

Merlin looked ready to start ranting, so Rhiannon quickly cut him off. "Sailor doesn't want to be alone, Merlin. She asked if you'd go over there and watch out for her."

"Of course," he assured her, already walking to the door. "What you girls need is a good dog."

Rhiannon stepped forward to open the door for him, but he was too upset for courtesy. He walked right through it, and when she looked through the peephole, she saw that he was heading toward the main house with a purposeful stride.

She turned to find Brodie standing directly behind her.

It was amazing, the response that an Elven, *her* Elven, could arouse in the human body. She'd thought that the reality of their situation would weigh so heavily on her that nothing could distract her.

She'd been wrong.

All Brodie had to do was touch her and her only thought became that all time was precious, and their time together rarest and most precious of all. He swung her easily into his arms. "I think we're alone now," he said huskily, moving toward the stairs.

"You know, I really can walk," she told him.

"Why bother?"

Later she didn't remember being carried up the stairs or reaching the bedroom. All she knew was that they were suddenly just...there, on the bed together, urgently kissing and trying to struggle out of their clothing at the same time. As soon as she was naked, Rhiannon looked up at him breathlessly.

"Did we teleport?" she asked.

"No...but we did travel at the speed of light," he said, smiling into her eyes.

And then he was kissing her again. She kissed him in return, breathing him in, and even the scent of him seemed golden. When he moved against her, she moved against him, her body curving to echo his every shift. The taste of his kiss was sweet and suggestive and erotic, and when they finally broke away they were both breathless, staring at each other in wonder for a long moment. And then they were touching again. She pressed her lips to his shoulders while he ran his hands along the length of her back and down to her hips. Her fingertips seemed to streak with fire as she touched him. And where his kiss fell on her bare flesh, her blood felt as if it was boiling beneath her skin. They hungered, as if they could never have enough of the simple taste and feel of each other, until the urgency created by that longing become unbearable. They melted together, suddenly one, in a movement as natural as breathing....

Rhiannon felt as if she were soaring toward the sun, his every caress erotic, and the feel of his flesh, the thrust of his body, wickedly abandoned and so, so real. She felt everything acutely, each slightest brush of his fingertips, the pressure deep inside as he moved within her, driving her ever higher.

Her climax burst through her. She relished it, drifted on the wave, clung to the wonder that filled her, as molten and sweet as release itself had been. And then she saw that the sun had risen and the day had begun, golden light seeping in between the curtains.

"It's morning," she murmured, snuggling again him.

"Morning," he agreed, and groaned. "Matinee today."

"We need to get a few hours' sleep," she said huskily.

"We do," he agreed, cradling her against him.

Moments later she felt the liquid fire of his kiss moving along her back.

She turned in his arms, looking at him with a curious smile. "This is how you sleep?" she asked.

"I'll sleep…soon," he promised as he studied her, a slight smile on his face.

"Are you reading my thoughts?" she asked him.

"Not the way you're suggesting," he said. "But I'm reading what I can from the way you're looking at me. What's your *real* feeling about sleep?"

She smiled. "Soon…" she whispered. And then her lips met his and time lost all meaning.

Chapter 12

Is a wannabe-vampire serial killer on the prowl in L.A.?

Rhiannon started reading the story underneath the headline. Barrie had done an excellent job. Her story wasn't front page, but at least it was the lead story for the local section.

Barrie had included information on all five murders, information credited to an "anonymous source" at the police department. She listed the victims and the dump sites, and included the detail that every victim had been drained of blood. She listed the number for the police hotline, urging anyone who had any information whatsoever to please call.

There was a tap on the door just as Rhiannon finished the article. She jumped up and went to answer the summons.

Barrie was standing there looking decidedly nervous. "Well?" she asked.

"It was excellent," Rhiannon assured her.

"Where's Brodie?" Barrie asked.

"On his way to the theater—matinee today. Have you seen Sailor?"

"I was just over there—she and I are going for a run," Barrie said.

"Wait," Rhiannon said. "I just need a minute to grab some sneakers, and then I'll go with you."

"I'm warning you," Sailor said when they joined her, "I'm not slowing down just so you can keep up with me."

"We'll struggle along as best we can," Rhiannon said, laughing.

Twenty minutes later Rhiannon was regretting her words. Sailor was in excellent shape and had no trouble with the hills, while Rhiannon was appalled to realize that she was quickly panting and sweating.

"Have mercy!" Barrie cried at last, saving Rhiannon from having to be the one to cry uncle.

Sailor paused, and Rhiannon bent over, gasping for breath. As she did so, she realized that they had reached the area where she had found the body in the pond.

"Cops walking around—look," Barrie said, breathing heavily between words.

Rhiannon looked. There were two patrol cars parked on the private road, and she could see two sets of officers knocking on two front doors.

Then she noticed that someone was standing on the sidewalk, a notebook in his hands, watching as the officers went door to door.

"Isn't that Adam—the guy from the club last night?" Sailor asked.

Rhiannon nodded and straightened. A pain shot through her rib cage, and she gasped.

They had to find the killer fast, she thought, or she would perish just from trying to keep up with Sailor.

Adam must have heard them talking, because he looked up and saw them, then smiled, waved and started in their direction. "Morning, ladies," he said cheerfully.

"Hi, Adam," Rhiannon said. "You working the streets now?"

He nodded, then looked at Barrie. "I guess I don't have to wonder who your source is, but don't worry, I won't tell anyone. Your article got the phones ringing, at least. We got an anonymous tip that someone saw a pair of lovers out here a few weeks ago, walking down toward the water. We're trying to find the tipster, see if he can't tell us more." He shook his head glumly. "It's just hard, you know? If coyotes could talk, we might get better information."

"If coyotes could talk," Rhiannon agreed.

"Well, ladies, have a beautiful day. I'm going to get back to work," he said, then met Rhiannon's eyes. "I'm surprised to see you out here. Yesterday must have been hell for you."

"It wasn't pleasant, that's for sure," she said. "Well, time for us to get going."

She waved and was about to start jogging again when something on the sidewalk caught her attention. She didn't want Adam to see, so she quickly paused to do some stretching, keeping an eye on him until he was safely out of range.

"What are you doing?" Sailor asked her.

"Stretching to pick up…this."

She reached down for the bit of white cardboard that had attracted her attention. It turned out to be a matchbook.

"House of Illusion," Barrie said aloud.

"Want to have a late lunch there?" Rhiannon asked.

"I don't know. We're going tomorrow night anyway, and Brodie will be with us then," Sailor said.

"We're just going to have lunch, not storm the place," Rhiannon said.

"All right," Sailor said. "Race you home!"

As soon as he finished with costume and makeup, Brodie stepped outside to the parking lot to call the station. He was surprised when he got Adam's voice mail and a message saying he was out for the day. Brodie hit "0" for the switchboard and asked to be transferred to Bryce Edwards, his werewolf friend in Vice.

"Hey, Brodie."

"Bryce, sorry, I was trying to reach Adam Lansky in tech assistance, and I thought you might know where he is."

"He's out on the streets, with the uniforms, going door to door by that pond you were at yesterday,"

Edwards told him. "The kid is trying to earn some brownie points with you, I think. So, how are you really doing on this case, Brodie? Do we need to start worrying that it's going to blow up on us?"

"I promise you, I won't let it get to that. Can you get me patched through to Adam? I don't have his cell number, since he's never away from his desk," Brodie said.

"I'll make it happen. That article in this morning's paper has brought out the crazies. Are you going to get in here to help sift through the tips?" Edwards asked.

"First thing tomorrow morning," Brodie promised. "And if anything comes in that you think I should know about..."

"I'll call you, anytime, day or night," Edwards promised. "Okay, hang on. I've got Lansky for you."

A minute later he was connected to Adam.

"Hey, Brodie," Adam said.

"What are you doing?" Brodie asked.

"Helping."

"That's great, Adam, but I need you on the computer."

"It's Saturday, you know. I'm working on my own time," Adam said. "I came in this morning to print out pictures for the patrol teams to show around. Head shots of the victims, stuff I found online. I know I'm a geek, but I'd like to make detective one day."

Brodie wasn't sure why he felt uncomfortable. Adam had been a godsend many times in the past, digging up all kinds of information on the internet.

He'd also followed Sailor the other night at the club. For her safety? Or for some other reason entirely?

"All right," Brodie said, seeing that he wasn't going to get Adam to back off, at least not today. "I'll give you a call after the matinee, okay? You can catch me up on what's going on."

"Sure. I'll do that. You going to the Snake Pit tonight?"

Brodie frowned, thinking quickly, and said, "Yes, I'll be there to watch over Rhiannon. I've got friends watching her, too, keeping her safe 'til I can get there."

"Good to know. Well, I guess your show is about to start. Break a leg. I'll talk to you later," Adam promised.

Brodie hung up, not happy with the situation.

He'd worked with Adam a long time. He'd seemed a good enough kid. But now...

Everybody wanted something. The kid didn't want to be a geek all his life. But how would that turn into a compulsion to kill?

"Hey, Mac!"

He looked up. Bobby Conche and Joe Carrie were standing at the cast entrance.

"Getting late," Bobby warned him.

"Places in five," Joe called, then added, "You all right, Mac?"

"Yeah, I'm great, thanks. I'm coming," Brodie said.

He was afraid it was going to be a long performance.

The story had broken, and something was going to happen—he could feel it.

Adam wasn't the killer. Brodie had been convinced from the beginning that the killer had something to do with the play, and he was even more certain of that than ever.

The killer was here.

But the killer had accomplices—he was convinced of that now, too.

But how many? That was the question.

* * *

Jerry was in the entry hall, chatting with one of his magicians when the cousins arrived. He seemed surprised to see them, but also pleased.

"How nice to see you," he said. "There's not much going on, but the lunch buffet is still open. Or I can give you a tour," he suggested.

"We'd love to have some lunch, Jerry," Rhiannon said. "And a tour would be great."

"Wonderful. I'll call ahead, have a nice table set for you—I'll make sure you have a view of the valley." True to his word, he pulled out his cell phone and called the hostess. Smiling, he hung up, but then his smile wavered. "I saw the paper today. Are you sure that was the right move?"

"We need help, Jerry, and that article could bring in crucial information. And thank *you,* by the way, for everything you're doing for us," Rhiannon said.

Jerry was visibly pleased. "All right, ladies, follow me."

The castle had been built in the late 1890s, and the generously proportioned main-floor rooms had been converted to both large and small showrooms, the dining room and what Jerry called the Magician's Cave, an intimate space where a magician was currently staging a demonstration for a group of his peers. There was even an outdoor stage with a patio seating area that stretched right to the lip of the canyon, with only a low concrete wall to stop the unwary.

"Downstairs, we have our staging area," Jerry said. "You know, trapdoors, secret passageways… all the good stuff. Would you like to see it?"

"The hidden underbelly? You bet," Rhiannon said.

"No spilling secrets," Jerry warned Barrie.

"My typing fingers are sworn to silence," Barrie promised.

Jerry smiled and led them through a small unmarked door. A sign on the other side read Magicians' Staging Area and pointed the way to a set of stairs next to an elevator.

"We need an elevator, and you'll notice it's quite large. Needless to say we can't make a 757 disappear in a venue like this, but some of our performers use large boxes, tall glass tubes—like the one the Count de Soir used at the Snake Pit the other night," Jerry explained, then gave them a wicked grin. "Come, enter my den of mystery!" he said teasingly.

They followed him down the stairs to a basement with a definite dungeonlike feel—at least until she looked around and saw the electrical outlets everywhere, not to mention the huge LCD monitors on the walls, each screen showing a different view of the rooms just above, most of them various angles of the stage in the large showroom.

He pointed out a series of dressing rooms to the left, and then Sailor asked, "What are those doors to the right?"

"Guest room for visiting performers, complete with coffins for beds. We get a lot of vampires, along with all sorts of Others," he said quietly.

"Is the Count de Soir on the program Sunday night?" Rhiannon asked, changing the subject.

"Yes, he is," Jerry said.

"Interesting," Rhiannon said. "We'll look forward to seeing him."

Jerry nodded. "I hope I can help you. You'll come here, you'll see who you see and you'll ask all the questions you want to ask." He smiled suddenly. "And now lunch!"

The audience loved the show. Every Saturday they ran a fundraiser for the local animal shelters, and that went well, too. As he stood with a basket and greeted people, Brodie thought about how much he'd learned by going undercover as an actor. Take the fundraiser, for instance. He loved seeing how willing people were to donate to support creatures who desperately needed the help.

He found himself thinking about dogs, wonderful creatures with a sixth sense about who was trustworthy and who wasn't, and an ability to be useful in any fight against the kinds of danger a stone wall couldn't keep out. The Gryffald cousins definitely needed to get one, maybe more.

As soon as he could, he put a call through to Adam. "Found out anything useful yet?" he asked.

"A couple of things, starting with a couple you may want to talk to yourself. They live in the house nearest to the pond where the last body was found. They saw a car parked out in front, some kind of dark sedan. They didn't think anything of it at first, thought it must've been someone visiting a neighbor. A couple came out, and they were laughing, seemed happy. Another car came along a few minutes later, but they didn't see it, they just heard the motor. They heard a lot of laughter coming from down by the water, loud enough that they were going to call the police."

"So did they?"

"No, the laughter stopped, and they didn't hear anything else. When the husband finally went out to look, both cars were gone," Adam said.

Brodie was silent. Yes, more than one killer. Someone calling the shots. Someone else carrying out commands. And one of them able to glamour the guard to let them through. But…what was the underlying motive?

"So, Brodie, more than one killer, right?" Adam asked eagerly.

"Yes, Adam, more than one killer." He took a deep breath. "So, you said you said you had a couple things."

"Yeah, I have a name for you. That newspaper article really got things going. We got a tip from a woman named Shirley Henson. She was friends with our last victim—Rose Gillespie. The last time she saw Rose was about ten days ago. They met for lunch at the Mystic Café. Rose told her that she was going to go to see *Vampire Rampage*. She'd heard they were going to be casting the touring companies, so she wanted to see it again. Which means you were right—she most likely disappeared right after the play."

"Please, Sailor, I know it isn't a hardship for you, hanging out at the Snake Pit," Rhiannon said to her cousin. "Now that Barrie's article is out, I'm really afraid. The killer is either going to be gloating because his work has been noticed or afraid because of it. Please, stick with us tonight?"

Sailor sighed. "Rhiannon, I'm just tired of Declan Wainwright being a—a dick. I'll be perfectly safe at home with Merlin. And all my windows closed, of course."

"Sailor, please? Can we just stick together for the next few days?" Rhiannon asked.

"What if you and Brodie don't find out anything in the next few days?" Sailor asked.

"We have to," Rhiannon said, desperation in her tone. "So, what do you say? Will you come?"

Sailor sighed dramatically. "All right. But you're both coming running with me tomorrow morning."

Barrie and Rhiannon looked at each other.

"Well, it is good for our health," Barrie said. "Though I'd rather be hiking or rock-climbing, or...

well, you know—doing something a little more interesting."

"And I'd rather be in an air-conditioned gym with earphones and a little television screen showing something entertaining," Rhiannon said. "But tomorrow we run."

Sailor grinned. "Then I'll go with you tonight."

Brodie took the few free hours between performances to talk to Shirley. She seemed unusually surprised to see him.

"You're...a detective?" she asked. "I could swear I saw you in that new play, *Vampire Rampage*. I'm an actress, too. I saw it about two weeks ago—I'd heard they would be casting the touring companies soon."

Brodie offered her a rueful smile. "I'm undercover. I believe someone associated with the play is responsible for Rose's death, along with the others you read about in the paper this morning. I'm even more convinced because of what you told Adam. Tell me about the last time you saw Rose Gillespie."

Tears instantly filled Shirley's eyes. "It was a Saturday—two weeks ago tonight."

Brodie felt as if there were rocks in his stomach. That had been his first show. He hadn't really known anyone, and he had tried to watch them all as they left. He hadn't seen any of them leave with an audience member.

The couple next door to the pond had said there were two cars, so presumably Rose had been in the first, part of that happy couple, and the other had arrived after. She had been lured to her doom and then killed...by the second party?

He stayed with Shirley a little while longer, listening as she rambled on. She obviously needed to talk about the friend she had lost.

But there was nothing else he could gain from her. When he left her house, he called Adam again, this time getting him at the station.

"I need you to go through the victims' credit card receipts. I want to know how many times they saw the play, and the dates."

"Once might not have been enough, huh?" Adam asked.

"Just find out for me, please," Brodie said.

He headed back to the theater for the night's performance. As he parked, he called Rhiannon, anxious just to hear her voice.

"We're fine," she assured him. "We went to

the House of Illusion for lunch and got a tour of
the place."

He frowned at that. "Rhiannon, I'm not sure that
was safe. We'd agreed we would all go together tomorrow night."

"We were fine. We stayed together. And now
we're home, getting ready to head to the Snake Pit.
We'll stay close there, too. Oh, I had to promise to
go running with Sailor tomorrow, so make sure you
have sneakers," she said lightly.

"Stay safe," he cautioned her.

"I swear I will."

"Everything is all right at home?" he asked, feeling anxious, though he told himself there was no
reason for him to be afraid. The woman were together, and Merlin was there to play watchdog.

He just didn't have a sense of smell—or teeth.

"You need a dog," Brodie said, and thought about
the ones that had been at the theater that afternoon,
looking for homes.

"I would love to have a dog, I told you that," she
said. "But let's get through this first, huh?"

"I'll be at the Snake Pit when the show lets out,"
he promised.

The minute he hung up, his phone started to ring.

He picked it up and checked the caller ID. Adam, and he sounded excited.

"Brodie, you won't believe this. They all saw the play three times. Every one of them went three times. Strange, huh?" Adam asked.

"All right, do your computer magic. Check out a woman named Penny Abelard. Find out how many times *she's* seen the show," Brodie said. "And check out Shirley, too."

"Will do," Adam said.

Brodie parked the car and saw that Joe and Bobby were at the stage door entrance. They waved, smiling, as they saw him. He waved in return.

As he started to get out of the car, his phone rang again.

It was Adam. "Penny Abelard has seen the show twice. She has a ticket to see it tonight for the third time. The dates of the performances are on the sales receipts."

Brodie felt an icy chill run up his spine. He didn't know why three was the magic number, but it clearly was. He thanked Adam and hung up.

Nothing seemed unusual. Joe and Bobby greeted him as he entered. Hunter Jackson arrived, and he and Brodie chatted as they did their makeup. Places were called. The show began.

Brodie saw Penny Abelard immediately; she was sitting in the first row, looking enthralled.

He couldn't wait for the play to end. When it did, he dressed with record speed and was ready before Hunter even made it to their dressing room. He ran past the director on his way out, dimly aware that he'd agreed to meet everyone at the Snake Pit later.

He found Penny waiting backstage.

"Well, hello," he said, pretending to be surprised by her presence.

"Oh, hey! Great to see you. You were brilliant tonight," she told him.

Wide-eyed hope and innocence, he thought. It was such an L.A. look, at least for so many new arrivals. All too often it was followed by a dull look of weariness, of exhaustion and lost hope, as the young and the hopeful became the drained and hopeless.

"Thank you," he said. "Who are you here to meet?"

"I'm hoping to see Audrey—she's been so nice to me, and so has Lena Ashbury."

Lena! How the hell could he have missed it?

Penny was still smiling and talking. "I'm hoping to bum a ride with Audrey again, maybe get a chance to hang out with some of her friends at the club, like Declan Wainwright, and maybe even Darius Simonides. She knows all the cool people."

Cool people who might be murderers.

He didn't know what to do. Take her with him so he could keep her safe?

Or wait to see who was anxious to give her a ride?

Audrey Fleur, Kate Delaney and Lena Ashbury came out of their shared dressing room, laughing together.

"Hey, Brodie, Snake Pit?" Audrey called.

"Definitely," he said.

"Penny!" Lena called in greeting. "I saw you out in the audience."

"Hey, Lena," Penny said, flushing happily.

Hunter emerged from the dressing room just as Bobby Conche came walking over. He looked as hopeful as Penny. "You all heading to the Snake Pit?" he asked.

"Absolutely, and I hope you're coming, too," Hunter said.

Bobby seemed to bask in the glow of Hunter's words.

"Hey, where the hell is Joe?" Audrey asked. "If we're going, he should be going, too."

"On three," Kate said playfully. "One, two, three..."

"Joe!" they all cried as one.

Joe popped his head out from behind the curtain. "What? What did I do?"

"Heading out to the Snake Pit! I'm taking the sheet music for the show. Maybe Miss Gryffald will play it for us."

"It's a plan," Joe said

Brodie gritted his teeth. With everyone there, he didn't know what his next step should be.

But he couldn't risk an innocent woman's life. "Penny, why don't you ride with me?"

"Don't be silly, Brodie. Penny can come with us," Audrey said. "You're taken, remember?"

"And Rhiannon trusts me completely. Stick with me, Penny. Audrey thinks she's filming *The Fast and the Furious* every time she gets in a car."

"Who cares who drives with who?" Hunter asked. "Let's just go."

Brodie took Penny's arm politely but firmly. "It will be my pleasure to give you a ride," he said.

Oh, yes, my pleasure—if I can just keep you alive.

Chapter 13

If it weren't for the possibility of a vampire serial killer and the attack on her cousin—okay, and the attack on her own car, too—Rhiannon thought, life would be pretty great. She was making a living playing music, and then there was Brodie. She didn't know where that relationship was heading or how long it might last, but she intended to enjoy every minute of it while she had the chance.

She noticed Brodie the minute he arrived with the cast and crew from the show, along with a young woman she didn't recognize, and she smiled at him, nodding toward the table where Sailor and Barrie were sitting. Sailor waved as he approached with the woman, while Barrie didn't notice him until Sailor nudged her—she was engrossed in reading something on her tablet.

Even from a distance, she could see that he looked troubled. She couldn't desert the stage, but she suspected Brodie would find a way to join her as soon as he could.

He did, sliding onto the bench next to her when she paused between songs.

"Sorry if I'm acting distracted, but I'm trying to keep my eye on a woman," he said.

"I don't think you're supposed to tell me that you're watching another woman while we're sleeping together," she told him with a sexy grin.

He grinned back. "Rhiannon, I found out that all five victims disappeared after having seen *Vampire Rampage* three times. And this woman—Penny Abelard—also auditioned for the show, and she saw it for the third time tonight."

Rhiannon nodded. They both had a clear view of the table where Penny was now seated. "I'll try to keep an eye on her, too. Plus you have help here, if you want it." She started playing again, but this time she let the piano speak for itself, so she and Brodie could keep talking.

"Who?" he asked, frowning.

"Well, Declan is walking around looking like an eagle on the hunt. Hugh's here, too, but mostly he's just staring at me as if I were a caged wolf someone suddenly set loose. I meant your tech buddy, Adam Lansky. He's at a table a couple of rows back from where my cousins are sitting. He's alone. See him?"

"Thanks," he said, but he was getting more and more curious as to why Adam was suddenly showing up in a lot of places where he didn't need to be. "I'd better get back to the table. Our murderer intends to kill again tonight, and I've got to—damn! She's leaving the room."

Worse, Adam Lansky was following her.

Without even taking time to say goodbye, Brodie stood and hurried off the stage in Adam's wake.

The minute Rhiannon reached the end of the song she announced that she was taking a break. Not even caring what people might think, she went racing through the club and out into the night.

She didn't see any of them.

Then she heard a groan coming from behind some bushes.

It might be a trap, she realized, but she had to do something.

Plunging into the bushes, she gasped.

"Rhiannon! Is that you?" It was Brodie's voice, coming from somewhere off to the left.

"I'm over here!" she called.

Brodie thrust his way through to her. "That little rat bastard. I was two steps behind. I can't find Penny—Adam has her somewhere."

"No, Brodie," she said. "Adam doesn't have her. Adam is here. Call an ambulance. He's bleeding."

Brodie had his phone out even as he hunkered down over the tech, who, judging from the blood, had been bashed on the head.

"Son of a bitch," Brodie cursed. "Get Humphrey out here until an ambulance comes. Then you get back inside with your cousins."

"I can't hide from what's going on, Brodie. I'm a Keeper. Finding a vampire killer is what I'm supposed to do."

He grasped her by the shoulders. "The killer isn't out for you tonight. He's out for Penny Abelard. I have to find her—quickly. It might already be too late. Please, watch out for your cousins. There's more than one person involved in this, and for all I know at least one of our killers is still inside. Rhiannon, please, go now."

Rhiannon called for the bouncer as she ran for the door. The minute she had his attention she sent him over to help Brodie with Adam, then hurried back inside.

"Rhiannon, I know there's serious stuff going on, but you can't just disappear every few minutes and keep your job here," Declan said, catching her as she entered the room.

"A cop was attacked just outside, and a woman is missing. I think that's a good reason for taking a break, don't you?"

Declan paled. "Go back to the piano. I'll go out and see what's happening."

Rhiannon scanned the room as she headed back onstage.

The entire cast of *Vampire Rampage* was now gone, except for Lena Ashbury, who was sitting with Darius and laughing. Then, to her surprise, she spotted Audrey, who was flirting with a tall attractive stranger at the bar. But everyone else was among the missing.

She sat down and started to play, glad that her

fingers could find the keys by rote, because her mind was racing.

Declan found her on her next break and told her that she needed to give a statement to the police.

"Is Adam hurt badly?" she asked the officer who sat down to talk to her.

"He was still unconscious when the ambulance left," he told her. "But the paramedics said his pulse was steady, so with luck he'll come out of it soon."

"Have you seen—" She broke off before finishing the question, remembering just in time that Brodie was undercover.

The officer smiled, then lowered his voice and spoke close to her ear. "Detective McKay is still looking for the young woman Officer Lansky was following."

He took her statement and her number in case of additional questions, then let her return to the stage.

Finally she saw that the crowd was thinning out. Eventually the only other people remaining at the club were Sailor, Barrie, the workers who were closing up and Declan Wainwright.

"I'll follow you girls home," Declan told her.

"We're together—we'll be fine," Rhiannon assured him.

Declan smiled. "I don't doubt it. I just don't want Brodie on my case, okay?"

Rhiannon nodded. "All right. And I'm ready to go. I'm exhausted. Of course, I probably won't be able to sleep after all this," she said.

"But you'll be home. I still have to drive to Malibu," he reminded her.

"Good point," she said, feeling guilty. They all stood, and she noticed that Sailor seemed a little unsteady. "What's with you?" Rhiannon asked, slipping a supportive arm around her cousin.

"Five cosmos. I mean, hell, we've been here for hours," Sailor said.

"Can she make it?" Declan asked sharply.

"Of course," Rhiannon said indignantly. "All she has to do is walk to the car." The man owned a bar, and now he was being insulting because Sailor had actually been drinking there.

Barrie moved around to Sailor's other side, and together they walked out to Rhiannon's car. Just as they got there, Rhiannon's phone rang. It was Brodie. "Hang on," she said as she pulled her keys from her purse.

"Toss me the keys," Barrie said. "I'll drive, you talk."

"Thanks," Rhiannon said, handing them over. She balanced the phone between her shoulder and her cheek while she got Sailor settled in the backseat. "Brodie?" she asked a moment later as she slid into the front.

"You okay?" he asked anxiously.

"We're fine. Declan is going to follow us home."

"I'll be there soon," he told her.

"Did you find her?" Rhiannon asked.

He sighed. "Oh, yeah, I found her."

Penny Abelard was alive. Just barely.

And she still had her fingers.

The killer—or killers—must have known he was on the trail, Brodie thought.

He'd headed for the nearest body of water—a lousy little rock pit beside the ramp to the 101. She'd been attacked, but the killer hadn't had time to finish the job.

He'd found her facedown in the water, and his heart had dropped—it had felt as if it were sinking right into the mud—but when he dragged her out and started to perform CPR she had spewed water into his face, then begun to cough and wheeze.

For a moment, a brief moment, her eyes had

opened and she'd stared at him. They'd been wide and filled with terror.

"It's all right. I'm here to help you," he'd said.

Her eyes had closed again then, and he'd called 911, then sat by her, waiting. Soon he heard sirens, and in moments the medics were there.

"She needs a transfusion—quickly," Brodie told them.

They were good at their jobs, and one of them was a vampire who opened his mind to Brodie.

I'll see that she gets blood, McKay. She'll be okay.

"I'm going to follow you guys," he told them.

He waited at the hospital. After forty-five minutes a doctor came out. "Miss Abelard is a lucky young woman. You found her in the nick of time. We've transfused her, and her condition is serious but stable."

"Is she conscious?" Brodie asked.

"No, and I don't expect she'll come around for hours. Why don't you get some sleep? I'll have someone call you the moment she comes to," the doctor promised.

Brodie decided to read the man's mind.

It's going to be days, at best, 'til that poor girl comes to.

Brodie's head ached; he was soaked, muddy and exhausted.

"I'm calling for a uniformed officer to watch over her, and then I'm going to get some sleep, just as you suggested," Brodie said. "I want to be informed the minute she wakes up."

He checked on Adam while he waited for the uniform to arrive, and he had better luck there. Adam was conscious, and the doctor told him he could have five minutes.

The kid had a black eye and a bandaged head. He looked contrite and utterly dejected.

"Who was it?" Brodie asked him.

"Someone taller than me, that's all I know. That girl—Penny—she got a call and nearly ran out of the place. That seemed weird to me, so I ran after her. I made it outside, I got hit and the next thing I remember, I'm here. I'm pretty sure it was a man who hit me, but that's all I know. I'm sorry. I suck."

Brodie grimaced, shaking his head. "You're all right, kid. But maybe you should stick to computers for a while."

"For the rest of my life," Adam vowed.

Brodie decided that he wanted someone watching Adam, too, and made another call. He waited until both uniformed officers arrived, and then he left, driving well over the limit to the Gryffald compound.

Rhiannon must have been watching for him, because the gate swung open as he drove up. She was waiting for him in the driveway, and ran toward him the minute he parked. "Is she still…?"

"Alive, yes," he said. "But in a coma."

"Adam?"

"Awake and aware, but he doesn't know anything other than that his attacker was tall."

"I know who wasn't involved," Rhiannon said.

"Who?"

"Audrey. She was flirting with some guy at the bar the whole time. And Lena Ashbury was talking with Darius."

"What about Joe, Hunter and Kate?" he asked.

She shook her head. "No idea where they were. Which may not mean anything, but…"

"It might mean everything."

"Oh, and you know who else was missing?" Rhiannon asked. "Bobby. You know—the security guy."

"Shapeshifter," Brodie noted. "I get the feeling we're being led in circles."

"Maybe. But we have to follow, don't we? At least, I do."

"Rhiannon, I'm a cop *and* an Other. *I* have to solve this."

"*We* have to solve this. *We*."

He stroked her cheek gently. "We," he agreed.

She nodded, smiling at him sympathetically. "You look like hell. No insult intended."

"A shower would help a lot. May I?"

"Of course. And how about some tea?"

"So long as you lace it with whiskey." He grinned.

Twenty minutes later he collapsed on her bed. The tea had helped, the shower even more so. She lay by his side, just there, supportive. He felt so drained, so tired.

She stroked his hair, then his cheek. He felt as if her energy was pouring into him, and he turned to her and smiled. "You can be a little more...energetic, if you want."

"You need to rest," she told him.

The scent of her seemed to invade his blood. The feel of her created life in limbs and loins. He pulled her to him. "Um, not so sure what I need right now is rest," he said, his voice husky.

She smiled, a beautiful slow smile that lit her eyes and seemed to brighten the night. The very air seemed alive with sensuality.

She kissed his lips and drew her shirt over her head, baring the fullness and beauty of her breasts.

"I'll sleep…soon," he whispered as he reached for her.

In the end, it wasn't really all that soon. But with her in his arms, when he slept, he slept deeply, and when he woke it was to find himself feeling fully restored.

Rhiannon managed to get out of running with her cousins, because Brodie needed to get to the hospital, and she wanted to be with him.

He didn't want Sailor and Barrie running around the Canyon alone, though, so he arranged for a couple of officers-in-training to go with them. Both women were more amused than upset. After the events of the previous night, it seemed no one wanted to take any chances.

Rhiannon and Brodie visited Adam, who was

still feeling down and looking forward to getting back to the safety of his computer.

Penny Abelard was still unconscious, though the doctor on duty told them that he believed she would recover. Her vital signs were growing stronger, but he couldn't predict when she would wake up.

Brodie seemed uncharacteristically depressed, and it hurt Rhiannon to see him so down, but even the reminder that he'd saved Penny's life didn't seem to help. "Brodie, we're close, so close, to figuring this thing out," she said.

"Joe Carrie, Kate Delaney and Hunter Jackson," he said. "They're my friends, Can it really be one of them?"

"I think that has to be the answer," she said. "I don't understand, though—why? Joe's a vampire, but this play, the film, the video game…they're going to make him rich. And Hunter Jackson, he's already famous and he's only going to get more so. Kate Delaney…she's human, like Jackson, but this play is going to open doors for her. And there's Bobby, too. One of them must be involved, because they were all missing in action when Adam and Penny were attacked, and the circle always comes back to the theater and the play."

"Or the movie," Brodie said.

"Jerry Oglethorpe is convinced we can learn something tonight at the House of Illusion. Who the hell else is involved in this?"

"It could be a trap," Brodie pointed out. "Maybe I should go and the three of you should stay home. It's as if your arrival, in particular, has been some kind of catalyst."

"The murders started before I took over," she reminded him.

"Yes, but your father's...promotion was already in the works, and the bodies were pretty well hidden, as if the killer knew they wouldn't resurface—literally—until your father was gone."

"A vampire is involved somehow, maybe more than one, but I don't think a vampire is pulling the strings. We'll find out something at the House of Illusion, Brodie. I know it."

"Then we'll go early, for dinner," he said. "But we have to be prepared for anything—including the possibility that you're wrong and it really is a trap. Call Sailor and Barrie, tell them we want to get there by six." He looked at her consideringly. "Three," he said. "Why three? Why did the killer wait until each victim had seen the show three times?"

Rhiannon shook her head. "I have no idea."

"What about Jerry Oglethorpe?" he asked.

"Jerry *is* a vampire, but he has nothing to do with the show. And the first magician who said we should go to the House of Illusion, the Count de Soir, is Elven, and he has nothing to do with the play, either. Getting back to vampires, though, the House of Illusion is where they meet, so maybe that's the connection to tonight. Have you ever been through the entire mansion?"

"No, I haven't," Brodie said. "I've been to shows there, but that's it."

"There are bedrooms in the basement for guest performers to use. And the beds are all coffins. I know it's a cliché, but a lot of vampires like that kind of thing."

"Interesting. We really need to be on the alert tonight, especially you, because I think the killer would like nothing better than to make you the next victim. Rhiannon—"

"Oh, Brodie, I love that you want to protect us— protect *me*—but it's our job to fight when there's trouble among our charges. You know that. I have to face this."

He drew her close to him and he held her for a

moment, then kissed her tenderly. "I know you do," he said at last.

"Everything was peaceful out here for so long. But now, when we—when *I*—have just arrived, all hell had to break loose."

"And that's exactly why it did."

"And why we have to prove ourselves," Rhiannon said.

At six o'clock, they arrived at the House of Illusion.

Jerry Oglethorpe had reserved a prime table for them, right in front, and they had plenty of time to eat before the featured performance started. In the meantime, while the audience waited for the main act—the Count de Soir—a series of young magicians took the stage.

Rhiannon watched them, but mostly she tried to keep track of everything that was going on *off* the stage. All the while she could sense Brodie's tension as he, too, made a point of watching everything while trying to appear not to.

As soon as he finished his meal he leaned over and whispered to her that he wanted to take the tour and see the basement bedrooms, then excused himself and went in search of Jerry Oglethorpe.

Thirty minutes later he was back, but before he had a chance to share his thoughts with her, the Count de Soir took the stage.

He performed some rather ordinary tricks at first, using scarves, rabbits and doves. But then he built up to a major routine, the music growing louder and a bevy of beautiful assistants gesturing dramatically as a huge glass case, something like the water tanks Houdini used to perform his amazing escapes, was wheeled onto the stage.

"First," the Count announced, "I will turn a beast into a beauty!"

And then, with great fanfare, he introduced a large wolf to the stage.

Jerry Oglethorpe, who was standing near their table, bent down to whisper, "Don't worry, it's real. Not a werewolf. Actually, it's a hybrid. Most magicians use dog/wolf crosses. They're not as volatile."

The Count de Soir continued with his act, ushering the wolf into the glass case before covering it with a red velvet drape and tapping his wand lightly on the top. When he pulled away the drape, one of his assistants was inside the case.

"But that was child's play," he said. "Watch." A second glass enclosure was wheeled on. "Beauty to beauty. In the blink of an eye, one beauty will become another. I will need a volunteer. You!"

This time he was looking at Sailor and not Rhiannon.

"Don't go," Rhiannon whispered. "He could be using us for some reason—baiting us."

"What's wrong with you, Rhiannon?" Sailor said. "You helped with one of his tricks."

"That was different. Something is happening here tonight, and we can't take any foolish risks."

"Rhiannon, the man hasn't done anything at all to make us suspicious."

"It's just that we have to be very careful. It's dangerous to trust anyone we don't really know. He's just…an unknown entity."

"I'll be careful, Rhiannon, so stop talking to me like I'm an idiot. Besides, he's the one who suggested we come here. Maybe he's afraid of something. Maybe he's trying to help us."

Without creating a massive scene—and perhaps sacrificing their chance to learn the truth—Rhiannon couldn't stop her, so she exchanged a worried look with Barrie, and then, with her heart in her throat, she watched her cousin go up onstage.

The three of them were ready. As ready as they could be.

Three!

The number three had to mean something. There were three new Keepers in the Canyon because three had been called to the council.

"I don't like this," she whispered to Brodie. "He's got her onstage, where there are all those trapdoors that lead down to the basement."

"I'll go down there, just in case," he said, but he looked worried.

"Before you go," she said, "I just thought of something. You said the victims all saw the play three times. And there are three of us. Sailor, Barrie and me. Three new Keepers."

"Interesting," he said, nodding thoughtfully. "But now I have to get down there. You need to watch up here." Jerry Oglethorpe was still standing nearby, and Brodie beckoned him over. "I'm going downstairs, Jerry. I just want to make sure nothing is going on down there, in case the count sends her down there as part of the switch."

"Whatever you want. But I'm sure Sailor will be all right. The Count de Soir is an Elven, after all."

"I know. Still…"

Jerry nodded, and Rhiannon watched as Brodie left, then returned her attention to the stage. The Count de Soir was escorting one of his assistants into one of the glass enclosures and Sailor into the other.

He did his bit with the draperies, waved his wand and pulled off the draperies.

The two women had changed places.

"And now…"

Once again Count de Soir covered the cubicles, but this time, when he whipped off the drapes, there were wolves in both cases.

Her heart pounding, Rhiannon jumped to her feet.

Barrie caught her hand and pulled her back down. "Wait—let's just see what he's doing," she advised.

"He's got Sailor in the basement," Rhiannon said. "Anyone could be doing anything to her down there."

"Just hang on."

The drapes went over the cubicles. The wolves turned back into the two women.

"See?" Barrie said smugly.

Rhiannon saw, but something wasn't right. She didn't know what, and she didn't know how she knew, but she did.

The count thanked his beautiful volunteer as he let Sailor out of her glass box. She walked down the steps from the stage, but instead of returning to the table she started to walk out of the room.

"What the hell is she doing?" Barrie asked, her eyes narrowing suspiciously.

"I don't know—yes, I do!" Rhiannon exclaimed, staring at Barrie. "That isn't Sailor! Come on."

By then "Sailor" was heading out the back door, toward the outdoor stage—and the sheer drop-off into the canyon below. Rhiannon, with Barrie close behind, raced after the shifter impersonating their cousin.

Outside, Rhiannon burst into motion and grabbed the faux Sailor, who turned to face her, looking startled.

"Rhiannon!" the shifter said in Sailor's voice. "Why do you look so worried? I just needed some air. Come on, let's walk."

"You're not Sailor," Rhiannon said. "And I'm not going anywhere with you."

"Sailor" stared at her, trying to wrench free and hissing. And then...

In seconds Sailor became Bobby Conche.

She dropped her hold, and Bobby Conche swung a fist right at her head. She ducked just in time.

She vaguely registered Barrie catching up to them as she felt adrenaline pulsing through her and her teeth...becoming fangs. She leapt on Bobby, slamming him to the ground and baring her teeth, ready to rip his throat to shreds.

"Rhiannon, stop!" Barrie said. "He has to tell us where Sailor is."

Bobby began to laugh. "The Count? He's an innocent pawn. He's busy congratulating himself on a great show. We rigged the set-up. It's so easy to manipulate people."

Rhiannon struck him—hard. "Keep it up and I just might kill you. You're a shifter, Bobby. And a vampire bite is pure poison to an Other. So tell me where my cousin is."

He started to shift again, squirming beneath her, thrusting her aside.

Barrie pounced on him, holding him firm as he

changed from form to form, until finally he was Bobby again, staring up at them.

"He'll kill me! Don't you understand? He'll *kill* me!"

"Who?" Rhiannon demanded. "Bobby, damn you, who? I can stop this, but you have to tell me— who?"

Brodie reached the basement just as the last of the young magicians was leaving. He raced toward the guest rooms—and their coffins.

The first yielded nothing.

The second was the same.

He could feel time ticking away.

He threw open the door to the third room and stopped, stunned. There was Sailor, lying motionless, eyes closed, in a coffin, arms crossed over her chest as if she were...dead.

Three. Three new Keepers. Destroy them one by one, and in the process destroy the entire system they represented and the laws that governed an Otherworld society whose members possessed legendary strengths.

"Sailor!" he shouted, and hurried toward her. She was breathing; she had a pulse.

He heard the sound of clapping and turned.

Three people stood in the doorway: Kate Delaney, Joe Carrie—and Hunter Jackson. Hunter and Kate were armed, their guns pointed at him.

Joe kept applauding as he walked toward Brodie. "We've got you just where we want you—cop." He practically spat the last word.

"Where? In a basement?" Brodie demanded.

"That's right. In a basement—where no one will ever think to look for you. As you've noticed, we already have Sailor here. And we'll have the other two within minutes. You were a bit of a fly in the ointment, Elven, but we have you now, ready to be packed into a magician's box, transported down to the port and sent on a long ocean voyage."

Brodie crossed his arms over his chest, staring at the three of them. Kate? Human. He could take her with one swipe of his hand. Hunter Jackson? Human—he wouldn't take much more. The guns might pose a bit more of a problem, but still, he could teleport.

Joe Carrie...

Vampire. Taking him out might require a little more effort.

"I'm armed, you know. If I shoot Kate and Hunter," he told Joe, "they're dead."

"They can shoot you, too, Elven."

Brodie smiled. "They don't have my speed. I can kill them before they even begin to pull a trigger."

"Whatever. Then it will be you and me," Joe told him.

"Joe!" Kate protested. "What are you saying?"

She and Hunter were both staring at Joe, dismayed.

They hadn't realized they were pawns, Brodie thought. Of course, neither had he and Rhiannon. They'd gotten everything backward, thinking a human was controlling the vampires instead of vice versa.

In the second when they were distracted, Brodie pulled his own weapon.

"Now, that's going to be interesting. You—shooting two civilians," Joe said.

"They're armed. Trust me, I can find a way out," Brodie assured him, trying to appear completely calm. They had a plan—he had to know what it was.

And quickly. He had to find Rhiannon and Barrie. He didn't fully understand it yet, but Rhiannon had been right. Three new Keepers. It meant something.

Before anything else, though, he had to rescue Sailor.

"Rhiannon and Barrie will be down here any second," Brodie said.

Joe started to laugh. "I told you—she and her cousin have been taken care of. And now I have both the Elven Keeper and the Elven cop. Give up, Brodie. Give up, and maybe, when I've gotten you boxed up for a nice sail, you'll figure out a way to escape before the sea kills you."

"Where is Rhiannon, then?" Brodie asked, playing for time. He had to believe that Rhiannon and Barrie would figure out what was happening and save themselves. And then there was Jerry. He knew where Brodie was...but when would he suspect that something was wrong?

"Rhiannon is busy dying," Kate said. "Your little Keeper and her other cousin are out chasing Bobby Conche—who, at this moment, looks just like that imbecile Sailor. And once he has them somewhere out of sight, he's going to turn into a grizzly or something."

"I wouldn't count on Bobby beating Rhiannon,"

Brodie said, praying that he was right. Then he turned to face the two humans. "Meanwhile, I want to know one thing."

"What's that?" Joe asked.

"Why? Hunter, you have Hollywood in the palm of your hand. Kate, you're beautiful. Your career is just taking off, thanks to *Vampire Rampage*."

Kate laughed. "Are you kidding me? The only way I even got this role was by agreeing to help Joe."

"Same here," Hunter said. "I was actually on my way downhill. It just hadn't hit the gossip columns yet. You really don't understand yet, do you? There's going to be a new world order, and Joe is going to make us part of it."

"Joe is ready to sacrifice you at any time for his own ends," Brodie said. "I thought you'd just figured that out. And...what new world order?"

As he spoke, he felt something creeping along his shoulder. He allowed himself a split-second glance. It was some kind of caterpillar.

Instinctively, he knew. Barrie was here. And that meant Rhiannon couldn't be far behind.

"I'm bringing down the Keepers—all of them," Joe said. "This has been ridiculous for decades now…all of us hiding what we are. There will be a new world order, and the vampires will be at the top. I couldn't have asked for a more perfect opportunity for starting the revolution. They took away the men who had strength for their grand World Council and gave us three inexperienced girls, no opposition at all. And, I must admit, it was fun watching you try to figure it out. Three, Brodie. Three new Keepers. So we threw you bread crumbs. Trace that number three. Don't kill people unless they've shown up three times. It's poetic justice, don't you see? Now, destroy the three new Keepers. Rid the world of the new international council and the annoying local ones all at once. Strike down the ridiculous order."

"What's wrong with order, Joe? Everyone just wants to live and let live. Elven, vampires, shape-shifters, human beings, you name it. We all want the same things."

"You're wrong. And this…hierarchy hasn't been natural. We should be able to dine on human chattel as we choose."

"Human chattel?" Brodie repeated, laughing. "That's you," he reminded Kate and Hunter.

"Shut up!" Kate screamed. She raised her gun and fired.

He moved in a flash, knocking the gun from her hand. "You're supporting the beast who would like to drink your blood," he warned her.

"The Keepers are going down," Joe told him. "By tomorrow morning I'll be ruling the Canyon." He walked toward Brodie. "A council? A world council? To rule over us? Oh, no. We are powerful, and we will rule the world. And I'm going to show you now just how powerful we vampires really are."

Joe suddenly grabbed Kate and shoved her away so that he could face Brodie. He hissed, his fangs lengthening, and flew at Brodie.

Brodie threw him, saying, "Get Sailor out of here. Wake her up—make her teleport."

"Who are you talking to?" Hunter cried out, backing away.

"He's not talking to anyone," Joe said. "It's a ploy. Now quit being such a sniveling coward or I'll kill you myself." He laughed. "Distract him, at least, you pathetic human beings!"

Kate rushed at Brodie head-on at the same time that Hunter attacked from behind. Brodie backhanded Kate hard; she crashed against the door and went limp. Then he spun and easily sent Hunter flying.

Both were out stone cold, flat on the floor.

But when he turned, Joe was standing over Sailor.

"Get away from her!" Brodie roared, throwing himself at Joe.

They were locked in battle, but finally Brodie managed to trip Joe, and they both went down, rolling.

Joe broke away and ran toward the coffin, his fangs dripping.

But before he could reach her, Sailor opened her eyes.

"Teleport!" Brodie shouted to her.

And she disappeared.

Joe let out a roar of fury, turned and ran toward Brodie again just as Brodie felt himself being kicked savagely in the ribs. He looked up from the floor to see Audrey Fleur staring down at him.

In a flash, he weighed his options.

Teleport himself? Stand his ground and fight?

"Enough!" The voice was strong, full of authority.

For a moment they all stopped.

Rhiannon, tall, confident and furious, had entered the room. She drew her lips back, displaying long fangs, as she came closer.

Audrey blocked her way. "I'll take you down in a heartbeat," she vowed.

"I don't think so," Rhiannon said, reaching out, clutching Audrey by the collar and throwing her to the side of the room. Joe flung himself furiously at Rhiannon, but she evaded him and rushed to Brodie's side.

"Trust me?" she begged him in a whisper.

He met her eyes and nodded.

"Then stay down."

"Bitch!" Joe screamed at Rhiannon. "Stop now, and maybe I'll let you live. But first I have an Elven to rip to shreds."

"I want to live," Rhiannon said. "I'll do anything. Let *me* kill him. I'll rip him to shreds for you."

"Really?" Joe said. "How fascinating."

"Don't trust her!" Audrey cried.

"Don't trust me?" Rhiannon asked. "Why not? You have the power—you have the numbers. I want to live, and it's obvious I have no choice but to answer to the strength of a real vampire. I'll help you overthrow the Keepers. I'll be your servant, Joe," she said. "I don't want to die."

"And you'll really kill your lover?" Joe asked her. "That I would like to see."

"I'll drain his blood and find him delicious," Rhiannon said.

Brodie knew he could fight her off, or he could teleport. But it was equally true that the last fight had taken a heavy toll on his strength. What was she playing at?

Trust me, she had said. She had a plan, even if he didn't know what it was.

She opened her mind to him, and he read her thoughts. *Trust me,* she pleaded again.

He nodded his acknowledgment.

To his amazement, she sank her fangs into his throat. And then, carefully hiding her actions from the others, she ripped a gash in her own wrist with her nail and forced the wound to his lips.

A vampire bite could be poison to an Other. And drinking vampire blood…he had no idea what that might do to him.

Inordinate strength seemed to rip through him. He leapt to his feet just as Joe came at him again, enraged.

"I warned you!" Audrey screamed. "She's done… something!"

Ignoring her, Brodie teleported, smashed the coffin, grabbed a shard of wood and thrust it into Joe's heart.

Audrey screamed and turned to run, but Rhiannon stopped her, picking up another makeshift stake.

"No!" Audrey shrieked.

"You're a killer," Rhiannon said. "I am the vampire Keeper—and I condemn you to die for your actions."

She impaled Audrey with a single thrust, never faltering.

Brodie looked at Rhiannon. "We've won," he told her. "But, Rhiannon, I'm Elven. A vampire bite will kill me. And if not the bite, the blood I drank."

She shook her head, beautiful beyond measure as she seemed almost to float over to him. "No," she told him. "Bobby thought the same—that I could kill him. But a bite from my fangs really isn't the same, and drinking my blood isn't the same at all. Because it's not real vampire blood. It was a *Keeper* bite. It won't kill you, and the power will fade from you just as it will from me."

He drew her into his arms, and they were both shaking.

But they were together....

And the enemy had been defeated.

A moment later Jerry burst into the room. "What's going on? Barrie came for me, and... Oh, Lord, what happened? I don't understand."

Before either of them could explain, Sailor and Barrie came running in.

"You did it," Sailor breathed to Rhiannon.

Rhiannon smiled and let go of Brodie to draw her cousins into her arms. "*We* did it," she said. She turned to Jerry, still holding tight to her cousins. "It's complicated, and we'll explain later, but let's just say it's a good thing we have Barrie at the paper. She'll see to it that everything's explained in a way that...makes sense."

"Sense?" Jerry asked. "In Hollywood? Is that really going to matter?"

Epilogue

Sailor found her new friend right away.

Or perhaps he found her.

As they walked through the kennels, their hearts bleeding for the unwanted animals waiting at the shelter in hopes of finding love and a home, a massive mix of golden retriever and…something jumped against the fence just as Sailor was passing. She jumped and then laughed, looking at the big yellow mutt.

"Well, hello," she said.

"That's Jonquil," the kennel volunteer said. "His owner died. Sad story, really. He sat by her bedside until a neighbor finally came in, worried because he hadn't seen the old lady in a week. The poor woman had no family, so there was no one to take Jonquil. He looks like a bruiser, but he's a kitten inside."

Sailor hunkered down by kennel, slipping her fingers through the wire. Jonquil proceeded to slobber on her fingers, and that was it, she was in love. She looked up at Rhiannon, Barrie and Brodie. "I've found my true love," she told them.

"He's beautiful," Rhiannon assured her, and kept walking. She paused near what she thought was an empty kennel, then realized that a huge dog was huddled against the back wall. "Who's that?" she asked the attendant, who had come up behind her.

"Wizard," the woman said. "He's mostly Scottish deerhound, I think. Kind of wiry, kind of gray and he doesn't trust people easily."

Brodie joined Rhiannon then, and she looked at him and smiled. "Hmm. I don't trust people easily, either." She knelt by the kennel. "Hey," she said softly.

The dog stared back at her with wide eyes, hunching a little closer to the wall.

"Rhiannon, he might not be the right dog," Brodie warned.

She looked up at him. "His name is Wizard. He's the right one."

He shrugged and hunkered down beside her. "Come here, boy. Come on."

"Wizard?" Rhiannon called softly.

At last the dog moved away from the wall. He was mammoth, Rhiannon realized. Standing on his hind legs, he would be her height.

He came slowly toward them.

"I promise you, he doesn't bite," the attendant said.

"If only I could say the same about me," Rhiannon said, looking sheepishly at Brodie.

"The occasional bite can be a good thing," he assured her with a grin.

Just then she felt something wet touch her fingers, and she turned to look back at Wizard. His big brown eyes were on her, and she could have sworn that she saw hope in them.

"I guess you've found your dog, too," Brodie said.

"Looks like we've got two dogs," Barrie said, coming over to see Wizard. "I'm going to find a cat."

"Right this way," the attendant said.

An hour later, animals in tow, they were back at the compound. On the ride home they'd decided to have a barbecue later. By evening the summer heat would slack off, but it would still be warm enough for everyone—even Brodie—to enjoy the pool.

But with the barbecue a few hours off, Brodie and Rhiannon were busy making Wizard comfortable, setting out his bowls and making him a bed in the kitchen out of an old comforter.

"I wonder if I should make him a bed upstairs in my room, too," Rhiannon said.

Brodie set his hands on her shoulders and said, "No. We already need to lock the door and hang up a do-not-disturb sign, what with your cousins and Merlin. We'll give Wizard plenty of love, and he'll be fine with that and enjoy his bed in the kitchen." He smiled knowingly at her. "In fact, I think we should give him a chance to try out his own bed in privacy right now."

He swept her off her feet into his arms, strong and secure. There really was nothing like an Elven for romantic gestures, she thought.

Wizard began to bark.

"It's okay, boy," Brodie said. "Your mama and I

may be looking at a future together, so you'd better get used to me."

Wizard sat and wagged his tail.

Rhiannon stroked Brodie's cheek. "It's hard to know *where* we're going," she said. "An Elven and a Keeper."

"True—even with fortune-teller machines all over the house," he agreed. "I do know that I've never been happier. We are what we are—but I know I want to be with you more than anything in life, even if it's going to be a journey strewn with obstacles."

"Yeah, vampires, shapeshifters, werewolves, Elven, even some gnomes and a fairy or two," she said drily.

He nodded. "But I believe we can avoid them all. As long as you're game?"

She smiled. "There's nowhere else I'd rather be than where I am right now. In your arms." Lest she get too sappy, she added quickly, "Especially since you're Elven and very unlikely to drop me."

"Not a chance," he told her. "And I can scale staircases with a single bound."

She laughed, and he set out to prove it.

In seconds they were falling on the bed together,

wrapped in each other's arms. Rhiannon was certain that the future that lay ahead would be hard, but equally certain that it would be worth it.

Then she forgot about the future, because she was too busy living in the present.

There was nothing in the world like making love with an Elven.

No.

There was nothing in the world like making love with *Brodie*.

* * * * *

A sneaky peek at next month...

NOCTURNE™

BEYOND DARKNESS...BEYOND DESIRE

My wish list for next month's titles...

In stores from 15th March 2013:

❏ Undercover Wolf – Linda O. Johnston

❏ Dark Wolf Rising – Rhyannon Byrd

In stores from 5th April 2013:

❏ Blood of the Sorceress – Maggie Shayne

Available at WHSmith, Tesco, Asda, Eason, Amazon and Apple

Just can't wait?

Visit us Online

You can buy our books online a month before they hit the shops! **www.millsandboon.co.uk**

0313/89

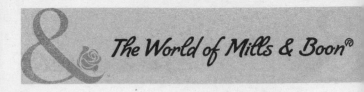

The World of Mills & Boon®

There's a Mills & Boon® series that's perfect for you. We publish ten series and, with new titles every month, you never have to wait long for your favourite to come along.

Blaze.
Scorching hot, sexy reads
4 new stories every month

By Request
Relive the romance with the best of the best
9 new stories every month

Cherish™
Romance to melt the heart every time
12 new stories every month

Desire™
Passionate and dramatic love stories
8 new stories every month